BEYOND

BEYOND

Catina Haverlock & Angela Larkin

SWEETWATER
BOOKS

An Imprint of Cedar Fort, Inc.
Springville, Utah

This is a work of fiction. The characters, names, incidents, places, and dialogue are products of the author's imagination and are not to be construed as real. The views expressed within this work are the sole responsibility of the author and do not necessarily reflect the position of Cedar Fort, Inc., or any other entity.

ISBN 13: 978-1-4621-2026-0

Published by Sweetwater Books, an imprint of Cedar Fort, Inc.,
2373 W. 700 S., Springville, UT 84663
Distributed by Cedar Fort, Inc., www.cedarfort.com

LIBRARY OF CONGRESS CATALOGING-IN-PUBLICATION DATA

Names: Haverlock, Catina– author
Title: Beyond / Catina Haverlock & Angela Larkin
Description: Springville, Utah : Sweetwater Books, an imprint of Cedar Fort, Inc., [2017]
Identifiers: LCCN 2017006050 (print)
    ISBN 9781462120260 (perfect binding : alk. paper)
Subjects: LCSH: Romance--fiction | LCGFT: Ghost stories
Classification: LCC PS3608.A8794 B49 2017 (print) | DDC 813/.6—dc23
LC record available at https://lccn.loc.gov/2017006050

Cover design by Priscilla Chaves
Cover design © 2017 by Cedar Fort, Inc.
Edited and typeset by Hali Bird, Casey Nealon, and Jessica Romrell

Printed in the United States of America

10 9 8 7 6 5 4 3 2 1

Printed on acid-free paper

Catina Haverlock: To Scott, who never doubted

Angela Larkin: For Nic, who gives me wings

"There's so much to love about this book! With a paranormal aspect filled with its own fascinating mythology, a main character in a refreshingly and non-standard role, an ending I couldn't guess, well chosen, vivid settings that made the story come alive, all packed with mystery and new love and heartbreakingly tough choices, this is a story that will hook you from the start."

—Peggy Eddleman, author of *Sky Jumpers* and *The Forbidden Flats* (Penguin Random House)

"*Beyond* is a beautifully crafted star-crossed love story that will keep you turning pages to see if there can be a happily ever after for Presley. In their debut novel, Haverlock and Larkin have woven an engrossing and touching tale of young love that reaches beyond mortal limits. A quick and satisfying read that is not to be missed."

—Katherine King, author of the award-winning book *The Other Side of the Stars*

"Beyond is a match made in heaven for readers wanting to immerse themselves in an all-consuming, ghostly romance."

—Nikki Trionfo, Author of the award-winning book *Shatter*

Contents

Contents

CONTENTS

The boundaries which divide life from
death are at best shadowy and vague.
Who shall say where one ends and the other begins?

—Edgar Allan Poe

Chapter One

Unforeseen

(Landon)

One hundred and twenty days since they pulled my body from the river. My four-month dead-iversary. Four months of tug-of-war with my exasperated guide, James. He was wearing me down.

"This isn't where you belong. Not anymore," he'd said. "It's futile."

"You know exactly why I can't go," I'd said. "You *know*."

Cut down at the end of my junior year. That was bad, but it wasn't the reason I refused to leave.

James was right, though. I was completely alone. No one could hear me. No one could see me.

Until someone did.

(Presley)

"Seriously? Eggs?" I'd meant that to remain a private rant. *Oops.*

Several nearby classmates watched me appraise my Jeep, which I could see even from across the parking lot, dripped with yellow slime. This was just the latest slap in the face of my first week at Truckee High.

My first day of school, someone was kind enough to smear a roast beef hoagie on my windshield. It took five bucks in quarters at the do-it-yourself car wash to clean off the mayo haze.

Day three. After PE, my clothes disappeared from the girls' locker room, forcing me to finish out the day in my uniform. These small-town punks made it hard to fly under the radar. I just wanted to get my senior year done and get out of this place.

Most people would be furious at these anonymous jerks. But I was madder at my mom for moving Chase and me two weeks before my senior year started.

"It's a great opportunity, Pres," she'd said. For who? I could live with the change, but this was going to be hard on Chase.

It wasn't that Truckee, California didn't have its perks. At the very least, it was different from Vegas. Towering Ponderosa pines covered the mountains and enveloped every structure in town like they gave permission for each building to exist. But they loomed, threatening to reclaim the real estate. I'd smiled at the first of many baby pine trees I'd noticed growing like weeds in the cracks of the sidewalks.

Truckee was pretty quiet with school back in session but I could tell by the rows of ski rental shops and paddleboard stores that winter and summer would be a different story. Lake Tahoe, with its freak-ishly clear blue water, was a pleasant surprise, since I'd spent the last several years in the Mojave Desert where the only nearby lake was a carp-filled stink hole. Cool town. Not-so-cool people.

Taking a deep breath and pulling my shoulders back, I walked to my Jeep. The tell-tale sting of tears betrayed me as eggshells crunched under my shoes. Trying to appear casual and composed, I pulled a hair band from my wrist and gathered my uncooperative curls into a top knot. I turned my back on a group of eager spectators, and hefted my bag onto an egg-free patch of hood to dig for my keys. My phone vibrated. I ignored it.

Of course my keys were lost in the black abyss of my backpack. I felt unwelcomed eyes on me as I searched. Finally, with keys in hand, I opened the door and hurled my bag onto the passenger seat.

Then, I caught sight of a face I hadn't seen before.

A good eight to ten cars away, he stood at the edge of the park-ing lot in the shade of the pines, arms folded across his chest, and studied me like some nightclub bouncer who was handed a fake ID (if bouncers looked like raven-haired H&M models). The boy was shameless. He stared, unabashedly, and the longer he looked at me, the more flattered I felt.

That is, until I realized what he was probably looking for: a reaction to my messed up Jeep. Wasn't that what the girls behind me were smugly discussing? Wasn't that why those freshman boys avoided eye contact when I walked by?

My cheeks flamed and I surprised myself by yelling across the lot at him, "What? What are you looking at?"

He flinched and unfolded his arms. His eyes locked onto mine and I matched him.

"Yeah, you!" I jabbed my chin in the air. *Bring it, dude.*

His eyes narrowed, and then he started toward me. An older man I hadn't noticed before quickly grabbed his shoulder and tried to pull him back. The boy became upset and jerked free. They argued. The man put both palms up in a gesture of pleading. The boy turned and glared at me once more, then charged toward me in strong, quick strides.

My gut seized at his fierce gaze and swift approach. A split decision of fight or flight. *Flight. Definitely flight.*

His gait quickened. I nearly dropped the keys, uttering a couple of son-of-a's before I got the key into the ignition. The engine growled.

I slammed the lock down with my palm and hazarded a look. With only a pane of glass dividing us, his gaze bored through me. But behind his intense stare I thought I detected more. Confusion? Distress?

Surprisingly, an arrow of sympathy pierced me. My hand gripped the shifter—frozen, unable to pull it into reverse.

His eyes held me, almost . . . imploring?

I wavered, but finally tore my eyes from his and accidentally hit the gas before pulling the shifter into gear. The tires squealed as I ripped out of my parking spot. A slouched boy yanked his friend's shirt back as I narrowly missed them. As I burned through the rows of parked cars, a few bystanders shouted something to the effect of, "Watch it, psycho!"

I looked for my pursuer in the rearview mirror, and saw his figure, distorted by the dribbles of dried egg on my back window. He stood there, the only still figure in a swarm of activity, and watched me drive away.

Chapter Two

Here We Go Again

(PRESLEY)

Maybe I was overreacting, but I kept checking my rearview mirror. That boy's face blazed in my mind. In comparison to some insane stranger chasing me down, roast beef hoagies suddenly seemed minor. I just wanted to drive straight home, run up the stairs, get in bed and hopefully be eaten by my mattress. But the humiliation of driving back to school in the morning in an eggmobile overrode my paranoia.

I loved my Jeep. It was only three years old with leather seats and chunky upgraded tires. My mom had bought it for me when she'd decided to move us from the dry black streets of Vegas to the high mountain roads of Truckee. I'd guessed she wanted to make sure I'd be safe on the snow and ice, so she'd traded in my decaying Civic for Romeo. The only stud in my life.

I rolled down Main Street and turned into the Buggy Bath. Coins still rattled in the cup holder from the last time I'd been here. After a decent amount of scrubbing with a foamy brush and a thorough rinsing, I knew Romeo was in trouble. Large faded patches appeared all over where the eggs had eaten through the paint. I kicked the front tire and threw down the spray nozzle. Sliding to the ground, I sat in a cold, soapy puddle, but wouldn't let myself cry. Not about mean people. Not because Romeo was all jacked up. Not even because I hadn't made a single friend. Even though no one would ever know the difference, I would not let myself cry.

—

I didn't expect Gayle to be there when I got home. She never was. I hadn't seen her for more than five minutes at a time since we'd moved here. We were more like roommates than mother and daughter. That's mostly why I always thought of her as "Gayle" instead of "Mom"—I only called her "Mom" to her face because she asked me to.

I looked in the fridge with a weak hope that there would be actual food and not just condiments and Diet Coke. I settled on a tub of chocolate chip cookie dough and a banana that had seen better days.

We didn't have cable or internet yet because Gayle had spent so much time at Truckee High getting established as the new principal. I was pretty much doomed as far as entertainment went, relying heavily on a cardboard box of *National Geographics* and my collection of zombie movies.

Upstairs, I peeled off my soaked jeans and put on some striped pajama pants. I pulled back my rumpled comforter, set my snacks on the bed and put on *Night of the Living Dead* (1968, not 1990). Curled up in my covers, I attacked the cookie dough. *Zombies would never egg my Jeep*, I thought. *They don't pull pranks behind your back if they don't like you; they just eat you. I prefer straightforwardness.*

I half-woke to the groan of the garage door. The clock glowed 9:45 and was the only light except for my small TV screen, which played the DVD menu on a loop. I groaned and closed my eyes. "I'm not brushing my teeth. I don't even care."

A minute later, Gayle flipped on my light. "Nice, you're lying in a banana peel."

I rose up on my elbows and squinted. "Where's Chase?"

Before Gayle had a chance to answer, I heard his size twelves stomping around downstairs, kitchen cabinets slamming. Instead of his usual husky and contented hum, aggravated screeches and high-pitched screams tore upstairs and into my room.

She leaned her curvy hip against the doorway and pulled a clip from her hair, releasing auburn waves. "He tantrumed the whole ride home," she said flatly.

"Yeah. Ya think?" I sympathized with the difficulty she must have had working while trying to manage Chase, but seriously, 9:45? The poor kid just pulled a fourteen-hour day. "You can't expect him to sit in your office for hours like that." I picked up the limp banana peel and tossed it toward the wastebasket across the room. I missed. "I would have picked him up if I had known you were going to be this late."

Gayle picked up the banana peel and dropped it in the wastebasket like a dead fish. "He was fine until half an hour ago. He had his tablet."

Yeah, probably zoned out on Yo Gabba Gabba *the whole time.* "I'll just bring him home with me tomorrow." A huge crash from downstairs. I felt the vibration of it from my bed.

She raised her eyebrows at me, completely ignoring the mayhem downstairs. "Well, I texted you several times. When you didn't answer, I tried calling." She tossed my phone to me. "This was downstairs."

Fingers of guilt crawled up my spine, punched through my back and into my chest. Squeezed my heart. *Squeeze, squeeze, squeeze.* Had I not been so absorbed in my own little pity party, I'd have known hours ago that Chase needed me.

I sat up and swung my feet over the bed and onto the wood floors, bracing myself for tantrum de-escalation. I had a few minutes; maybe less before Chase would storm up the stairs, looking for help to calm down.

Chase. My five-foot-eleven, nothing-but-muscle baby brother. His nut-brown hair hadn't been cut since summer and curled up at his ears. He was fourteen but looked much older—a *generally* gentle giant with autism. He was mostly sweet and content, unless he was neglected or pushed beyond his ability to cope. That was definitely the case tonight. And it was both Gayle's and my fault.

Gayle unbuttoned her jacket and announced, "I'm going to bed." She pushed off from the doorjamb, headed down the hall, and closed her door.

Several sickening thuds from downstairs. Chase was banging his head against the wall. I'd waited too long.

Chase was red-faced, yanking at the front room door knob. I was relieved that Gayle had touch-pad locks installed our first day here. We may not have unpacked our dishes and silverware yet, but every door was secured.

I gave him a minute longer, knowing he'd eventually give up on the idea of escape, and took the moment to close all of the kitchen cabinets and fridge and freezer doors which were hanging wide open.

His favorite songs soothed him most of the time, but my heart hammered in its cage. *What will I do if it doesn't work this time?* Like the Pied Piper, I started singing the "Yellow Song" in the tune of "If You're Happy and You Know It":

Y-E-L-L-O-W spells yellow. Y-E-L-L-O-W spells yellow . . .

He gave up on the door and darted over to me, grabbing my forearm and banging it brutally against his forehead. People were always astonished at my purple bite bruises, but it was the head banging that hurt worse.

Despite the crushing pain in my arm, I used my free hand to stroke the back of his sweat-drenched hair. "It's okay, buddy. Sing with me. You know the words."

Chase struggled to sing along, his voice strangled with agitation:

Like the early morning suuuuuun . . .

"That's right—good singing, Chase . . . keep going, sing with me."

. . . when the day has just begun . . . Y-E-L-L-O-W spells yellow.

I cursed Gayle, and then sang through red, purple, orange, and brown before Chase was calm enough to climb the stairs with me. He started to sob, and my heart slowed to its usual rhythm. He couldn't verbally communicate his remorse, but his tears meant that he was sorry and that the rage was over.

In my room, I led Chase to his table, turned on the lamp and dumped out his favorite *Toy Story* jigsaw. He'd had too much screen time and needed technology detox before he would fully relax. I sat at the table with him and helped flip upside down pieces. He bent over his puzzle while his hands worked busily.

People would never guess our relation. His skin was tanned, even in winter, whereas mine was usually pale and prone to freckling on my nose and cheeks. Thick lashes hooded his brown eyes. The only thickness to my lashes was a coat of drugstore mascara. We both got curly hair from my dad's gene pool, but Chase merely dipped his toe in, whereas I dove in deep and ended up with coils that plagued me.

Chase had been my enthusiastic shadow. Then, right after his second birthday, autism took him. I was only five at the time, but I've never forgotten how it came like a greedy thief and stole his smiles, his words, and his ability to play with me like he used to. I felt like my brother died. His body was still there, but it was like his soul had been abducted.

Twelve years later it still sucked. If he didn't have autism, we'd have each other's backs. We could commiserate over Big Macs about Truckee High and having to leave our lives behind in Vegas.

He finished *Toy Story* and reached for a 200-piece SpongeBob from his materials shelf. It would be hours before the adrenaline and video overload were out of his system. Good thing I'd had a nap.

With Chase on his way out of crisis mode, I should've relaxed too, but instead grew more restless as I replayed the parking lot incident. I'd been feisty with people before, but never had anyone chased me down. I knew I should've been scared of that boy, and I was . . . at first. But something about the need in his eyes fueled my curiosity. He was after something, I was sure of it. And it wasn't just to confront me for telling him off.

So, what could he possibly want with me?

Chapter Three

HEADWAY

(PRESLEY)

I wished I could have spent lunchtime with Chase. Too bad his autism class had first lunch. Today, however, I resolved to not eat lunch in my car.

The lunchroom looked more like a resort than high school dining commons. Instead of rollaway tables and benches like the ones my old school had, these kids noshed at tall pub tables on leather stools. The entire south side of the room was framed in a giant window that peaked at the top. Outside I could see the green, wooly, tree-covered mountains that I guessed would soon be covered in snow.

Settling in near the window, I basked in a sunbeam and lifted the bun off of my burger. *Dang. I forgot ketchup.* Circling back from the condiment table, I sat down again and prepared to doctor my burger, but when I lifted the bun, I found a bright blue wad of gum squashed into the pickle. Instant loss of appetite.

I scanned the room to see if anyone was watching me. The bulk of the student body milled around in their respective crowds like cattle—indifferent and occupied. In a stereotypic scene that was almost laughable, some cheerleaders in their matching game-day uniforms, shamelessly flirted with a couple of upperclassmen. One girl with muscular thighs and a stubby ponytail reached across a table and slugged the cuter one in the arm. Laughing, he leaned back and rubbed his fake wound.

Finishing my senior year online was becoming more appealing every day. I didn't need to sit around with these dirtbags anyway when I could hit up the courtyard vending machine and score a perfectly suitable lunch of peanut M&M's. I glanced outside toward the vending machine and startled when I saw the hot psycho guy from the parking lot seated on a bench in the middle of the court-yard. He studied me and made no effort to look away.

With each second that passed, the blood ran warmer in my veins. Emboldened by the thick glass window between us, I returned his stare. It didn't seem to bother him; he simply rested his elbows on his thighs and supported his chin on the steeple of his fingers.

Why are you always hanging out on the fringe? And why do you seem to pop up after something bad happens to me? What, are you some kind of godfather of high school pranks?

"It's just because you're so pretty, you know." I whipped around and saw a sober, yet lovely face contemplating me (and my ruined burger) through stylish tortoiseshell glasses. "One of the downsides of a small town, I guess. Some people just can't handle competition."

I let my eyes flicker for an instant back to the courtyard, but the boy was gone. She sat down across from me along with another girl I'd seen around but hadn't met. "I'm Violet. You okay?"

A great gush of breath came out of me which I wasn't aware I had been holding. I didn't want to seem like a freak to the first person who took the time to get to know me, so I lied and said I was fine.

She took a plastic knife, cut her hamburger in half, and handed me a piece.

"Thanks." I accepted her offering gratefully as I covered my own burger crime scene with a white napkin.

"So Vegas, huh?" Violet took a dainty bite from the end of a fry. "Our little mountain town must be quite a culture shock then."

"It's a little different," I admitted, disguising the sarcasm in my voice. I certainly didn't have to deal with daily pranks and mysteri-ous stalkers at my old school.

She looked at the girl who'd sat down with her. "This is Sam."

Sam had a padded layer of plumpness to her, but without appear-ing heavy. Her shoulder-length blonde hair was parted in the middle, and she appeared to have a genuine reason for smiling as she greeted me.

"Hey girl! Good to meet you." Her face was brighter than Violet's, and it was easy to see why someone would choose her for a friend.

I took a big bite of food just as Violet asked, "So, what year are you?"

I chewed as fast as I could and swallowed with the help of a swig of milk. "I'm a senior, but if I really hustle, I think I can graduate early."

"That anxious to get out?"

"Yeah—I'm kind of done with the whole high school thing, you know? I mean, I've moved five hundred miles away from all of my friends, I only have a year left . . ."

"I know exactly what you mean. The year has just started but I'm totally looking forward to getting it over with." Violet and Sam smiled knowingly at one another.

Eager to keep the conversation going, I grasped and reverted to senior citizen conversational topics. "So, I've heard it gets pretty cold here."

Violet smiled and nodded with Sam. "That's kind of an understatement," she said. "But at least we have the rest of September before it gets too bad. Still swimming weather, if it doesn't snow like it did last year. This is actually the perfect time for hiking."

"Who's going hiking?" An alarmingly cute boy with black hair and an interested expression pulled a stool up next to Violet. He reached his large hand across the table and gave my hand a warm squeeze. "Hey, I'm Reese. It looks like you've met my cousin, Vi—she's school royalty you know." He wrapped his arm around Violet's shoulder and planted a solid kiss on her cheek, then let her go before she could protest.

"Violet." She corrected him as she wiped the kissed cheek with a wadded napkin. "And please quit with the whole royalty thing—it's lame."

"What, you didn't introduce yourself as Violet Blackwood, Truckee Student Body President?" Reese pretended to be shocked.

I smiled at their banter. "I'm Presley."

"Presley, huh?" A tiny fluttering sensation winged through my stomach as he repeated my name.

"Her mom is Dr. Hale," Violet said.

He raised his dark eyebrows. "Seriously? Your mom's the principal? More school royalty. You two should get along well."

I wrinkled my nose. "Don't tell people though. I'm trying to blend."

"Good luck with that." Reese gave a crooked smile.

What was that supposed to mean?

"So, do we really have to call her *doctor*?" Reese made quotation marks in the air with his fingers.

"Only if you want to graduate. I'll tell on you if you don't."

"Nark." Reese bit his lip and smiled at me.

I shrugged and returned his smile.

"Too bad we can't be friends, Presley. I was just about to invite you along with all of us to go down the mountain on Friday, but you can forget it now, sister. No narks allowed." He winked adorably.

Confident much? This boy could be trouble.

Reese linked arms with Sam and Violet. "Are you ladies game? Kade's mom is letting him take her mom-mobile so we have extra seats."

I was sure I wanted to go, no matter where it was. "Down the mountain?" I said, trying to divide my eye contact evenly between Violet, Reese, and Sam, but failing miserably.

"Yeah, we're all going down to Reno for the night—bowling, out to eat," Reese said.

"Let's do it," Sam said to Violet. "You'll have fun, I promise."

"Fine," Violet answered.

"What about you?" Reese said to me. "You in? I promise to protect you from Violet the whole time." He flashed a smile and nudged Violet with his elbow.

I needed little convincing, but Sam said, "You should come. It can get a little claustrophobic up here if you don't get out of the trees every now and then."

I concentrated on sounding casual. "It sounds cool." I finished off my milk, then watched happily as the three of them programmed my number into their phones—a gesture that solidified my first real friends in Truckee. Which would have made for an absolutely perfect day. But after school, I found my Romeo slumped and sagging with four slashed tires.

Chapter Four

DOWN THE MOUNTAIN

(PRESLEY)

Gayle was so ticked about Romeo's tires. It was like she blamed me for it, and said I shouldn't have parked outside the view of the security cameras. At least she said yes about going "down the mountain." Of course there was one condition—I'd have to take Chase. It wasn't that Chase hadn't tagged along with me before; it was just that I barely knew these people. What if they were annoyed by him? A good litmus test for genuine friends, I supposed.

The ride to Reno turned out better than expected. Reese and his alpine ski buddies, Garett and Kade, along with Sam and Violet all met Chase and me at the Truckee River Rafting parking lot. Chase jumped in the shotgun seat right away, buckled himself in and tuned the radio to his long-time favorite, the Latino station. Kade, who reminded me of Shaggy from Scooby Doo, seemed happy to have Chase as copilot. He bumped fists with him and ordered the rest of us into the back. I didn't have to employ any strategy to land a seat by Reese. When Garett sat down next to me in all of his linebacker glory, Reese noogied his blonde curls and shamelessly wedged himself between us.

I relaxed a little about Chase when I could tell my friends weren't bothered by his shenanigans. Even though he slapped Kade's hand away any time he tried to change the station. And even though he reached around and snatched Reese's Big Gulp and downed it in three swallows.

We pulled up to an old casino on Virginia Street –the main drag. I knew that Reno was a gaming city like Vegas, but it seemed eons older. If any place in Las Vegas even hinted toward being dated, it was demolished with some grand implosion to make way for something taller, sexier, and more expensive. The opposite was true here. Some buildings looked nearly a hundred years old next to the newer, flashier hotels. The sidewalks were smaller and more uneven than the thoroughfares designed for large Vegas crowds. Towering palms lined every street back home, but fluffy shade trees dotted Reno's streets. I wondered what the allure could possibly be for this dingy dive the group chose for dinner.

Inside the dim casino, my ears were assaulted by coins dropping into old-school slot machine trays. Chase, enchanted by the music and bright lights, had to be pulled off a few machines and steered through the gaming floor. The ceilings were much lower than in the cavernous casinos back home. Even the smell of the cigarette smoke seemed aged—almost greasy, like the stench of fried food had taken up permanent residence in the gaudy carpet.

Violet seemed to sense how underwhelmed I was by the place.

"Don't worry, I know it's not the Bellagio, but they don't ever card us here. I think they just need the business. It's only ninety-nine cents for a massive shrimp cocktail, and the karaoke is rockin'. You should hear Reese's Michael Jackson repertoire. Truly inspiring."

Reese, a couple of steps ahead, obviously heard Violet's compliment, slid into a moonwalk and sang, "Shamone!"

Chase and I followed the hyper group of boys as they put each other in headlocks, jumped on one another's backs, and engaged in every other juvenile behavior. Violet and Sam walked behind them like two chaperones. Soon we were all seated in a sticky vinyl booth under a keno board.

A waitress whose nametag read, "Bev," balanced a tray loaded with ice waters and menus. She set the drinks down on the table and teased, "Oh, not you guys again." Her smile said that we were the best part of her night. "Let me guess, three specials," she said, pointing a stubby pencil at the boys. "A Cobb salad," pointing at Sam, "and a shrimp cocktail for little miss thang," she said pointing at Violet.

I ordered for Chase. Bev stood poised with her pencil stub ready for my order. "Um, the special I guess," I said, looking around at the group for affirmation. The boys cheered and Violet huffed in disgust. Bev spun around in her well-worn tennis shoes, disappeared into the kitchen, and screeched the order in Spanish to some unseen cook.

"I guess I should have asked what the special is before I ordered it," I said.

Violet leaned over in earnest, "Yes, you should have. It's revolting. They bring out a platter of the biggest hunk of pig you ever saw, alongside a mountain of eggs and potatoes. It's called 'The Lumberjack,' and if you eat the whole thing you get your picture on the wall." She gestured toward a wall of fame that featured a lot of green looking Lumberjack victors, each holding up a golden pig trophy.

The boys suddenly turned somber. Kade had a faraway look in his eye and said, "I just gotta win me a Golden Wilbur." He reminded me of some sappy kid from a '50s movie. Somebody who'd use terms like *gee whiz* and *mister*.

Violet continued, "Nobody in our group has ever done it. And Kade's barfed twice trying. He tries to bribe Beverly to give him a trophy every time we come. Shameless."

Dinner arrived quickly in a steaming heap. I'd honestly never tasted better ham and eggs. Not completely full, I stopped eating when my plate was about halfway empty. The boys groaned, leaned back and patted their stuffed bellies.

Violet tipped her purse and emptied its contents onto the table. "Crap," she moaned. "I forgot my phone in the van. Kade—give me the keys please." Kade reached in his pocket and tossed the keys across the table to Violet, who was already standing.

"I'll walk with you," Sam said. "I want to get my jacket anyway." The girls edged past Bev who had just arrived with another jumbo shrimp cocktail for Chase.

As the two girls trotted to the exit, Reese seemed obligated to explain.

"Aunt Afton, Vi's mom, is a little paranoid since the accident. She freaks if she can't get a hold of Violet. That's why she won't be without her phone even for a minute."

"What accident?"

He looked at me with sad brown eyes that reminded me a little of Chase's. "I'm guessing you haven't heard anything about Landon yet."

"Landon who?" I asked.

"Landon Blackwood." Reese dropped his gaze to focus on the table. "He was Violet's twin brother."

"Was?" I instantly dreaded Reese's explanation.

He looked up and appraised my face with caution. "He died in April."

Everyone at the table watched with wide eyes as they shifted their attention from me to Reese, then back again to me.

"I had no idea. That's horrible. I'm so sorry." I barely knew Violet or Reese, but already felt some affection toward them and this news made me sick to my stomach. Violet had lost a brother and Reese, a cousin—and so recently.

"Yeah—it's been a rough five months for everyone. Especially for Violet. They were so close." He half-smiled but it didn't reach his eyes. "It's funny, because they were complete opposites, but they were practically attached at the hip. Landon kind of kept Vi from being too serious, and I think Vi kept him from getting kicked out of school."

I imagined how hard it must be for them to do their senior year without him.

"Surprisingly, Vi came back to school, just a week after the accident, like nothing ever happened," Reese said.

"We all thought it was weird that she was back so soon," Kade chimed in. "We were barely back ourselves. Don't let her strong front fool you, though. One night after practice a couple of us cleaned out Landon's locker so no family would have to. When Violet found out the next day she went totally ape."

Reese shifted his attention to the group. "I haven't told you guys, but Aunt Afton told me she's not so brave at home either. I talked to her just a couple of days ago. She said she still hears Violet crying in her room—never breaks down in front of the family though. Even when they try to talk to her about it, she just shuts down. That's gotta suck . . . never talking to anyone about something like this."

I swallowed hard. "Poor Violet." The faces around the table seemed to wait for my inevitable question. I felt uncomfortable asking, but also sensed that everyone expected it. "Do you mind me asking how he died?"

"It's probably best that you hear it from us anyway," Reese said. "There's still a bunch of crap going around about how it really happened." He took a deep breath and a quick look toward the exit— making sure that Violet and Sam weren't on their way back in, I guessed.

"A bunch of us were at the river down by the railroad overpass. When we were kids we tied a rope to the bridge—we've always hung out there in the summer. We should have never been out there in April. Way too early in the season. It was raining like crazy that day too." Reese shifted his weight in the seat. "The thing that kills me the most is that we've been there probably fifty times and never had anything happen. We don't really drink—don't smoke—nothing like that. But we were stupid that night. A buddy of ours had snuck a bottle of vodka from his parents. At first, we were like, 'you're such an idiot, dude—just put it away.' Especially since Coach Rancati kicks anyone off alpine if he even hears a rumor that we've been drinking. But then someone took a swig and started passing the bottle around. We all knew we were buzzing but we thought we were fine."

Reese rubbed at one eye hard. "So a buddy swings into the river. Such a moron. The water was practically frozen. He makes it back to the bank, dripping wet and shaking, and then dares the rest of us to do it. Like total fools, we all accept the challenge. I don't know how many times we did it, but by the time the sun was down, I bet we were all on the brink of hypothermia. We'd finally had enough when I noticed that Landon was missing. Just like that, he wasn't anywhere. We looked all over the bank and even up on the tracks."

Reese paused. The crease between his brows looked foreign compared to his usually vibrant and mischievous expressions. I knew he wanted me to have their version, but I was still surprised, given the short time I'd known him, that he'd share such painful details with me.

His voice cracked. "Then it hit me that he must not have made it out. We all jumped back in and looked for him 'til we knew we had to call 911. It was two hours before they pulled Landon from the river." Reese closed his eyes and the muscles in his jaw flexed.

Garett squeezed Reese's shoulder, his blue eyes round and rimmed in moisture. "It was an accident."

All of a sudden the smell from the cigarette smoke and the food on the table turned my stomach, and I felt an immediate need for fresh air.

"Presley—are you okay? You're really pale." Violet and Sam had returned, a flush of pink on their cheeks from the chilly air.

"I'm fine," I assured them, fanning myself with a menu. "Probably just ate too much."

We all agreed to skip bowling and everyone was pretty chill on the way home, especially Chase, who was snoring in a shrimp coma. I'm sure Violet thought we were all just tired, but a heaviness hung in the air that had nothing to do with sleepiness.

Back at home, I dropped my purse softly on the floor and slid the pink Converse from my feet. Gayle was crashed on the couch, CNN droning in the background. Chase ran in, stripped down to his underwear and made his way to the fridge to rummage for a snack.

He filled his arms with a jar of green olives and a full jug of orange juice, then clomped and hummed all the way up the stairs. Gayle didn't stir. Content with his snack stash, he bolted for his room and turned on the TV—a sure sign he was set for the night.

I collapsed backward on my bed with thoughts of Reese and Violet. They were so kind and unselfish. Their lives were a nightmare but they still made time for me.

My mind was active, but my body exhausted. I fell asleep thinking of a dark river and a boy who wasn't just hallway gossip, but my new friend's brother.

Chapter Five

HUGGING AND HITTING

(PRESLEY)

Sharing rides to school with Gayle was getting old, but I didn't have the money for new tires since I'd just spent my life savings on a paint job. On the way, Gayle stopped to gas up. Chase sat in the back seat, clutching his iPad, and rocked back and forth with such force that the whole car shook. An annoying kids' show blared from the speakers, but he still held the device right next to his ear and insisted on rewinding a song about healthy snacks over and over. I searched the console hoping a pair of Chase's headphones might be there. They weren't.

Instead I found a quasi-cache of secrets, as if Gayle's car was her own safety deposit box of gross. A couple of self-help CD's about dating in your forties, a cheesy looking romance novel, and some printed-out emails from someone named Emilio who wrote in very poor English. They were sent to my mom's email address, but he called her Sylvia, not Gayle. I didn't want to know.

The gas hose clicked so I hastily folded Emilio back into a square and tucked him behind a CD titled, You Are All Woman, Own It! Flipping the visor mirror down, I acted like I had something in my eye.

My mom, in a black pencil skirt and red silk blouse, sat behind the wheel and flipped down her own mirror. I looked at her through the corner of my eye while she applied red lipstick to her thin lips.

She pressed top lip to bottom, gave herself a smoldering appraisal in the mirror, and then noticed me for the first time. "What?" she asked, as she tucked the gold tube of lipstick into her oversized purse.

"Nothing. I just . . . um . . . my eyes were burning for some reason." It wasn't a lie. My eyes were about to melt out of their sockets after watching "Sylvia" apply her lipstick while thinking of her cyber-beau, Emilio. Definitely not a lie.

"Well, quit rubbing them, you'll make it worse." She started the car and pulled onto Main. "What are your plans for lunch? I've got plenty of food if you want to come to my office," she offered.

I knew from the hours of mind-numbing loafing I'd done around her office for the past week that her mini fridge was stuffed with three things: microwavable taquitos, generic ketchup and Diet Coke. Greasy paper plates and crushed soda cans always overflowed her waste basket. The student body would never know that behind Gayle's perfect posture and iron fist lurked a woman with the nutrition sense of a ten-year-old.

"No, it's okay. I'm hanging out with some of the kids I went to Reno with now."

"Violet Blackwood was one of them, right?"

"Yeah."

"That girl's going places. You ought to nurture that friendship." Her smile faded. "But I wouldn't say the same for her cousin, Reese. He has a file three inches thick. He'll be lucky to graduate this year. Hard to believe they come from the same family."

"I'm pretty sure he's harmless, Mom. He's just goofy. Likes attention."

"He's certainly captured mine. Barely a week goes by that I don't get a complaint about him from the staff. I've already had him in the office twice and school's not even been in a month." Her mouth turned down at the corners. "Don't let that handsome face fool you into bad choices, Pres."

My stomach turned. I did not want Gayle noticing who was and who was not handsome among my peer group.

I pushed the thought from my mind by starting a fight. "It's not his face I like, Mom. It's more his bod."

She didn't take the bait, but struck back below the belt. "Hmm. Sounds like we need another talk about the birds and the bees." She

23

knitted her eyebrows and spoke in a voice that sounded like the drone of a documentary narrator. "You see Pres, when a man and a woman are truly in love, they give each other a very special type of hug . . ."

"NO! It's okay. I'm good. Really." I considered how much injury I might sustain if I leapt from the car right then. Tuck my body, protect my head. It couldn't be that bad.

Her painted lips curved into a victorious smile. "Change of subject then."

"I'm okay with that."

Chase's seatbelt clicked. We both looked back to find him unbuckled and attempting to open his door. I laughed. "Sorry bud, that's what child locks are for." He gave a screech of frustration.

———

Two girls who'd had it out for me the last couple weeks were standing near my locker when Chase and I came around the corner. My money was on them for the eggs and the tires. I made up my mind to ignore them as usual, but they moved their bodies in front of my locker.

"Look, it's Princess and her retard brother," the dark-haired one sneered.

I guessed her aggressiveness stemmed from embarrassment. Before she knew Chase had autism, she, like many girls at Truckee High, was smitten with his good looks and aloofness. After a few days of not-so-subtle crushing on him, she found out that he had autism. Although she tried to deny ever being interested, it was too late. People had already teased her about it. So, to clarify to the entire student body that she never liked him, she'd stooped to this kind of drama.

My heart beat against my ribs and my stomach rolled like it did every time someone was cruel to Chase. I never tried to reason with willful ignorance.

"Excuse me. I need to get in my locker," I said flatly. The whole thing suddenly felt ridiculous. Her blocking my way, throwing jabs toward my autistic brother. What were they going to do? Slap my hand if I tried to open it?

The girl's eyes were small. "You're not excused."

"Wow," I read her name that was embroidered on her cheer jacket, "Megan. Just wow." I couldn't help but smile. It was just so sixth-grade. "Nobody blames you, you know. He is really handsome."

And then she shoved me. Hard. I fell back against Chase and we tumbled to the floor in an awkward heap. My landing was cushioned by Chase but he wasn't as lucky; his head flung back and cracked sickeningly against the floor. He let out a shriek of pain. Blood streamed from the roots of his wavy hair and down one side of his face. He frantically rubbed his injury and then wiped the blood on his T-shirt.

Megan's eyes widened and her mouth hung open. I could see the retainer on her teeth.

I pushed off the floor with one hand and threw my fist across Megan's face with my other. I felt a dark elation as her head jerked to the left. Before she could react, I slammed her up against my locker, cop-style. Wrenching her arm behind her back I seethed, "Is your life really so pathetic that you have to pick on kids who can't defend themselves?"

Bullying Chase crossed the line.

"Does it make you feel good to see him cry like that?" Chase rocked on the floor, weeping.

A crowd of students stood by and gawked. Megan struggled against me, and clawed at my arms with her fake nails, leaving deep scratches as she attempted to free herself from my hold.

"What's going on here?" The voice startled me from my rage and I turned and looked into the very developed pectoral muscles of Reese Blackwood. Reese looked at Megan and then back to me. My anger with Megan gradually evolved into humiliation as Reese assessed the situation. "What happened? What did you do, Megan?"

Inside, I crumpled. I wanted Reese's attention, but not like this. I released Megan and she stumbled back, rubbing her neck and breathing noisily. I just wanted to get Chase to the school nurse, and get as far from the train wreck as possible.

Megan opened and closed her mouth like a pony-tailed fish, and Reese put his thick arm around my shoulder. I had the urge to turn my face into his chest.

"I swear," he said, offering Chase a hand and pulling him to a standing position. "What is your problem with Presley? Give her a break, eh? You and your little mob have been nothing but hostile toward her since she got here. And now you're picking on Chase? I have to say, it's not attractive." He gave my upper arm an affectionate squeeze, likely adding insult to Megan's injury.

Her face turned a hot shade of purple. "I don't have a problem with her. She seems to have a problem with us. In case you didn't notice, she practically broke my arm." The crowd lingered despite the approaching tardy bell. I could only imagine the versions of the fight that would circulate.

"You're a bad liar," Reese countered, disgusted. "Don't think everyone here doesn't know you're the one that ruined the paint job on her Jeep with your little egg stunt." Reese performed a cursory examination to find where Chase was bleeding from. He shook his head. "And I hear the police are looking for the ones that slashed her tires last week. Now you assault a kid with autism?"

Megan's painted eyes widened. "Screw you, Reese!" She turned on her heel and stalked off, trailed by her friends who looked over their shoulders in mock shock from Reese's accusation.

Perfect. That was the exact thing I needed to diffuse the situation with those chicks—exposure of their crimes in front of the whole school by a disapproving heartthrob.

The group of bystanders finally disassembled, and Reese wrapped his other arm around Chase's shoulder, in a comforting gesture. Chase continued to whimper and wiped a smear of blood on the sleeve of Reese's T-shirt. Reese didn't even acknowledge it.

"You guys okay?" His voice was sincere, and his dark eyebrows showed concern.

I shook my head. "Not really. I know this looks insane." I studied the gouges on my arm. "But, people are rude to Chase all the time. Just the other day a grown man told him off at an ice cream shop. At an ice cream shop! Because he misunderstood Chase's hand flapping as a threat. But even that guy backed off once I explained that Chase has autism." I shook my head. "I just can't stomach that Megan knows he has autism and still treats him like that."

"I know," Reese said. "She's a piece of work."

Chase stopped crying and wiped his nose with his arm.

"Get your stuff and let's get him to the nurse," Reese said.

After a thorough examination, the nurse determined that Chase merely had an abrasion and told me and Reese not to worry—that head wounds often bled a lot even if they weren't serious. I was sure Megan would be nervous I would rat on her. She deserved to be ratted on. But, I was also worried she might twist our little hallway tumble to be my fault, so I told the nurse that Chase tripped. You would think having your mom as the principal would have some perks in the avoiding punishment department, but I could see Gayle being extra harsh just to appear impartial in front of the staff. Besides, Reese told me not to worry. He had some ideas on how to get even with Megan.

Chapter Six

(PRESLEY)

I loved and I hated Mr. Price's government class. With a voice that could be heard three doors down, he was at least 6'4", and he arranged our seats according to grades—bad grades up front, good grades in back. He hated the president, and we heard his reasons why almost every morning. His was the hardest class I had; we were expected to absorb twice as much material than in my other classes. I dreaded and appreciated the challenge.

I sat in the back row with Violet and Sam and a tall jock with an extra toothy smile everyone called "J." Reese sat two rows in front of me, a little to the left. We were late today as was Mr. Price, which was nothing short of a legitimate miracle. Looking disheveled, Price hurriedly stalked into the classroom and threw his newspaper on his desk with a whap. Squinting over the rim of his cup, he took a sip of his steaming coffee and draped his Laker's jacket over the chair. He grabbed a stack of transparencies that were obviously our notes for the day and barked, "J—hit the lights!"

"J" obediently jumped up and turned off the lights just as the overhead projector clicked on. I smirked to myself. I'd never even seen an overhead projector before Price's class. The man was old school. He still used a typewriter to hen peck his tests and quizzes for the class and seemed to shun any technology post-1985.

We started taking notes on how a bill becomes a law. Three pages in, I glanced out the window for a break. I never noticed before that this window looked straight out over the parking lot where I had yelled at that scary hot guy. Whom I'd never met. Who then chased

28

me down. The memory of him at the tree line was clear and the wild intensity in his eyes after I called him out was unnerving. I couldn't help feeling he would materialize any moment to finish unsettled business. I had to admit I was a little disappointed when he disappeared from the courtyard at lunch. I'd looked around for him at school too. He was a mystery.

"Learn it, people!" Price boomed, jerking me from my thoughts. "There will be no multiple-choice or true-or-false. Learn how your nation functions so that when you grow up and get a joker of a president like we have now, you'll have something to say about it." His thundering pulled me back to my notes, and I scrambled to copy the last few lines before he switched the transparency.

By the sixth page of notes my arm and hand muscles ached. In front of me, I saw Garett pass a note to Reese. He read it, suppressed a laugh, then looked back at Garett and whispered, "You serious?"

Garett flashed a wicked smile, gestured to Mr. Price with his head and whispered, "I dare you." They considered each other for a brief moment and I could tell by the impish grin on Reese's face he had decided to do whatever it was Garett had dared him to do.

I refocused on my notes but realized I'd missed too much just as Price switched the transparency again. Violet noticed my panic and whispered, "It's okay. I'll catch you up after school. Library."

"Thank you," I mouthed.

Garett and Reese kept trading mischievous glances and it became harder for me to pay attention. Reese raised his hand. "Excuse me, Mr. Price?"

Price turned around on his stool by the projector, scowled at Reese and gruffly inquired, "Number one or number two?"

"No, I don't need to go to the restroom, sir. I just need to ask you a question." He stood up and started to walk toward Price who looked all what the heck. Reese closed the gap between him and Price, with every eye in the classroom watching.

"Spit it out, Blackwood."

"Sir, can I give you a hug?" Before Price could respond, Reese crouched over and gingerly laid his head on Price's shoulder, nuzzled his nose into his teacher's neck, and tenderly embraced the most abrasive man I'd ever met.

Mr. Price rocked back on his stool and bellowed as his coffee spilled all over his slacks and splashed onto the projector. The veto process suddenly blurred from Price's block-like script into a brown blurry puddle on the screen. The class roared.

"GO! Get out of here, Blackwood!" Mr. Price held his arms up like a ticked off scarecrow and shook droplets of coffee from his fingertips onto the cringing students next to him. Reese knew the routine. He turned and walked to the door to pay a visit to my mom at the office. He winked at me on his way by, and as he opened the door to leave, I heard Garett mutter through a strangled laugh, "So worth it, dude."

I didn't see Reese in English or at lunch. Apparently he was spending the day in the office. When the last bell rang, I headed to the library to catch up on my notes with Violet. I found her already bent over some books at a table near the reference section. I took the empty chair across from her and began to hunt for my incomplete government notes. "Thanks for doing this."

She looked up at me and I was struck by her beauty. Not a conventional beauty, but she had an understated, effortless glow to her. Her black hair was pulled back in a sleek ponytail and the way her glasses framed her eyes was a perfect meld of trendiness and class. She smiled at me, then picked up her vibrating cell to read a text.

"Reese is still in the office," she sighed. "Since it's his third detention, he may get sent home for three days." She rolled her eyes and texted something back. Then she threw her phone into her bag. "He's such a cabbage."

I checked my phone to see if Reese might have texted me too. Nothing. "You have to admit though, that stunt was pretty classic."

Violet's smile never reached her eyes. "Funny, yes. Stupid, absolutely. Boys just don't think about consequences, I guess."

I had the feeling she was thinking about more than just Reese's stunt.

"Boys," I agreed.

Violet straightened. "Have you started your paper for Price's class yet? It's not due for another week, but the resources in this library are sometimes limited, so I would get a jump on it if I were you, before all of the good material is taken. He's so archaic; don't even think about citing an online reference. He won't accept it."

"Yikes."

Violet flipped to the back cover of her book and took out a piece of paper with some titles written on it. "Here, these were pretty good. I had enough material without needing to use the last two if you want to start there. I'm pretty sure they are all shelved in the back. You go find what you need, and I'll flip through your notes and fill in the missing spots."

Walking past rows of books, I studied the paper and headed to the back of the library. Although this library was much smaller than the one at my old school, it was no easier to navigate because of the confusing layout. The further back I traveled, the more quiet and musty it became. I had little luck finding the books, which tempted me to go back and get Violet, but I didn't because she was already helping me with my notes. I'd been through the section three times and could only find one of the books. "Humph. I'm going to need some help," I mumbled.

As I walked back toward the main aisle, I poked my head out to see if there was anyone who could assist me. I was surprised to see Reese walking away and around the corner to where Violet was. "Reese," I called, and jogged after him. He didn't answer.

Disappointedly, when I made it back to the front, there was nobody there except the librarian, who was shutting off her computer with keys in her hand. On the table, Violet had left me a note:

> *Presley, Sorry I had to go. My uncle called me and he was pretty mad at Reese.*
> *He actually towed his truck and told me to go get him out of the office and take his butt home. I left your notes in your bag.*
> *See you tomorrow,*
> *—Vi.*

I was a bit confused at Vi's note because hadn't I just seen Reese?

The librarian startled. "OH! Oh, honey you scared me!" She pressed her flattened palm into her chest. "I thought I was the only one left in here! I'm glad you came out when you did or I would have shut the lights off on you. The library closes thirty minutes after the bell, you know." She readjusted the twist of hair at the base of her neck and pinched it with a plastic clip.

"Oh, I'm sorry," I said. "I must have lost track of the time." My eyes scanned the room for Reese. "I didn't think it was that late because I saw other students still in here."

"Other students?" She examined me more closely and then looked around the empty room as if to demonstrate her point. I followed her gaze. It was true, there wasn't anyone in the library but her and me.

"Well, I'm pretty sure I just saw my friend a second ago walking by here, and that's why I came out—to catch up with him."

"Well, I'm sorry, but I don't know anything about that. I locked the main doors ten minutes ago and if your friend was here, he would need my key to get out." She held up her clump of keys and then walked over to the doors and unlocked them for me. She held the door open with an expectant expression. I grabbed my bag and left, more confused than I'd been in the reference section.

I wandered down the hall toward Gayle's office; my mind struggling to make sense of what just happened. I knew I had seen a boy. I thought it was Reese, but from what Violet had said in her note, that couldn't have been him. But someone was there. Whoever he was.

A movement in my peripheral startled me, but it was only my reflection in the glass of a trophy case. I walked closer to the wood cabinet and examined the photos inside. A diversion, even if it was a small one. Dropping my bag at my feet, I leaned in for a better look. There were pictures of championship teams from when the school opened back in the fifties all the way up to last year. Baton twirlers in knee high boots and flipped up hair smiled at me in black and white. In 1956 the boys won the state championship for basketball. The best part of that photo was how the coach held a pipe in his teeth. I laughed out loud at how ridiculously high the shorts were on those poor boys' uniforms. A group in cardigans and horn-rimmed glasses held a trophy for Academic Olympics. I had a habit of searching for interesting faces in photos. There was a leggy girl with blunt cut bangs and a tight tank top who'd won the 100-meter hurdles in 1972. Proud football teams with serious faces held game balls and muscle bound wrestlers flexed and held their hands behind their backs. Over the decades, girls' hairstyles went from fluffy to flat and back again. Near the end of the cabinet and the timeline, I eventually began to recognize people.

The middle shelf displayed a photo of the champion alpine ski team from last winter. "J" was standing in the back row with a nose so sunburned it almost matched the red team jackets. To his right was Reese, holding his arm straight up in the air, hand frozen in an eternal hang loose sign. His hair was cropped close like I knew it to be, and he hadn't bothered to take the snow goggles off of his eyes. In what I was sure would be a fruitless effort, I scanned each face looking for one that would be as beautiful as his. To my surprise, I didn't have to look long. Kneeling front and center and holding a gleaming golden trophy, was the crazy boy from the parking lot, looking so gorgeous it hurt to breathe.

Even if I wanted to, I wouldn't be able to not study his face. In many ways, he looked like Reese. They shared the same thick black hair, though this boy's was longer—similar gleaming teeth and dark eyebrows. Reese's eyes, from the handful of times I'd looked into them, were warm, brown and friendly. This other boy had penetrating blue eyes which looked happy enough, but flatly demanded notice. They each shared broad shoulders, tall frames, and an attractive angled jaw, Reese's being a bit softer around the edges.

I searched for more photos of the boy. Could he have been in more than one sport? My eyes quickly passed over faces, eager to see his again. Finally, gratefully, on the top shelf sitting next to a set of black and red goggles was an 8x10 photo of only him. Glad for the deserted hallway, I was free to ogle this new face for as long as I wanted. I searched for a name to identify him, but could find nothing. As if he wasn't mysterious enough already. I scanned the hall in both directions to make sure I was alone, took out my phone and snapped a picture of his portrait. The result was perfect. I smiled in spite of myself. "So we meet again, psychopathic ski stud. You're hot; I'll give you that."

My phone rang, startling me. "Hey Mom, what's up?"

"Where are you?" Her voice sounded tired and impatient.

"I just got done in the library. Are you done for the night?"

"Not really, but I'm going home anyway. Ready for some mind-less TV and taquitos."

Translation, I'm going to crash while you take care of Chase.

"Don't forget the Diet Coke," I added derisively.

"What do you take me for? I'm drinking one right now."

"You need to lay off the sauce."

"Meet me at the car."

"Be right there." I rolled my eyes and slid my phone into my back pocket. As I took my first step toward the door, the hairs on the back of my neck rose up—charged, just a heartbeat before somebody screamed my name.

Chapter Seven

CLASH

(LANDON)

I have to talk to her," I whispered. It was thrilling to contemplate the possibility of communicating with someone other than balanced, fixed, unbending James. His inability to become excited over anything was often maddening. Especially today.

James stood before me, gray eyes steady. His thick straw-colored hair always seemed like it wanted to stand on end, but it was parted on the side and grudgingly allowed itself to be tamed.

"The dead don't speak with the living," James said unemotionally. The corner of his mouth twitched. "This is, in my opinion, a moot point."

We stood together at the south end of the junior/senior hall, hidden in shadow. Hiding felt foreign and somewhat restrictive after months of complete freedom. Presley was a short distance away, oblivious to our presence, studying some photos in a glass trophy case. Occasionally, she'd giggle to herself.

"James!" I whispered in a strained voice. "How is this a moot point? You know she saw me. She yelled right at me."

James considered my face, a patient smile on his lips.

"Well?"

"Oh, I'm sorry," he said, his eyebrows raised. "Was I supposed to respond?" Someone else may have mistaken his comment as sarcastic, but knowing him the way I did, I was sure he was sincere.

"I'm not so convinced it was you she insulted. There were several people in the parking lot, Landon."

"Why are you playing games with me? You saw how she reacted to me. Tell me why, and I'll drop it."

James hesitated. "The truth is . . ." He paused. "I don't know why."

"But you do admit she saw me."

"Possibly." James scratched his chin stubble.

"And I have to know why."

James' forehead wrinkled. "I've never experienced this with anyone else." He hesitated, and then his face brightened a bit. "Of course, you are by far the most unique and stubborn case I've had."

I shifted my attention back to Presley and inched a little closer to her. She was engrossed in one of the displays.

Reaching in her pocket, she pulled out her phone. James started to say something, but I motioned for his silence. "I think she's taking a picture of something." With an electric elation, I realized what she was doing. "I think it's my picture."

Presley smiled dubiously and stared at the glowing screen. "So we meet again, psychopathic ski stud. You're hot; I'll give you that."

I spun around to James triumphantly.

James's face clouded over, dampening my excitement. "Do not approach the girl," he ordered. The force of his command made my stomach clench.

"But—you just saw that! What is your problem?"

"Landon, listen to me. Our dimensions are not meant to mix. They are separate for a reason. Do not approach the girl," he repeated.

Our conversation was interrupted by the chorus from one of my favorite songs, her cell phone ringer, I realized. She placed it to her ear, "Hey Mom, what's up? I just got done in the library . . ."

"She's getting ready to leave!" The chance to speak to her was slipping away. And what were the odds I'd ever find her alone again?

My eyes cemented onto Presley, who retreated toward the glass exit doors. "I'm sorry, James. I know I'm supposed to listen to you, but I can't let her get away this time." Without waiting for permission, I started on a dead run and screamed with all I had, "Presley!"

She whipped around to face my way, but a second before our eyes met, a strong set of determined arms wrapped around me, locked over my chest, and pinned my arms against my sides. My equilibrium rolled. The hallway and Presley became one dizzying swirl, like riding the Tilt-a-Whirl at those cheap carnivals. To my surprise, I felt nauseated.

The warm, dank hallway dissolved into crisp, cool air. I struggled to free myself from James's grip.

"Why the hell are we here?" I demanded, jerking my shoulders left then right. "Let me go."

But James kept me in his ironclad hold, forcing me to stay. To stay at a place I hadn't been in five months. Somewhere I refused to visit or even think of. We stood on a patch of grass framed in concrete. At my feet were wilted flowers, pictures, and half-burned candles.

The headstone read:

LANDON KREW BLACKWOOD
BELOVED SON, BROTHER, UNCLE, AND FRIEND
UNTIL WE MEET AGAIN.

My grave.

Chapter Eight

(PRESLEY)

My name still echoed, bouncing off the hard surface of the floor and rows of red lockers. Flyers on a bulletin board fluttered as if startled by the sound of that voice. The hall was empty. I slowly backed up, scanning for a sign of someone. Anyone.

—

Gayle sat in the driver's seat, digging in her purse with a taquito hanging out of her lips like a greasy cigar. "It's like I'm completely senile. Did you notice if I had my sunglasses on when we got out of the car this morning?"

I knew I should have answered, but my ears still rung with that voice from the hall. Gayle looked at me expectantly, her mascara smudged after a long day.

"I don't remember. I don't think you did," I finally offered, detached.

She sighed and bit off the end of the taquito. "Maybe they're in my briefcase. Will you grab it out from behind my seat?" she asked through a mouthful.

I reached back to retrieve her case, but it wasn't there. Only Chase, unsurprisingly rocking out to the same song from that morning. "Your case isn't back here, Mom."

"It's not?" She groaned. "Run back to my office and grab it for me. I have to have it. And look on my desk for my glasses, please." She took the keys out of the ignition, found the master key and held it out, pinched in her rosy nails.

They dangled between us, but I couldn't bring myself to take them from her. I was not going back in that building alone. I didn't want her going in alone either, for that matter. "Come with me," I said, feeling sheepish.

"Come with you? What, are you like five years old? Come on." She dropped the keys in my lap. "I'm tired Pres, and someone needs to stay here with Chase."

"He can come with us." I didn't pick up the keys.

"What's the big deal? Just run in. You know your young legs are yearning for the exercise," she whined.

"They really aren't, Mom."

"They are yearning, Presley." She squeezed my thigh, and I brushed her hand away.

"I'll just take Chase in with me," I posed.

"No," she said, the patience waning in her voice. "He's going to get frustrated if we make him go back in there. He thinks his school day is already done." Gayle tipped her loose French roll back against the headrest, closed her eyes, and spoke through a yawn. "Is this about the girls who screwed up your Jeep? Nobody is going to mess with you. Everyone's gone home," she added wearily. "The school is empty."

Right.

The metal handles on the heavy glass doors were hot from the afternoon sun. I pulled my sleeve over my hand to open one. Once inside the dark hallway, I looked over my shoulder and tried to quiet the thumping in my heart. I hurried to Gayle's office. Once inside, I flipped the light on and locked the door behind me, bringing my anxiety down a notch. The scuffed leather briefcase was open on her desk with papers half spilled out. She must be tired. I gathered what looked important and stuffed it in the case. A hiss of air escaped the cushion on the rolling chair as I sat to hunt through the drawers for her glasses. I didn't find what I was looking for in the first drawer, but I found something even better. A glossy 3x5 photo of Reese Blackwood was paper-clipped to a dog-eared and over-stuffed folder.

His own high school mugshot attached to his rap sheets. I'd just found my entertainment for the night.

The photo was obviously of a much younger Reese. I guessed he was probably a freshman, judging by his thinner neck and less developed jaw. Still, the cockiness and good looks were abundant. My phone rang. Geez Gayle, give me a minute. I answered without checking the number. "I'm coming," I said, a slight edge to my voice.

"Can I come too?" I should have checked the number. Reese's voice was playful, but a spark of embarrassment flickered in me as if he knew what I was up to. You know, stealing his personal information so I could stalk him in the creepy privacy of my own home.

"Hey. Where are you? The slammer?" I said, trying to make my voice sound natural.

"Just about; my dad's pretty ticked off. He's all worked up about me soiling the family reputation. It's not like the entire town doesn't know I'm a monumental screw off."

I hefted his fat file and tucked it under my arm, its weight proof of his statement. Then I gathered up the briefcase and glasses that were lying in plain sight the whole time.

"That stunt with Price was quite heartwarming. I didn't know you cared for him so much." I said.

"Yeah, we're basically BFFs."

"It shows."

"So anyway, if my dad will let me out of the house, do you mind if I stop by a little later?"

It was heartbreaking how at ease he seemed, while my guts were flip-flopping.

"Um . . . kay. That should be fine," I said, failing to match his easy voice.

"I have a little surprise for you, and I think you'd be glad to get it sooner than later."

"Um . . . okay." *Idiot!* Did I have any other words in my vocabulary?

I heard the smile in Reese's voice. "All right. Well like I said, I'm not even sure my dad will cooperate, but hopefully I'll see you tonight."

I managed to hide Reese's file by stuffing it in the back of my jeans and covering it with my shirt. When I got back to the car, Mom was passed out in the driver's seat—mouth gaping. So much for supervising Chase, who thankfully had not climbed into the front seat and escaped through a child-lockless door. Slipping the file into my bag was so easy it was silly.

When we got home, I offered to take Chase up to my room with me for a while. Gayle, still tired, eagerly accepted my suggestion. In part, my overture was out of kindness—to give her a rest. Admittedly though, a larger part was to go somewhere private where I could look into Reese's file.

Chase flopped onto my bed and wrapped himself in his pricey fuzzy blanket from one of those new age stores at the mall. He pulled up a puzzle game on his iPad and hummed contentedly as he worked to construct an airplane. I hefted the file from my bag and opened the cover of the folder. The stack of papers inside was thick. Like Gone With the Wind thick. They were arranged chronologically, and I thumbed through them starting with his earliest infractions. Unavoidable laughter erupted. The crap this boy had pulled.

Filling the fountain in the school courtyard with soap—an attached picture of bubbly foam mounded up to such heights, it spilled out onto the ground and covered most of the courtyard. Also attached was an invoice for the cost of draining and cleaning the fountain.

Next, an account of the hallway so thickly webbed with string tied from locker to locker, nobody could walk through. In his sophomore year, he and his cousin—a pang of sadness at reading the name, "Landon,"—had covered the entire principal's office in aluminum foil. Everything coated in wrinkly silver—the chair, the desk, the walls, even the pencil sharpener.

Reese and Landon, Landon and Reese. They were quite the dynamic duo—the pattern of their joint pranks clear. It wasn't hard to wonder how much Reese must miss him.

I turned to the top of the stack—the most recent documentation was a page of handwritten notes from the school counselor. I scanned the information. Reese's grades had dropped at the end of his junior year. He'd missed two weeks of school after his cousin's death. He'd refused to train with both the football and alpine ski teams over the summer, a decision, according to the counselor, to avoid activities that would painfully remind him of Landon. A couple of warnings from some teachers that he would face suspension if he didn't clean up his language and exercise more patience with his classmates. That last bit surprised me; I'd never witnessed him be anything but likeable and charismatic.

Guilt spread slowly like poured honey. I took the file to entertain myself and learn more about him. But now, my spying felt cheap and uninvited. I stashed the file back in my bag and lay back, one hand patting Chase's leg, wondering what I'd gotten myself into.

Chapter Nine

GRAVE INTENTIONS

(LANDON)

I wrenched my shoulders, this time throwing my chest into it, struggling to break James's grip. He remained still, arms clamped around my torso. No matter how much I fought, his steel vice would not loosen.

"I'm not letting you go until you give me your word that when I do, you will not leave." James spoke softly but firmly, his jaw parallel with mine, his voice close to my ear.

"But you know I don't come here," I seethed through clenched teeth.

"Yes, I know. But you are walking the line, Landon, and I think a reminder is in order this evening. Do I have your word?"

"I don't come here."

"Your word."

"Fine," I said, shaking free of him and swallowing hard.

I faced the choice of staring at my headstone or at my guide who was hugely disappointed with my disobedience. The choice was easy. I looked at James.

The usual pleasantness gone from his face, he stood with his hands stuffed in his pockets, and appraised me with sad and tired eyes.

"Why did you bring me here?" I asked. James was upset, but I didn't think my actions warranted such an extreme maneuver. I spoke coolly, attempting to stifle my aggravation. James knew that this of all places. My eyes warily scanned a large swath around the cemetery. The sun was low in the sky and a pinkish haze filtered through the towering pines. Long shadows extended from almost everything—the cast iron fences, the statues and headstones; everything had its shadow but James and me. "Why are you punishing me?" I asked. "It's not like I . . ."

"You nearly stopped the earth from spinning, my friend," James interrupted. "That's what you did."

"That's a bit melodramatic, don't you think?"

"Maybe." James smiled but it was fleeting and quickly gave way to a grieved expression. "It pains me that you think punishment has anything to do with this." He shrugged, and shook his head, looking weary. "I have done my best these five months, but this girl has thrown a wrench in your progress. It's almost as if you've forgotten that you drowned in the Truckee River last April."

"I haven't forgotten; I assure you."

"Yet you seem to have. Why, when I've repeatedly warned you, would you attempt to speak to her? To what end?" James reached up and raked his hair back. "I don't understand it. Your course for progression was locked. You committed to leave. Because she can see you does not change that you are dead."

I contemplated his words, but they held little weight. Everything was different now. It was like his counsel expired the moment she acknowledged me in the parking lot.

I hated disappointing him though, because he'd been nothing but kind and supportive.

"I'm sorry," I said. But the words were mostly hollow and James knew it.

"You need to understand that I'm here not only to guide you, but to protect you."

"From what?" I snorted. I motioned to my grave, frustrated. Because what could be worse than dead?

James's eyes didn't follow my gesture. Instead, he deliberately looked across the cemetery, his gaze landing on a handful of graves in the shadows. The tombstones were adorned with perched gargoyles.

"What?" I questioned impatiently.

"Look closer, Landon."

I focused more intently. Other than a few ravens roosting in the trees, I couldn't guess what James could be referring to. Then, I realized what had appeared to be lifeless statues on the headstones were actually moving human forms. Horror crawled through me.

Clothed in shades of ash and ink, their skin was pallid and translucent in the poorly lit cemetery. The largest of the group dismounted his stone and appraised me—clearly aware that I was informed of their presence.

"What are they?" I asked James, repressing a sick feeling.

"Vigilum. The watching dead."

Like cats, they slid from their resting places and paced with whitish-blue eyes fixed on me. Their continual movement made it hard to decipher their number, but there were enough of them.

I turned to James. "You've got my attention."

He looked over my shoulder toward the spectral horde and studied them suspiciously.

"Your death was unexpected. By the time I sensed it and arrived at the river to support you, they were only seconds behind me."

His words overpowered me. Before this moment, I thought James was the only person keeping tabs on me.

"It's a race, Landon. It always is when the death is unforeseen. As your guide, I knew when your death was imminent. That's my right.

"The Vigilum sensed it as well," he continued. "They hunt it like a shark would pursue the scent of blood. The careless behavior you exhibited the night of your death was like a siren call to them."

A pang of regret. I had been careless. A cold fact I wished I could change every day since my death. The amount of if onlys was heaping. But what a bunch of freaky dead guys wanted with me or why they cared that I died in a reckless way was beyond me. James said it was a race. But a race for what?

He must have sensed my confusion. "Think about the night you died. You went from drunk to dead in a matter of moments. You never expected it. Once your soul was separated from your body, you were confused. Understandably it was difficult for you to process the reality of your death. That made you the ideal prey."

My mind revisited those first moments after I died. How I'd watched in baffled horror as my friends and Reese frantically thrashed through the freezing river, looking for me and screaming my name. "What do you mean by prey?" I demanded. "Just tell me what they want."

"Your passage," James answered grimly. "They want it and they will do anything to get it."

"What's a passage?" I probed, feeling like James was speaking a foreign language.

"Your passage is a decision. It's like a ticket, Landon. You only have one. You use it to travel from this life to the next. They are Vigilum because they gave their passage away. Having done such, they are now imprisoned in this realm with no opportunity to move on."

"Why would they do that?" I watched them as they moved, more like animals than humans—restless and predatory.

"There are many reasons," James said cryptically.

I steeled myself to make eye contact with one. The tallest one, a lanky man that looked to be in his early twenties, gave the impression of being the clear leader.

"What's his story?" I asked James, subtly gesturing to the man.

James hesitated, but then yielded. "His name is Liam." James searched for the right way to phrase something. "He lived a very dark life."

I questioned James with my eyes and reluctantly, he continued. "When he died, the realization of all his misdeeds became unbearably clear. An experienced Vigilum seized the opportunity to deceive him. She convinced Liam that punishment in the next life would be much harder to endure than to stay. She was wrong, of course, but he believed her and so he granted her his passage within hours of his death."

Like observing a gruesome accident, I forced myself to look at him for the third time. In life, I can't imagine he'd have drawn much notice. His features were weak, his hair mousy beige, and his body too thin for his tall frame. But his eyes, washed pale and icy, were lethal. I sensed the hunt acutely.

James exhaled forcefully. "All Vigilum have their reasons for staying, Landon. I fear Presley will be yours."

Chapter Ten

GIFT

(PRESLEY)

Reese called at 4:47 to say he was on his way to my house. At 4:49 I panicked at what a pigsty my room was. I hadn't considered he could end up in there until it was too late. Small patches of dark wood floor were visible under the heaps of clothes, shoes, books, and papers strewn all over my room. I took a quick moment to triage the situation, and decided first to target the dirty socks and pajamas crumpled next to my bed—and the bra hanging on the doorknob. Deciphering what was clean and what was dirty was taking too long, so I opened the mirrored closet door and began to push, snowplow-style, the entire contents of my room onto the already cluttered floor of my closet. I hastily made my bed, not bothering to straighten out the sheet that was wadded at the foot of it before parachuting my wrinkled comforter over the mattress. Good enough.

I replaced my leggings with my favorite pair of jeans and pulled a snug long sleeved tee over my camisole.

Smooth tones of an R&B song and the crunch of gravel announced Reese's arrival. I hadn't devised a casual way of telling Gayle that her archnemesis was paying a social call, so when she answered the door before I could get to it I wasn't surprised to see her turn around—face like an over-stewed prune. She sucked her teeth in a way that made her look like she was adjusting dentures and said, "Your friend is here." Reese stood still in the doorway, eyebrows raised and lips clamped shut. He wore a red plaid flannel, rolled to the elbows.

A soft current of air swept through the open door and carried his spicy, clean scent that made me dizzy. Gayle put a hand on her hip and waited for me to say something. Before I could, Chase saw the usually locked front door open and took the opportunity to make a run for it. Reese caught him around his middle and playfully tried to wrestle him back inside. But Chase wasn't having it. He pulled Reese's arm to his mouth and bit down hard.

"Oh, hey!" Reese said, jerking away and rubbing the spot.

Chase took advantage of the brief moment Reese let go of him and bolted down the porch stairs. Then Reese quickly turned, leaped down all of the steps at once and caught up to Chase, who was trying every door on Reese's truck. Finally, he found the driver's side unlocked, jumped in, and began fiddling with the radio buttons.

I joined them at the truck, my face pulsing with heat. "I'm sorry," I said to Reese. I squeezed myself between Reese and the door and pulled Chase's hand from the buttons. "Come on, Chase. Back to the house."

"No, it's cool," Reese laughed. "What kind of music does he like?"

"Anything, really, but he's a huge Taylor Swift fan. Oh, and he loves Patsy Cline." *Shoot me now. Somebody just please shoot me now. I can't believe he just bit Reese.*

Reese pulled out his phone, activating the Bluetooth in his truck. "Well, I don't have Patsy Cline, but maybe I can help you out with the Tay . . ." Before Reese could finish, Chase snatched the phone from his hand, opened the music app and started scrolling through songs.

"Brandon Flowers, eh? Good taste, bro," Reese gave a friendly slap to Chase on the back, and I noticed a purple oval bruise already forming on his arm.

Oh, geez. Could this have gone any worse?

If the bite was throbbing, Reese gave no indication. He turned to me and said, "It's totally cool if he wants to hang in my truck for a bit and listen to music."

I looked back at Gayle, who was still standing in the doorway.

"I'll watch him. Give me a second," she said. She disappeared inside and then quickly reappeared with a blanket and her laptop. She settled into a wood rocking chair and looked at us over her glasses frames. "You two go do whatever." She shooed us with a flick of her hand.

"You wanna take a little walk with me?" He pointed over his shoulder toward the fence line.

"Sure." *Anything to put this mortifying situation out of my mind.*

His brown eyes smiled through dark lashes, and he reached out and hooked a finger through my belt loop and pulled me toward the forest. We found the trail that followed the fence line, a narrow ribbon of matted grass, worn down by my morning runs. I had run this path dozens of times since our move to Truckee. Runs were my favorite part of the day because it was okay to shut off the two heaviest things I carried: school, and the weight of providing much of Chase's care. This was the first time anyone had ever joined me on the trail, and we soon discovered the path was too narrow to walk side by side.

"Ladies first," he said.

I led the way westward, down the slope heading toward the river. Even though I couldn't see the water through the trees, I could taste the cool dampness in the air.

"Presley," Reese said.

For the second time that day, someone called my name, causing the hair on the back of my neck to rise up and tingle. I stopped abruptly, and turned to face him. I felt like I was back at the trophy case. That voice. The tone was so familiar, but the desperation in it, obviously absent.

I blurted out, "Were you at the school today? After school, I mean. Were you still in the building?" The accusatory tone in my voice was plain.

His eyebrows pushed together. "For a little bit. But then I left with Violet."

"Did you . . ." I looked in his eyes and saw no flicker of comprehension of what I was talking about. "Never mind." I turned around and started walking again, this time faster as my mind replayed that voice again and again. I stopped once more so unexpectedly that Reese didn't have time to slow down before bumping into me. I turned and searched his face with all the discernment I could muster. He had to be lying. I saw him in the library. At least, I thought I did.

"Are you sure you weren't at the school?"

"No. I was not at the school. Ask Violet, she's the one that drug me out of the office by my earlobe."

"You're not messing with me? You weren't messing with me earlier today, in the library and in the hall?"

Tears pooled in my eyes. I'd had enough of people tormenting me for entertainment. The face of the boy in the parking lot flashed across the stage of my mind again. I closed the curtain on him.

Reese's face melted into concern and his voice softened. "No, Pres, I wouldn't mess with you. Come here." He gathered me up into a hug so quickly I didn't have time to think about how to feel about it. He softly pressed my head to his chest with his hand and laid his cheek on the top of my hair. "Look, I know it hasn't been easy for you, coming here. Some people at school have been straight up piranhas."

"It has pretty much sucked." My voice was thick with emotion.

"Aw, Pres, don't cry! Don't let them make you cry. You won't have to worry about them anymore. I've taken care of it."

"What does that mean?"

"Don't worry about it."

Then he held me and started to sway back and forth like a slow dance. Of course it wasn't just the crazy girls at school that were upsetting me, but I couldn't very well tell Reese about mystery voices and the disappearing boy in the library. He took me by the shoulders and pulled me to face him. I pushed the last of my tears out with my fingertips and used the back of my hand to dry the ones that had collected under my jaw. He took my hand and led me the rest of the way down the path to the river's edge.

My running path ran alongside a thin stretch of rocky shore. Luckily, there was a boulder smooth and wide enough for us to sit next to each other. I'd sat on it many times, but never with anyone else. The lodge pole pines had a warm, sweet smell from baking in the last of the afternoon sun. The fragrance collided with the cool freshness that blew across the surface of the water. Hot day, cold night. We sat between them, two quiet observers of an Indian summer.

The water lapped at the gray, round stones. "So, tell me more about you," Reese said, out of the blue. "What's your story?"

I laughed nervously. "I don't know that I have a story, per se." I thought about my life back in Vegas. It was likely the opposite of Reese's life. I didn't have a lot of close friends I'd left behind, because, let's face it, there aren't a lot of teenage girls who want to cruise The Strip with Chase rocking out on his iPad in the back seat. And since much of my time was occupied with taking care of him . . .

"Everyone has a story." He smiled.

"Eh . . ."

"Start at the beginning," he casually encouraged.

I flushed with shame. Because I'd snooped in his file, I already knew a lot about his story. How he had lost someone so close to him, how he must hide that pain to get through each day. I wrung my hands in my lap and avoided his gaze.

Reese broke my thought, "If you don't want to, it's no big deal."

"No. I mean, I'm just trying to think what would be worth sharing." I lied. I didn't want my life to sound like a sob story, but it kind of was. And as much as I liked Reese, I wasn't about to make up a bunch of crap so he would like me. So I just decided to go for it.

"I was born in Las Vegas. I had a pretty normal life. My mom stayed at home with us. Then, my dad left when I was five and Chase was two," I said flatly.

"I'm sorry," Reese said.

"I'm not," I replied. "He couldn't take the stress of Chase. Those early years were crazy. Chase never slept; he was sick and unhappy a lot. It was an around-the-clock marathon to care for him, so he bailed on them," I said, hard-shelled.

"And you," Reese added, softly.

A tiny spurt of pain. "Yeah." I shook it off. "I say he doesn't deserve Chase anyway. Chase can make you experience love on a whole other level, and I'd hate for him to waste it on someone so undeserving."

"Well said." Reese leaned back and held himself with such ease, he made it easy to share.

"Anyway, after he left, my mom went to college to become an educator, and when Chase and I weren't at school or in a crappy day care, we spent most of our time with my aunt who had a lot of cats."

"This is a terrible story," Reese chided.

"Lighten it up?" I asked.

"Please. Not for my sake, but for yours." He laughed. "So where did you hang out in Vegas? What would you be doing on a Friday night?"

"I warn you. I was kind of geeky. I spent a lot of time in libraries. Chase loves it there. There are puzzles and puppet shows and fountains. All kinds of free entertainment. I could take him there and he'd be happy and I could read or could get lost in a magazine for a few minutes or whatever."

Reese smiled, a charitable smile. A smile someone gives when they feel sorry for you.

"I'm not always boring though." I sat up a little taller. "Chase loves the energy of The Strip. Neon lights, water shows, pyramids, and castles. We spent more time with tourists and drunk frat boys than I care to admit."

I imagined how Reese must spend his Friday nights. Judging from the female attention he got at school, I wagered many of those nights were spent in the company of his groupies. Parties and the like. There was an awkward silence. "Oh dang. I am boring, aren't I?"

He shook his head and grinned warmly. "No. The total opposite, actually."

Not knowing how to take that or what to say next, I picked a piece of tall grass that had accidentally found root in the crevice of a rock and wound it slowly around my finger. "So your turn now,"

I said finally, anxious to shift the topic of conversation from me to him. "Give me the Reese Blackwood lowdown."

He took a deep breath and exhaled through his nose. Then he casually drew one knee to his chest and looked out over the water that had begun to shimmer pure gold in the waning light. "Well, I've lived my whole life in the same house. It's just me and my dad now. My mom died when I was little."

"That's awful," I offered, not knowing what else to say.

"Yeah, it sucked." Reese's jaw clenched as he stared straight ahead. He turned to face me. "I have a brother who is ten years older, so I basically grew up an only child." He smirked. "I'm sure Violet would tell you I'm spoiled, and in a way, she might be right."

I thought of his shiny black truck, tricked out with custom rims and stereo system. A chuckle escaped. Reese noticed.

"Hey, I'm not a total brat," he defended. "I've worked every summer for my dad since I was able to turn a wrench. And whenever I'm not at football practice, I'm at the shop. This is actually one of the first nights I've taken off in a long time."

"So why did you?" I asked, winding the grass even tighter around my finger, enough to make it turn purple.

He nudged my arm with his knee. "To come see you. Silly girl." I liked him touching me.

"Okay, so you are Reese Blackwood, tireless laborer, fancy truck driver, starting quarterback, and alpine stud," I teased.

"I'm only playing football this year because my dad wants me to. Said he'd take my truck if I didn't."

"Senior year burnout?"

"I guess."

"Tell me how you got into skiing. I saw your team's championship photo in the trophy case from last season. You must be pretty good."

Reese almost sounded annoyed. "If you grow up in this town, you automatically ski. Everyone does it. I'm not really into it anymore, though." He picked up a flat stone and skipped it once, twice, across the water.

I recalled his jubilant face of celebration in the championship team picture. It was polar to his current expression. I learned through his file that in addition to pulling pranks, skiing was another activity he'd shared with his cousin, Landon.

"So, are you going to go out for the team this winter, then?"

"Nope." Reese slammed the door on the topic.

"Hmm." I should have just dropped the ski thing. It was obvious this wasn't a comfortable subject.

"I'll probably just work and save up for school." He picked off a tiny piece of fluff that had floated from some tree onto his bottom lip. He examined it with much more interest than it deserved. The silence was noticeable. "Maybe go on a few dates," he added at last, with the tiniest grin.

Again, Reese groupies stampeded through my mind. "I'm sure you'll have more than a few dates. They all want a taste of you."

He laughed a mirthless laugh and then looked at me with meaning behind his eyes. I then realized he hoped those dates would be with me.

A frigid breeze picked up and penetrated my clothing, causing me to shiver. Reese stood up and unbuttoned his flannel shirt. "Here, wear this. I wouldn't want you to have to endure these subarctic Truckee temps of sixty-five degrees," he joked as he draped it over my shoulders.

His smell! It should be bottled and sold on the black market. Under his flannel, he wore a fresh white T-shirt no longer bearing the smudge of Chase's blood from the hallway incident earlier. The material stretched tightly over his chest and around his thick upper arms. I made myself look away.

Darkness fell quickly, but my feet knew the path well as I led the way back up the hill. By the time we reached my yard, the glow of lamplight in a couple of windows left a patchwork of golden light on the lawn.

I started up the porch steps when Reese said, "Hold up for a sec." It was just then I recalled he had a surprise for me. I stood there feeling more awkward than a de-feathered flamingo.

He trotted back to his truck and using the rear tire as a step, slung his leg and climbed over the side of the bed. I heard some sort of shuffling and scraping, but in the darkness, I couldn't make out what he was doing. He returned with a wide smile on his face and a new tire slung over each shoulder. "I brought these for you. There are two more in my truck."

"Reese! You can't buy me new tires!" I wailed.

Growing up without a dad in the house, my mom and I were forced to learn basic auto maintenance. We'd purchased tires before and on our shoestring budget, I was very aware of the cost of them. These were thick and heavily treaded—ideal for Truckee winters. And I knew they had to have cost a small fortune.

"It's okay, don't even worry about it. I get them for cheaper than wholesale from my dad's shop."

My mouth gaped open and then shut. I didn't know how to express my gratitude because I wasn't sure I could accept them.

"Pres, I wanted to do it. I can't believe somebody slashed all four of your tires on top of the egg thing."

I stared at the tires and struggled inside with emotion.

"Consider it a welcome present." He set the tires on the ground and walked back to his truck to get the other two.

"Thank you," I called after him. "This is . . . ludicrous generosity. I don't know what to say."

He came back holding the last two tires, looking so manly, like some stubble-chinned guy in a deodorant commercial. "Pres, seriously, you don't have to say anything. That's not why I did it. You just . . . deserve to be treated better than you have been, that's all." He set the last two tires on top of the first, making a leaning tower of his affection for me.

"Give me a call when your paint job's done and I'll come over and put them on for you."

I was perfectly capable of putting them on myself, but I wasn't going to tell him that. "Okay, I will."

"It's a date, then." He winked at me, which I usually found abysmally cheesy, but it was anything but, coming from him.

I bit my thumbnail, hoping to suppress the insane giddiness bubbling up inside me.

"I'll see you tomorrow," he said over his shoulder as he walked toward his truck. Then he stopped abruptly. "Oh! Hey! Actually, I won't. I'm suspended for the next three days. Oops," he chuckled.

I laughed at the memory of Mr. Price soaked in his own coffee, murderously yelling at Reese to get out of his classroom.

"See you sometime soon then. I'll call you when I get my car back." A smile spread on my lips.

He walked away and as I watched him go in his jeans and white T, I knew two things. First, his body was strong and a pleasure to view from the back. Second, he was definitely not the boy from the library.

Chapter Eleven

MISSED

(LANDON)

Just because you can jump back in time, doesn't mean that you should." James sat on the bleachers next to me and watched Truckee's football team captain count off push-ups.

I'd traveled back to this particular summer practice a handful of times. At least it broke up the monotony of hanging out at home.

"I thought if I stayed away from Presley you'd leave me alone. Can't you even give me some peace in the past?"

"You shouldn't even be in the past. None of my other cases have stayed long enough to figure out time jumps are possible."

"Guess I'm your star pupil." I kept my eyes on the field.

"I'm concerned. You're obsessing. This is the fifth time you've jumped back to this particular practice." James slid a little closer to me. "What's going on?"

"This new receiver sucks, that's what's going on." I gestured at the players. Reese threw a pass as my replacement ran for it. He turned too late and missed it. "See, he's not ready for the ball. He doesn't expect it to come to him. He's not anticipating it soon enough."

"Well, this is the first week of practice," James said.

"This guy's a benchwarmer, not a starter. I can tell. Look, even Reese knows it." We both watched as Reese cursed and then directed the kid to get back in position.

I could feel James studying me.

"I think I see what's going on here," James said.

"Whatever, Obi-Wan." The receiver fumbled again. I could tell his mistakes were getting to him. "This guy's fast, but he's got butterfingers. And there's no way he'll be tough enough to take the abuse." I turned to James. "Receivers get tackled more than anyone, and he's gotta be strong enough to break through the line to get open."

James listened patiently, but the look on his face made me uneasy.

"This is more than interest in the game. Your team is feeling your absence and you like that."

I hadn't thought about it in that way, but the instant flare of defensiveness I felt signaled James was right. Every player on the field had to be wishing I were still there. Every time that new kid dropped the ball, my teammates had to have missed me. "So what's so wrong with that, huh?"

"It's not wrong to want to be missed—and you are. But your fixation on traveling back here so frequently is not helping you."

I could feel the creeping, slipping pull of time approaching, and I knew this moment was nearly over. I'd be yanked back to the present by a force beyond my control. No matter what. No matter how hard I tried to stay. It was like this every time.

"I don't care if it's helping me. It feels good, okay? And these days, not much feels good."

"It could if you'd trust me."

"Not going there, James. Not today." None of it mattered anyway. My time was up. Again. The field blurred, the hopeless pressure bore down on my body and James's voice distorted and eventually faded.

I was swept away in a tidal wave I couldn't fight, and I knew Time would take me back to exactly where it thought I belonged—five months dead.

Chapter Twelve

VOICES

(PRESLEY)

I was restless and starving. Gayle swore we'd go home after school, but it was nearly five hours after the bell and by the looks of things, we weren't leaving any time soon. She was barefoot in her office, insensible heels kicked to the side. She knelt on the floor surrounded by stacks of files, and stretched her arm up to grab another huge pile of paperwork from her desk. Chase sat in the black leather chair behind her desk and rocked happily back and forth clutching his tablet. Thankfully, he was wearing headphones.

"Mom! I thought you were almost done!" I called from the secretary's office.

"I just got a second wind and am sort of on a roll."

Gayle held a paper between pinched lips and squinted over the top of her glasses at another. I'd finished my homework two hours ago and had spent my time coaxing Chase away from his iPad with puzzles and handwriting practice. When he grew weary of me and my phone battery died, I'd resorted to chipping old blue nail polish from my nails, making paperclip art (the turtle turned out quite well), seeing how far I could roll in the secretary's desk chair with one hard push, and trying to hack the password of said secretary's computer with random words. No success.

Aside from the creak of Gayle's chair rocking back and forth, it was so quiet I could actually hear the buzz of the fluorescent lights above my head. Time for a field trip. I didn't bother to tell Gayle I was leaving because she would say something like, "Where are you going and what are you going to do?" Then I would have to be honest and say something like, "I'm going to look for unlocked lockers to snoop in." I didn't really know what I was going to do, so I just started walking.

Walt the janitor was vacuuming in Price's room as I moseyed further down the hall toward the library. I told myself I was in search of a *National Geographic* or something else to keep my attention, but in truth I was more interested in replaying my experience earlier that week. It gave me a sort of dark thrill, thinking about the boy that seemed to materialize in the rows of books. When I got to the door, a light shone through the windows. I peeked in and then sagged when I saw Megan and her minions sprawled out on the floor making spirit signs.

I turned to go, but the hall was dark. The janitor must have shut the classroom lights off and gone home for the night. I couldn't see the end of the hall or much of anything else. I felt my way along the wall, not finding a light switch anywhere.

The biology lab was only a few doors down from the library, and Mrs. Freeman had a pretty cool container garden going, and a truly gruesome display of pickled creatures in glass jars.

The lab tables stretched in a straight line, the black surfaces shining with a greenish glow from the exit light above the door. I flipped a switch and let my eyes adjust to the light while meandering along the rows of vegetables. The tomato plants bloomed with yellow flowers, almost ready to grow fruit. I plucked a leaf of basil and pierced it with my thumbnail, smelling the spicy sweetness.

The glass jars of dead stuff were a little depressing, and for some reason I was drawn to the eyes of each creature. The sealed skin over the fetal pig's eyes looked waxy and pale and the frog's eyes, shriveled and black. I was grateful the sheep's brain had no empty eyes to stare at me with. Disappointingly, it looked flaky and the liquid surrounding it was too cloudy to examine much detail. Just as I was about to cross over to the bookcase for something to do, the lights went out leaving me in near blackness. Then, something rattled and scraped outside the door.

"Hello?" More clattering sounds came from the door and the pound of footsteps retreated down the hall. Was it Walt locking up? I felt my way to the doors. They wouldn't open. I fumbled at the switch but the lights wouldn't turn back on. "Wait!" I yelled. "Wait! I'm still in here!" No one answered. I tried the doors again, confused at how they could be locked as they were simply swinging doors like the kind in hospitals or operating rooms. I recalled the handles on the outside, but these doors didn't have any turning knobs, keyholes or mechanisms that would allow them to lock.

I checked my pocket for my phone but remembered it was dead, so I used the only option I had. "Mom!"

I yelled her name a handful of times before I admitted to myself that her office was too far away for her to hear me. I drew in a big breath and tried once more. "Mom!"

"Presley?" My heart jerked. The voice, though muffled from behind the locked doors, was a voice I knew. It wasn't even that I recognized the tone of it exactly, but my body somehow knew it because every nerve I had was alert and humming exactly like that day in the hall. The trophy case voice.

"Presley, it's okay. I'm sorry. They locked the doors and I can't open them. I don't have a key."

Something felt wrong. My hands explored the door again, confirming what I knew. That this was not a locking door and this person, whoever he was, was lying.

But, why would he lie? And who was he? The rectangular windows on the doors afforded little information when I looked through them because the darkness obscured his features. The seed of dread in my belly grew and curled through me until my skin prickled with adrenaline and my breath came in a shallow, quick rhythm.

I had only felt fear this consuming twice in my life. Once, in a truck rollover, and once when a horse bolted wildly and I could barely hang on. Both times I'd wondered if I was going to die.

Instinct warned me to stay silent. Like a kid hiding under the sheets from a monster who knew exactly where I was. Why was my breathing so loud? I eased backward, away from the door, but bumped into a table, tipping a metal stool over in a clattering ruckus.

"Presley, I know you're in there. Don't be afraid."

He used my name with such familiarity. It was both unsettling and comforting. My mind vacillated between the two reactions, wondering which to feel.

"A breaker must have flipped. The power's off in the whole wing. Listen to me, I can help you. There's a window in the back of the room above those plants you were looking at."

How did he know what I had been doing? Had he been watching?

"Who are you? How do you know my name?" My voice came out thin and weak.

The voice ignored my questions. "Go back to where you were. If you move the containers and stand on the table, you can open it and get out."

Slowly, my eyes adjusted to the darkness. I could see the window he described, though it looked too high and not much bigger than a cereal box. Not an option. And there was little point in hiding; I'd already opened my mouth. But I surely wasn't brave enough to re-approach the doors. Was he really trying to help me or was he just coaxing me out a window for his own purposes?

The hairs rose on my arms wondering what awaited me outside the window. Did he have an accomplice? Foggy episodes of America's Most Wanted replayed my mind. Maybe he was herding me to a greater danger.

With that in mind, the doors seemed less frightening. I didn't know who was on the other side of them, but it was more than I knew about what was outside of that window. I leaned back against a lab table and looked toward the voice. Even in the dark, I began to discern the form of a man through the two small windows on the swinging doors. He was tall with cropped hair—his head bowed and resting against the window. His posture gave the appearance of weariness.

He shifted his weight to the other leg. "Presley, please." His palm reached up and rested against the window. The gesture looked so tender, and he said my name with such softness that my fear thawed. But in the absence of fear, a surprising surge of anger took over.

"What's your problem?" I shouted. "Let me out right now or I'm going to call 911," I bluffed. "This isn't funny!" As an added measure of bravado I added, "JERK!"

He laughed at me. He *laughed* at me. And it was like he waved a red cape in front of a bull. I charged the doors, kicking a lab stool out of my way. It slid across the floor and knocked into the glass cabinet that housed the dead stuff. Glass shattered and a chemical smell suffocated the room. I didn't care. I took hold of the metal handles on the double doors and yanked back as hard as I could, feeling the tendons pull in my shoulders.

"Let me out right now! Right now!" The last two words punctuated with hard yanks on the doors.

My hands ached. The room stood quiet except for the sound of my labored breathing. I peered through the window. He was there—pacing, with his hands latched behind his neck. I studied his figure, frustrated that still all I could see was a dark silhouette.

He continued to pace. "Just calm down and listen to me. I can't let you out." He lifted his head and gestured frustratingly with his hands. "I would if . . ."

My insides shifted a bit more. I needed to know who he was.

"What's your name?" I asked. My voice was completely composed. A flickering light appeared behind him. A weak, blue light.

"Presley? Where are you? What happened?" It was Gayle. She was running down the hall with a lame keychain flashlight our realtor gave her.

The boy had disappeared. I was distracted by Gayle's approach for no more than a couple of seconds and he was gone.

"Hang on!" Gayle yelled. "I called Walt and he told me the breaker panel is right around here somewhere." Gayle huffed as she shined her wimpy light around, looking for the breaker box.

A moment later the computers hummed and the lights flickered back on. I couldn't see the boy anywhere. I'd hoped with the lights on he would have been revealed, but he was gone. All of a sudden the smell from the broken specimen jars overwhelmed me.

"Mom, hurry. It stinks in here." I covered my nose with my sleeve and slapped the door with one of my sore palms.

Gayle easily opened the door. "Why would it stink . . . UGH! What is that smell? What is that?" She mirrored me by covering her own nose with her sleeve. I nodded to the fetal pig lying on its side in a puddle of broken glass and liquid.

She dropped her sleeved arm and waved her still shining flashlight at the mess. "Oh Pres! What did you do? What a mess. Mrs. Freeman is going to love this. I'd better call Walt again. What were you even doing in here?" Her annoyance at my predicament was plain.

"Mother! I was locked in. I couldn't get out. It's not like I meant to break anything. It was totally dark in here, and I was scared. How did you get the door opened, anyway?"

She stalked out of the room; the staccato sound of her heels accented each step and returned with a yellow broom in hand. "Someone put this through the handles of the doors."

"A broom?" Things made even less sense. I was embarrassed that I couldn't trust my instincts. Gullible.

He had sounded so sincere.

"Well, was it really wedged in there?" I asked. "How did you get it loose?" I tried to compute how a large boy couldn't do what my mom was able to do with her chicken arms.

"It wasn't wedged in there at all. In fact it was half-way fallen out."

As much as I didn't want to admit it, the guy was a liar. An amazing liar. I felt tremendously duped. And angry. He'd found a way to torment me. Again.

Gayle covered her face again with her sleeve. "You know, on second thought I'm not going to call Walt back over here." She handed me the broom. "You can take care of this. The custodial closet is the door directly to the left of the ladies room. You'll find the mop and trash bags in there." She turned and left the room—the sound of her shoes clacking down an empty hallway.

"Don't you even want to know who did this?" I yelled after her, hurt that she'd left me there with this mess after what I'd just gone through. After all these years, I still expected her to be a mother.

"It's just a stupid prank. Can't worry about it now," she shouted without looking back. "Too much to do. I'll look into it tomorrow. Clean that thing up before the smell spreads!"

I went to the sink and grabbed a wad of paper towels. Somehow, sweeping that little pig up with a broom felt cruel. As I stooped down to bundle it up, the reflections of two people appeared in the remaining intact glass cabinet door, their forms framed by the doorway. Obviously my mom and Janitor Walt. Gayle's hovering could be so tedious. She didn't care enough to help me, but decided to stick around to make sure I didn't embarrass her? The impatience in my voice was cutting. "I'm on it, guys."

Their silence was evidence that I was too harsh. Too guilty to turn around, I chose instead to address their reflections. But something wasn't right. My mom had been wearing a cream suit and the reflections were both dressed darkly.

He was back. Maybe that's why he left in the first place. He'd returned with someone else—the accomplice outside the window. Even though I had been angry just moments earlier, that feeling vaporized and the paralyzing fear returned as I contemplated them wanting to harm me rather than just tease me.

People do two things when terrified. They either freeze or they flee. I froze. And studied the reflections to convince myself that the chemical fumes weren't causing me to hallucinate. Their figures *were* there, and unnaturally still. No escape.

My memory flashed to a desert path. I had been walking with Gayle when we encountered a rattlesnake, coiled tail buzzing and ready to strike. She'd told me to stay motionless. "It will strike if you move," she'd warned. This felt the same. I fought to keep my breath steady, but couldn't.

A rushing sound, like water swirled around me and my blood turned cold when I realized what I was really hearing was whispers. Dozens and dozens of whispering voices breathed around me, crawled through every hair on my head, increasing in volume until they penetrated my every thought. Electrified with horror and no longer able to hold still, I whipped around to confront the strangers, but found nothing but an empty doorway. Not a person. Not a sound.

Nothing.

Chapter Thirteen

BAD DREAMS

(PRESLEY)

I was up all night wondering what exactly happened in that lab. I knew I heard whispers. I knew I saw reflections. But when I'd turned to look, there was nothing. I couldn't argue with nothing. I couldn't tell anyone about nothing. I watched a documentary once that said people can hear voices if their heads aren't right. Maybe that was my problem.

To top things off, I think I dreamed of Landon.

In my dream, there was a river.

Men with somber faces gathered at the edge of the shore and searched the surface, looking for something I instinctually did not want to see. The railway bridge above, which spanned the river, was a poor shelter from the pitiless rain. A silent ambulance stood parked with its tires sunk in the mud, dim headlights struggling to assist. I wanted to leave this place.

The water finally stirred from some disturbance beneath the surface. Ice flashed through my veins and stopped the breath in my throat. The men took clumsy steps forward and stretched to improve the miserable view. I tried to turn and leave, but invisible weights lay on my feet.

A diver in a glistening black wet suit surfaced and an instant later, so did the mop of dark hair he cradled in the crook of his arm. The diver swam, towing his human cargo alongside him until he attained footing in waist-deep water. Alone, he struggled to heft the corpse, which revealed its skin, too pale against the dark—slick and ghastly.

An unconcerned train thundered overhead, leaving behind only the trembling bridge and a calloused whistle. The solemn men on the shore, issuing vaporous breaths in the cool night air, hesitated for an instant and then forged into the river, soaking their stiff jeans to their hips. One man with a ruddy face and a radio on his belt bent to pull the body's shoulders out of the water while two more hefted the legs and feet onto the sodden, rock-strewn shore. The diver, now hunched over in the mud, labored to breathe under the heavy tank on his back.

A gurney clattered as it was taken from the ambulance and navigated down a small hill; it stopped inches from the body, but no one lifted him. He was missing a shoe and the muscles and tendons in his foot appeared strained as if he still tried to swim. His body lay unnaturally against the earth. A man spoke into a cell phone and turned his back on the body.

They unrolled a black bag on the shore, lifted his body on top, and uncooperative limbs were tucked inside. The only sound I heard were the closing teeth of the zipper as it slowly enveloped feet, legs, the torso, and finally his head. Gratefully, the face had been turned away, obscuring features that were surely ashen and stone-like. The gurney clanked once more and was lifted into the ambulance. The doors closed and the men hiked, dejected, over the small rain-soaked mound and out of sight. No lights. No siren. Only empty footprints in the mud, which filled with water. They would vanish before long.

Chapter Fourteen

READY AND WAITING

(LANDON)

I knew the path well. I'd watched her athletic figure race through this forested trail almost every morning since she'd seen me in the parking lot. I'd memorized her coiled hair, white running jacket, and turquoise running shoes. She was incredibly predictable and always made it to this point right around sunrise. The horizon glowed with an eager sun. I counted every second and contemplated heading her way on the trail to close the gap.

"Spying again?" The familiar and increasingly annoying voice drifted from somewhere behind me. Without turning to face him I countered, "You mean, you are spying on me again?"

"Can't fault a man for doing his job. We've been over this."

"Look James . . . I'd love to engage in another philosophical debate with you about why I shouldn't have contact with Presley and how you know what's best, etcetera, etcetera, but it's only minutes until she heads down this trail and I'm not going to miss it."

"And how is spying on her every morning helping you?" James eyed me skeptically.

"It's just something I enjoy. That's all. Starts my day with some good energy. Let's just call it my morning cup of Joe." I tried to hide my sarcasm; it was too late. James was a cool guy and the last thing I wanted to do was alienate the only person that I could actually talk to, but this whole over-my-shoulder, micromanaging routine was getting old.

"I sense something different in your demeanor today," James commented coolly. I continued to face the trail but could tell that he had emerged from the trees behind me and was approaching. "I can't quite place it," he continued, "confidence, maybe even arrogance? I'm worried you've got something up your sleeve."

I ground my teeth. I really, really didn't want him here.

James moved to my side. "Tell me why you won't let this go."

"Okay James, I'm down to five minutes max, so I will humor you with what we've already discussed a hundred and one times. For starters, the girl yelled at me. You know it and I know it. She sees me. I want to know why. You're not giving me answers. Next, she hears my voice outside of the lab and we engage in conversation. So, it's apparent to me that she also hears me and again, you shed no light on the situation for me. All this time I think you're the last one on Earth I can communicate with, and now someone else comes along that I can hang with and you're against it, and you won't even tell me why this is happening. So . . .."

"Landon, she is alive and you are dead. Do you really need more than that?"

His words were rocks thrown at my head, but I wasn't giving him the satisfaction of knowing it.

"Yes! I do. I'm sick of playing by your rules, and I'm sick of being left in the dark."

James grimaced. "I would be incredibly remiss if I did not urge you to stop this exploration at once. I strongly suggest that you push Presley from your mind and continue the course you and I were traveling before that unfortunate day in the school parking lot."

"What? Unfortunate because she talked to me? That was the best day of the past five months."

James groaned.

I cocked my head, heard her footfalls approaching. I rounded on James. "She's going to be here in about thirty seconds, so as much as I'd like to stay and chat with you, I'm going to have to exercise that free will you always talk so much about and say good-bye for now."

"You know you can't keep stalking her."

"I know," I said, trying to hide a smile. I locked my eyes with his. "Today I'm going to meet her."

Chapter Fifteen

THE PATH

(PRESLEY)

I dreamed of Landon again. The memory of death snaked thick around me. A black body bag closing over his cold, pale skin. A cruel train speeding by with its thunderous noise, insensitive to the reverence it should have observed at a moment like that. But most unsettling was the new appearance of the dark figures from the biology lab.

They stood on the bridge ominous observers to the macabre scene, surely not mourners. So, why were they there? And why did they occupy the shadows of my sleep?

I caught a glimpse of myself in the mirror. Purple shadows hung under my eyes. My hair, disheveled and my expression—desolate. I didn't look like me. Didn't feel like me.

I rolled out of bed and fumbled with my iPod to find a playlist to help jumpstart my mood. Settling on one with ample electric guitar and drums, I slammed the iPod back into its dock and took a deep breath as the music exploded into my room. I pulled open the curtains, letting the first of the sunrise flood the space and dug through my laundry basket for some running clothes. It felt good to prepare for my run, familiar at least. The snugness of my leggings and the tightness of my tank top felt comforting and secure. Pulling my nest of curls back into a hasty bun, I washed my face, not bothering to wait for the water to turn warm.

After searching under a few piles on the floor I finally uncovered both running shoes. I tied my white fleece running jacket around my waist and tucked my iPod into the strap of my sports top. Eager to get going, I padded down the hall, guessing that Gayle and Chase were still asleep. I slowly turned the black antique knob and opened Gayle's door a small crack. She was out; sprawled on top of the bed in the same red suit she'd worn to school the day before. Chase had found his way to her room during the night and was lying next to her, the entire mess of blankets to himself.

Even though I got a little laugh out of her absurd sleeping arrangement, I still couldn't shake the restless feeling. I closed her door, wincing at the creak caused by its antiquity, and blocked out a childish, edgy feeling that something watched me from behind. I jogged down the steps as quietly as I could, bypassing the kitchen. I knew I'd need an extra-long run to feel halfway normal again. Maybe try out a new trail. There were plenty of them. That was one thing I loved about Truckee. Less than a minute from my front door, I could be buried in postcard-like beauty. I was grateful for the distraction.

I stood in the shade of my front porch and kneaded a few tense areas in my neck and shoulders. I folded over, and relished in the burn it provided to my hamstrings. A few black crows condescendingly watched me from a bare branch above. It knew it was stupid, but I hated them watching me. Even though they were just animals, their gaze felt too knowing, and that was enough to lead me over to my Jeep to dig the mace out of the console. Pocketless, I tucked the cold aluminum tube in the waistband of my pants.

No matter what level of fitness I had achieved, the first mile was always the hardest, especially at this ridiculous altitude. My lungs filled with thin cold air and my muscles protested the strain of the uphill trail. I cranked the volume on my iPod and it helped me reach the top of the hill with a little burst of energy. With the second mile under my belt, my muscles began to work in harmony allowing me to lengthen my stride. My breaths grew strong and rhythmic, and I took pleasure in the swell of power as my body carried me.

I decided against trying out a new trail, thinking it might be wiser to stick to familiarity. Running this four-mile path for the last several weeks, I'd memorized each turn in the road. I knew at the bottom of the slope I would round a corner and find a barbed-wire fence that stretched alongside a meadow. It was beautiful, with its clean grass moving like liquid in the breeze. It wasn't unusual this early to spot deer feeding. The grass had turned dry and straw-like, but I still appreciated the meadow's quiet vastness. It was the only area of my run where the trees broke open, and the surrounding mountains became visible.

As I reached the bottom of the slope, I quieted my breaths and footfalls to avoid startling the deer, if indeed there were any to see. I rounded the corner expectantly searching for them, but a guy was planted squarely in the middle of my trail. There was something off about his attitude, as he wasn't observing the meadow and he wasn't walking the trail. He simply stood there.

It was too much. The freak in the parking lot, the voice in the hall, reflections that whispered, the nightmare and. . . this. This trail was my last haven. I wanted to pretend he didn't exist—to simply jog by as if he were a weed growing on the side of the road, but the closer I came toward him, the more firmly he seemed planted exactly in my way. Adrenaline saturated my bloodstream as I prepared to face this unwelcome stranger. I rested my fingers over the tube of mace at my waist. A stone's throw away from him, I stopped short because I recognized his face.

He shifted his weight to his resting leg and watched me. He had no intention of moving out of my way so I remained planted. Using my free hand, I plucked the earbuds from my ears and appraised the human obstruction.

"Hello," he said with an intensity that stole my breath.

Chapter Sixteen

SURPRISE, SURPRISE

(PRESLEY)

Many pieces of the scattered puzzle finally came together. I'd recognized his face immediately from the "incident" in the parking lot, the nameless picture in the trophy case, the bench in the courtyard. And it was too easy to pinpoint exactly where I'd heard his voice before—the boy from the hallway and the bio lab. My tormentor's identity was no longer a mystery.

He was dressed in a blue collared shirt—impeccably fit, sleeves rolled to the elbow, leaving his bronzed arms bare. I noticed a woven leather bracelet hung from his wrist. His hands were casually tucked in the pockets of his pricey-looking jeans and he stood before me, cocky and expectant. How fitting that he'd chosen my private sanctuary to come and plague me once more.

"You!" I cried, taking several steps in his direction. My voice filled the meadow and a few birds fled their hiding spots in the tall, dry grasses.

All of the insulting stunts aimed at making me feel stupid, unwelcome, and hated pounded into my mind like metal spikes. Obviously I'd pinned Megan as guilty a little prematurely. I recalled all of the embarrassment and tears he'd caused me—walking through crowded halls in my PE clothes. Chewed gum buried in my hamburger. The disappointment of my Jeep being defaced and rendered un-drivable. And perhaps the worst part, being terrified and tormented in a dark, locked room. The cause of it all, stood here boldly, waiting to dish out more.

I gripped the can of mace and strode forward, aiming it directly at his face. I pictured myself spraying that smug look right off of it. My eyes narrowed and my jaw flexed. Just as my finger was about to apply the perfect amount of pressure to start the stream of pain, he flashed a charming smile. "You won't need that with me."

I tried to comprehend why this angel face appeared so delighted to see me. My mouth hung open, eyebrows drawn in confusion. I blinked several times. It was all wrong.

I stammered over what I wanted to say, settling again on what I'd chosen in the beginning. "You."

A flash of recognition glimmered in his eyes, spreading his impossibly perfect smile even wider. That smile, though narcotic, was a direct insult to all he had put me through. I gathered strength as I revisited the memories of my humiliation.

"It was you the entire time. You locked me in the biology lab. You shouted my name in the hall. You've been teasing me and embarrassing me for no reason! I don't even know you, and you've been making my life a nightmare." My fists balled. "You messed up my Jeep!"

He lowered his head and smiled. "Presley, I know you are upset, but, you have the wrong guy." He paused, shook his head and laughed out loud. It sounded in my ears, musical and baffling. His eyes held mine. "You have every right to be angry, though."

His expression made no sense at all. It's like he was privy to the world's best joke, and I wasn't in on it.

"Quit smiling!" The acid in my voice was clear, but it made no difference. He continued to beam at me like a groom at the end of a long velvet carpet. "What is wrong with you?"

He seemed to struggle to dim the bright lamp of his face. His smile didn't budge, but the excitement in his eyes receded in the smallest degree. He took a long breath in through his teeth. "Okay, first things first. I know what has happened to you, and I swear to you, I'm not the cause of it. Please trust that."

My face crumpled, bewildered. He was unequivocally the best liar I'd ever encountered.

"Next, I am just so . . . so glad to meet you. You have no idea." A crease appeared on his forehead giving the immediate effect of sincerity.

Questions surfaced in my mind. He didn't seem to be gloating, rather genuinely pleased. Against sound judgment, I gave him the tiniest benefit of the doubt. "You have some explaining to do," I warned.

A strong looking hand gently covered his heart and honesty warmed his features. "I know," he answered simply.

"Who are you?" I began with the first and most obvious question.

"Umm . . . Krew."

"Krew what?"

"Just Krew." He smirked, but then seemed to think better of it.

"Hmm. So, why did you lock me in the biology lab, just Krew?"

"I didn't. I found you there, but I didn't lock you in."

"It's a little early to start with the bald face lies isn't it? Kind of puts a bad taste in my mouth."

His eyes moved to my lips and his own parted slightly.

"I wouldn't want to do that," he said, his voice low and velvety.

Unbelievable. His ability to so easily knock me from my resolve to hate him was humiliating. I struggled to extinguish the flush I felt spreading through my cheeks.

My mind called back the yellow broom so sloppily wedged into the handles of the biology lab doors. "I know you're lying to me. I saw the broom in the handles. It wasn't locked at all, and you could have let me out. Yet you stood out there and led me to believe you couldn't help me. You lied." My face composed itself with the unarguable facts I'd laid before him.

His eyes were patient and searching. "I wanted to let you out, but I wasn't supposed to be in there and I was afraid that . . . if I opened those doors you would tell someone I was there. I tried to get you out though. Remember?"

I remembered. I remembered thinking I was craftily being herded to a crime show–worthy death.

"I may not have gotten you out the way you wanted, but I tried my best. I didn't want to upset you." His voice lowered into a soulful huskiness and he punctuated his statement with, "I promise."

"Who locked me in, then?" I asked, hoping he had an easy answer. One that would shuffle the confusion into some semblance of order.

"I'm pretty sure it was the girls from the library," he explained. "They were laughing and bragging to each other about something. So I looked for you."

Again, the more information I received, the more confused I became. "What were you doing in the library to begin with? I saw you in the parking lot and the courtyard before that day, but I've never seen you in school. Are you a student?" My mind flashed back to the day I found his picture in the trophy case—the image of it captured by my phone. I fought to assemble my face into an expression that demanded answers.

His eyes were fixed on mine, but I could not perceive the reason for the weight of his gaze.

"I don't go to Truckee High. Not anymore, anyway. I do carpenter work on the side to pay for school. I had been at the library earlier that day working on some remodeling. I left my, um . . ." he paused and his eyes flickered to the ground as he seemed to search for words. "I left some tools there by accident and while driving by the school I saw cars outside and lights on in the library, so I thought I'd run in and see if I could get my tools for my job the next day."

His story explained why I saw him in the library the afternoon Violet helped me with my government notes. It explained how he could be there after hours. It did not explain, however, why the librarian didn't seem to have noticed him.

He searched my face. "I do owe you an apology, though."

My eyes narrowed in skepticism. "For what?"

"For worrying about my self-interests more than yours that night. I really needed that job at the school and I was sure if anyone caught me roaming the halls after hours with teenage girls hanging around, they wouldn't be happy about it. It's a poor excuse, I know. You must have been terrified in there, and not letting you out immediately was unforgivable." A mask of pleading washed over his features. "It was a horrible choice, and I'm truly sorry. But I swear, that is the only offense I'm guilty of."

The slightest trace of a smile reached his eyes, thawing in my breast any antagonism I held for him. He seemed to notice the change and his eyes became teasing.

"Not that it excuses anything, but you actually sounded like you were doing a fine job holding your own in there. You are quite feisty. I was impressed with how you behaved . . . under the circumstances." He smiled crookedly.

My face grew hot as I recalled the insults and threats that I screamed at him that night. I smiled shyly, "Yeah, well under the circumstances."

I didn't know what to make of this beautiful person. Another question surfaced and my face puckered. "There's one more thing I want to know, though. What are you doing out here? It's like, 6:30 in the morning." I held my arms out and gestured to the obvious isolation.

He swallowed hard and a flash of something flickered in his eyes. Was it hesitancy? Before I could decide, his mouth curled into a wide dazzling smile. "I didn't know you'd be here. I was just lucky, I guess."

A small, sensible voice in my head warned me he was lying, but I offered him my hand anyway. "Friends then?"

He looked at my hand without touching it and his eyes rose to mine. I wondered if I should've felt rejected.

But then he smiled, took a couple of steps backward, and said, "I would love nothing more."

—

He walked the way I'd came from and I continued my run in the direction I'd been heading when we met on the trail. I didn't feel the ground beneath my feet as my mind swam with combatting deliberations. Was I stupid for trusting him so quickly? I replaced my earbuds and adjusted the volume to the highest level I could without bursting an eardrum.

With my mind so occupied, my legs carried me farther and farther into the enveloping forest. Happy it was Saturday and that I had no tardy bell to worry about, I passed the outermost point I had ever run to and the terrain no longer held landmarks I recognized. I wasn't afraid; the trail was worn enough that I knew I could find my way back, but there came an instinctive uneasiness with the exploration of new ground.

I wanted to run forever. Exhaust myself, mind and body. I estimated the distance I had run. It had to be about five miles. By the time I ran home I would have gone over ten—the furthest I'd ever run. The sun was higher in the sky and I found myself wishing I would have applied sunscreen to my already freckled nose. Though my muscles and body were warm, the frigid breeze nearly froze the sweat I produced. I paused to throw my jacket on. Pushing my head through the opening of my top dislodged the earbuds from my ears. Surprisingly, a sound almost as loud as my music reverberated off the trees around me. Its power had a disorienting effect and it took me a moment to realize that what I was hearing was water. Quick-moving water from the sound of it. A sickening wave rolled through me as dark images re-emerged. A too-clear picture of dark, wet matted hair. A black body bag. A silent ambulance. My head became the reluctant host to unwelcome callers.

I stood fixed on the trail. Part of me wanted to run home. Part of me wanted to find that water. I don't know how much time passed before I stomped off the packed, pebble-strewn trail onto the virgin ground of the lonely woods. Dried, yellowed pine needles crunched under my shoes and I was grateful I'd worn long leggings as the undergrowth scraped at my calves. I took the path of least resistance by walking downhill as much as possible. I knew water ran downhill and if I continued descending like spring runoff, it wouldn't be long until I found the source of the menacing sound.

I felt it before I saw it. The air turned cold and the energy around me pulsated from the force of so much moving water. The trees diminished almost completely as I reached the shore of the river. I took care not to twist an ankle as I navigated through chalky round river rock. The occasional insect avoided its undoing and scurried into cracks and crevices in the egg-shaped stones. The river coursed before me in feral brawn, making me feel small.

Hesitantly, I approached the edge of the water. A flicker of gold caught my eye from somewhere near my feet. A shallow pool, protected from the current by a ridge of mud, lay tranquil and glassy on the wet earth. Exactly in the middle of it was a ring. I stooped down to retrieve it from the water. It was a class ring, a lot like the one I remembered my dad wearing when I was a child. The square stone was blood red and cut with perfectly symmetrical facets. The ring felt heavy and cold in my hands as I examined it. On one side, two skis crossed to make an X. Under the X read the word Alpine. The other side had a simple block T. I slipped it onto my index finger; it was at least three sizes too big. I removed it and upon closer inspection discovered there was an inscription along the inside of the ring. It was one word: Fortis.

I contemplated what that might mean to someone. Strangely, there was no year on the ring to give me further clues as to who that someone was. I held the ring between my thumb and forefinger and pressed the cold stone to my lips as I watched the current force its way over the rocks—tireless and supreme. More crows perched on an adjacent tree and called to companions in the distance. Why did I feel like those birds were always following me? I followed the gaze of their glassy black eyes that were fixed upon an iron bridge. There was no mistaking it. The rusty brown tone of the aged metal, the angles of the support braces, its span over the water resting on familiar banks. The rope knotted three times that drifted lazily over the water.

It was the railway bridge from my dream.

Chapter Seventeen

KING'S BEACH

(PRESLEY)

I'd seen it in a movie, but had never tried it myself. My hair whipped wild and free in the wind as I propped my body up through Reese's sunroof—one foot resting on Reese's seat, one on Violet's. Reese had called and woke me up this morning to inform me that we were all ditching school since the weather was going to be in the eighties. It wasn't like me to ditch, but as crazy as things had been lately, I looked forward to the distraction.

We weaved down the highway, through the shadows of towering trees. Sunlight flickered warmly on my closed eyes as I tipped my head back and breathed in adventure and the unexpected.

Not even Violet could argue with Reese's idea to ditch school. The weather really had turned unseasonably warm overnight. It took little effort to convince Sam, Garett, and Kade to simply walk out the front door of the school instead of going to class after lunch. Reese drove with Violet and me as shotgun cocaptains with Sam, Garett, and Kade in the cab's backseat. We laughed and joked with music blaring and cups of convenience store soda in our hands. I slurped the last of my soda through a straw. I slithered back down into the truck and wedged myself back between Reese and Violet.

"Where we going?" I asked, feeling like they could have said "the moon" and I wouldn't have argued.

"Kings Beach," Violet said quickly, a tentative smile on her lips.

Reese looked at her, a mix of surprise and confusion on his face. "Are you sure, Vi? There are other beaches . . ."

"I'm sure," she said, more decidedly. She faced me, warmth in her eyes. "It's where we used to go with Landon," she explained. "We haven't been back since. . ." She swallowed.

"Oh." I spared her from finishing the sentence. "I see."

"It's time," she continued lightly. "It's one of our favorite places and I'm sure Landon wouldn't want us to stay away on his account."

Garett raised his soda cup. "To Landon." Each person in turn raised their cups and tapped them in a caffeinated, carbonated toast, Reese and Violet stretching their cups behind them to meet their friends'. My cup was gone, so I didn't join in. An ironic manifestation of how I felt. I'd never known Landon and it often made me feel like an outsider in the group. Reese brought me out of my private thoughts.

"You girls are all getting thrown in the lake. Don't try to fight it. It's happening," he stated matter-of-factly, as if he were declaring the contents of his suitcase at the airport.

Violet rolled her eyes. "You guys are so juvenile. Can we not go to the beach one time without you doing that? We don't even have our suits."

"Don't care. It's happening. Leave your phones in the truck if you don't want them ruined," Reese said, chewing on his straw through the sides of his perfect mouth.

In the rear-view mirror, I saw the boys in the back fist bump each other, at which Sam giggled.

Reese made good on his promise. At Kings Beach, he pulled nonchalantly to the side of the road, got out, walked around and tore Violet from the passenger seat. He threw her over his shoulder, with Violet kicking and punching, and deftly marched through the sand until he reached the shore. He didn't wade deeply; he simply set her in knee-deep water and pinned her down until she was thoroughly soaked and gasping from cold. Then he sprung from her and ran away inhumanly fast. It was pointless for her to try and catch him. Garett and Kade had also drug Sam from the back seat, Garett holding her under the shoulders and Kade holding her feet. She drooped obediently—throwing her head back, laughing. I took my opportunity to run and hide like the coward I was. Lake Tahoe water was no more than barely melted snow, even in the dead of summer. I couldn't imagine how freezing it would be in October.

I bolted at an angle down the beach and found a thick pine trunk to hide behind. I could hear Reese yelling.

"Presley! Where did you go, you wimp? I'll find you!"

He made his way in my direction and I fused my back to the trunk, tucking in all my limbs, attempting to become as invisible as possible. It was quiet. I waited for a stretch of time that felt too long. Maybe he had given up. I hesitantly peeled myself from the tree and peeked around the corner.

"GOT YOU!" he yelled, startling me.

I screamed and tried to run, but his iron arms were already clamped around my middle. He threw me over his shoulder and jogged toward the water, but instead of taking me to the area where he pinned Violet, he went a bit further to the sun-bleached pier. The end of the wooden walkway came more quickly than I hoped.

I gave him my biggest puppy-dog gaze. "Please Reese. Please no," I pleaded. He held me now, cradled in his arms like a honeymooner.

He smiled. "Aww, look at you. Such a sweet little girl begging for your life."

"I am. I am begging. I hate cold water. I hate it so bad." I giggled nervously. "Please, I'll do whatever you want," I added.

He cocked an eyebrow. "Whatever I want?"

"Yes!" I gasped.

"As in, I'm the total boss of you?" he teased.

Stupidly, my pride got to me. "No man is the boss of me."

"Oh, I think I am your boss. I think I'm your total boss if you don't want me to throw you in that water."

I stared incredulously at him. "You are not the boss of me."

"Say it," he beamed. "Say I'm the boss of you or you get it," he warned.

Our eyes were welded to each other, one daring the other to make a move. His eyes were brilliant with life, his face flushed with jubilance and playfulness.

I'd made up my mind. "Reese Blackwood, you are not the boss of me. Nor will you ever be." I cocked my eyebrow this time and waited.

He considered my statement, his face smooth. "Is that so?"

"Yes it is," I said, more confident now.

"Alrightly then," he said lightly. Then he jumped with me in his arms into the rib-cracking cold of Lake Tahoe.

Chapter Eighteen

GREEN-EYED MONSTER

(LANDON)

I couldn't remember ever feeling jealousy like this. It boiled, hot and filthy inside me. I watched from a distance as Presley giggled behind a tree, hiding from Reese. She was bubbling. She was laughing. Her eyes, animated and bright. This is how he made her feel.

My gut lurched as I watched him find her, then pick her up and hold her so easily. His hands were strong against the softness of her body. A slap in the face. I knew my hands could do nothing like that. Not anymore.

Her hair came loose and fell forward in soft brown curls, bouncing with each step he took as he toted her to the water. He slowed at the pier and flipped her around in his arms to hold her like a baby or worse, a lover. I couldn't see his face, but I didn't need to. I'd seen it enough in situations like this. His power to intoxicate girls was undeniable. His magnetism was a force of its own.

I wasn't sure why my feelings were so strong. I'd only met her once, well twice, really. It wasn't like I was in love.

She was beautiful, undoubtedly. And I'd seen the sweet way she treated her brother, many of the ways she spent her time. She was different than other girls I had known. If I were truthful, she wouldn't have caught my attention in my former life. I gravitated toward the party girls. Anyone Violet couldn't stand—that was my type. I would've never slowed down enough to even notice Presley. I was surprised Reese had.

Put her down, already. You don't need to hold her that long. Throw her in and get it over with.

Finally, after minutes of banter that I hated to watch, Reese jumped in with her. He'd never done that before.

The memories I had of King's Beach with this group weighed like lead in my heart. I missed my friends and family. But I had dealt with those demons in a lot of ways. So much that just a month ago, I was ready to move on with James. But now, a new yearning burned in me, consuming my thoughts. As selfish and crazy as it was, I wanted to be with Presley.

She trudged through the water, laughing and calling Reese names I agreed with, and finally collapsed on the sand. He stripped off his soaked shirt and lay next to her, covering his bare stomach with large scoops of sand. She joined in the effort and kneeled next to his legs, shoveling handfuls onto him, until only his toes, shoulders and head were exposed. What were they talking about? They appeared so relaxed—natural around each other.

Just as I couldn't stand another minute of watching the two of them and was about to leave, Garett and Kade threw insults at Reese, calling him a pansy and a wuss. It was enough to entice Reese from his warm mound of sand and Presley's company. He ran into the water and dispensed justice on his teasers. Presley jogged over to the girls and explained something to them. Her fingers formed a phone near her ear. She needed to make a call, from the looks of it.

Everything tightened inside me as I watched her walk back up the slope of sand toward the road. In a matter of seconds she would be alone at Reese's truck—out of view from the others.

Deciding quickly to seize the opportunity, I laced my hands behind my head and conjured some labored breath. I heard the soft pad of her bare feet on the concrete as she approached the truck. She opened the door and soon after, slammed it.

"Krew? Is that you?" Presley called from the truck, still wet with a cell phone in her hand.

Bingo.

I looked up, forcing my face into some natural appearance. "Oh, hey! What are you doing following me again?"

"What?" she laughed.

"If you keep doing this I'm going to start thinking you're creepy," I warned.

"I know exactly what you mean," she said, a mix of amusement and misgiving on her face. "What are you doing out here?"

"Running. I'm a runner. I like to run." *Way to stay cool, idiot.*

"Okay."

"What are you doing here? Shouldn't you be in school or something?"

"Yeah, I'm just here with some friends. You know, the weather was so nice we decided to skip. One last hurrah before winter sets in." She glanced back at the beach. "Do you know Reese or Violet Blackwood?"

A punch to the gut. " We didn't really run in the same circles."

"Oh." She looked at me skeptically.

"I hear they are cool, though," I offered. "For the most part."

"What's that last bit supposed to mean?" She quizzed me, but still looked happy enough.

A small tinge of guilt. Easily swept aside. "Well, some of my friends . . . that are girls, don't like Reese much. I like him as a dude, but as a chick . . . yeah. That's all I'm saying. Bro code."

"Think I get it," she said flatly.

I hated to do it, but I knew the only way to keep girls interested at first was to act like I wasn't. Even death hadn't changed that rule. "Well, it was good seeing you, Presley. Have fun."

Her posture changed immediately.

"Where you running to? I mean, what's your route today?" she asked, looking shy.

Her cheeks bloomed pink under a light sprinkling of freckles. I wanted to touch her face and watch her blush more.

"I don't know. Until I get tired, I guess. Usually four or five miles," I lied.

"That's how long my route is. I think it's the perfect distance. Long enough to call it a legit workout, but short enough that I can walk the next day."

"Exactly. Perfect." Surely she thought I was commenting on running routes, but I found myself inwardly commenting on her eyes, which were liquid and alluring.

"We should run together sometime," she blurted out. She turned a little pale, probably regretting her forwardness.

I smiled inside, stoked that what I hoped would happen actually did.

"Oh Presley, I couldn't do that to you."

Her face deflated.

I continued. "I mean, guys can't even keep up with all of this." I gestured to my body. "Enough to make a grown man cry, let alone a girl like you. But if you insist on embarrassing yourself . . ."

"Oh, I see," she teased. "You're afraid that your geezer self can't keep up with my young spry legs. It's okay. I totally get you have to save face. Lots of old people do that."

Accidentally, my eyes traveled to her legs. Clearing my throat, I broke the spell. "Well, we'll see then. I know you like using my trail by the river; perhaps that would be a good meet-up spot?"

"Your trail?" she laughed.

"Yes. My trail. I love it and I run on it so it's mine," I reasoned.

"You can't own . . . nature."

"Oh, I own pretty much anything I want."

Her eyes narrowed. "Really."

"And I'll own you if you try to run faster than me. But, no need to brag I suppose, you'll find out soon enough." I had her. I was sure of it.

"How soon?"

"Tomorrow, if you want. Sunrise?" I said casually, though a leaping, thrashing feeling struggled in my chest.

"I'll be there," she said with a crooked grin, like she was scheming. "I'll meet you right where you were stalking me the first time. Just remember to bring your tissues for when I send you home crying."

"You're a sassy little thing, aren't you?" I said through a smile.

"Only when provoked." Her hands rested on her hips.

"I'd hate to see how you'll react tomorrow when you realize you can't keep up."

She took a few steps closer and I found myself narrowing the gap with a couple steps of my own. We were a person apart and I was startled by the smell of her—vanilla, mint, and something else I couldn't identify. But it made me want to close the gap and breathe her in up close.

"Oh, I can keep up," she said, her chin set in defiance, but her eyes spirited.

"I think I'm in trouble, after all," I said.

"I think you're right."

She didn't know how right she was.

Chapter Nineteen

PARTNERS

(LANDON)

The sun was near rising. I stood where I'd met Presley just two days before and contemplated the complexities of what was about to take place. First and foremost, I couldn't give myself away. She could not learn under any circumstances who or what I was. For a moment, I considered the opposite—indulging in a mini-fantasy of telling her the truth. I imagined the comfort of someone from the living world knowing I was still here, that I had not left forever.

Ridiculous. She could not know. It was selfish to even think it.

But we would be talking to each other. And this was the perfect place for it. I'd chosen it purposefully because I had to be sure she wouldn't be seen talking into thin air. Next I'd have to make sure we didn't touch. That wouldn't be a problem. A girl like her probably wouldn't expect a guy to touch her on the first date. Date? Could I even call it that?

Eventually I'd have to gauge whether or not she'd learned anything about my accident. Thankfully at the end of last school year, they'd taken down that enormous memorial in the main hall. It was hard to admit, though, that for most Truckee students, my death was old news by now.

I'd have to be vague about my family—avoid speaking specifically about Violet. No mention of Reese either.

I knew it was impossible, but I could actually feel my palms getting clammy. I vividly remembered all of the physical sensations of being human, so much that I think my mind often took over and convinced me that I was still actually experiencing, not just remembering. Because, of course, my palms could not be sweaty.

What if I couldn't pull this off? What if something gave me away? Since the day in the school parking lot, James had warned me how ugly it could get if Presley found out the dead walk among the living. It wouldn't be fair to scare an innocent person that way. But if I were careful, scaring her would never happen.

I couldn't help but feel a little entitled to her. There had to be a reason why she could see me. I deserved to find out.

Birds called to one another and the shadows retreated. The sun was up. Maybe she wasn't coming. Maybe she was on to me and realized our two meetings weren't by chance. Maybe she was more into Reese than I thought. My spirits sank contemplating that possibility.

A head of cinnamon curls emerged from the trees and relief washed over me. I waved to her and was surprised at the simple thrill of her waving back.

She saw me. She waved to me.

I studied her as she approached. Her unruly curls were pulled back in a messy knot at the nape of her neck, which allowed better scrutiny of her pixie-like face. She wore an outfit suitable for the cover of a runner's magazine—sporty, but feminine. Though most people would probably not rank her as supermodel status, there was something wholesome and tempting about her that I couldn't exactly explain.

There was a lightness to her. Her face, her body, her expression— it all suggested ease. The images struck me as foreign, but so welcome it ached. In the months since my death, naturally, much of my time was spent around Violet and her carefully controlled emotions.

She paused for a minute, kneeling; I thought she was tying her shoe. Instead she stood up with a pinecone in her hands and held it to her nose. "This never gets old."

"What?" I laughed. "Sniffing pinecones?"

"No," she retorted. "Living in the mountains," and she playfully tossed the pinecone at me.

I dodged it, thankfully. A pinecone traveling right through me might put a damper on our morning. "I hope your aim is better with snowballs," I teased.

"I guess we'll have to wait and see."

The possibility that I would be with her when the snow fell was small, yet exciting. Her eyes sparkled, playful and confident. Freckles, tiny ones, dotted the bridge of her nose and soft apples of her cheeks.

"Ready?" I asked, though I would have been content to stay there with her all day.

"If you're sure you're okay with humiliation," she said, not missing a beat.

I spent the first five minutes of our run wondering if she would notice my footfalls making no sound. But it soon became obvious that our conversation was the focus of her attention. And why wouldn't it be? Why would she have any reason to listen for the sound of my feet? I resolved to not think of it anymore.

"So, where do you go to school?" she asked.

"Just down the mountain," I said. "UNR."

She revealed that she'd already made the drive and I could only guess it may have included some Lumberjack gorging.

"Are you there full-time?" she asked between breaths that were barely labored.

"Nah, just twice a week," I said. "I get all of my classes done on Tuesday and Thursday." I swallowed back the bitter taste of the lie that came too easily.

"So what do you do in the summer?"

"Mostly work and hang out at the lake. My family has a pretty cool boat, so we ski a lot. You really only get a few months of warm weather here, so we try to come out as much as we can."

"I water-skied, well *tried* to water-ski once. It wasn't pretty." She grimaced.

I glanced at her toned, shapely legs. "You? You um . . . seem like you could get up on skis pretty easily."

She raised an eyebrow and looked knowingly at me. *Whoops.*

"Well I did get up. That wasn't really the hard part. It's just that once I was up I looked around and sort of spazzed out. I'm not a speed demon. I may or may not have cried when I got back in the boat."

"Wow."

"I know. You didn't know you'd made such a cool friend did you? I'll give you my autograph later."

"Lookin' forward to it."

"Probably get some cash on eBay for it."

"Oh, I would never part with it."

The distance passed too quickly and a sort of sadness bled into me as I realized it wouldn't be long until our miles were covered. I feigned fatigue and slowed my pace hoping it would prolong our time.

"What?" she goaded. "Ready to quit when you haven't even broken a sweat?"

"Okay, I admit it. I'm a weenie." We slowed our trot to a walk that brought my arm only inches from hers as we matched steps. The proximity immediately brought on the buzz of physical awareness. Ironic, since I no longer had a physical body.

"As long as you admit it," she smirked.

Presley was a generous conversationalist. "I'm assuming that because you live in this place and you water ski, you also snow ski?" she asked.

It took all of my superpowers not to smile at that. Of course she knew I skied. She only took a picture of me on her phone from the trophy cabinet. It felt good to have a girl into me. "Yeah, I did in high school. It was definitely my thing. Loved the speed."

"Mmm . . . good for you. I could never."

"No. You could. You'd probably love it once you got into it. You just have to psych yourself out and not really think about how dangerous it is, how steep the mountain is, how fast you're going."

"See! Why must sports be dangerous? I do not understand this concept. Death is not fun to me."

My face dropped. Death definitely wasn't fun. There was no way she could have known why I suddenly darkened, but in response, she lightened up a bit.

"So water skiing in the summer and snow skiing in the winter." A crease formed between her eyebrows and she wrinkled her nose. "I'm afraid I'm not going to fit in very well here."

"Of course you will." My need to assure her overtook my common sense. "I'll give you lessons. Snow and water, if you want." I knew I could give her neither, but it was impossible for me not to be me when I was with her. If I were alive still, that is exactly what I would have offered.

I was still me in every way, except the body. I felt the same, I loved the same, I saw and heard the same. I still had desires. With a dejected clarity I realized that the only difference between being dead and alive was the ability to physically act upon my inclinations. And my inclinations definitely pointed toward Presley.

I loved my time with her, and not just because she was the only person who'd spoken to me in five months. Well, there was James, but he had such an agenda, it felt like he didn't count. Presley was different. With her, it was the first time in so long I'd had the chance to be myself. Or as much of myself as I could be.

She stared at me skeptically, but somehow affectionately too. "Why are you so nice to me? You don't even know me, and you'd give me lessons?"

I shrugged. It wouldn't take much convincing for any guy to want to get to know her. "A new town for your senior year, that has to be rough."

"So, you feel sorry for me, then?" she teased, and without warning reached out to playfully slug my arm. I dodged with success.

"Whoa, girl. Why all the violence?" I laughed. "First the pinecone . . ."

"I'm sure you deserve everything I dish out." She smiled and pulled two granola bars from a zippered pocket. She ripped one open and offered the other to me.

It was like she'd offered me a poisonous snake. I had to think fast. Of course I'd have to refuse an offering of food. Disappointment weighed heavily as I realized the simplest thing like her asking me to hold something, could bring down this entire thing. I'd have to get used to smoothly navigating between our separate worlds.

The pause grew awkward, so I collected myself and reasoned that saying no to a granola bar was not incriminating. "I'm good, but thanks. Made an omelet right before I came."

"Oh my gosh. Hot food actually cooked on a skillet. What's that like?"

"What do you mean?"

"Hales don't cook. Ever."

"Not your mom or your dad?"

"My dad might, but I wouldn't know." She chewed her granola bar slowly and kicked at the pine needles until they formed a small mound at her feet.

"So your parents aren't together anymore." It was a careful statement.

"He left when I was five."

"That sucks."

" It really messed things up, you know?" She shoved her crumpled granola bar wrapper in her pocket and started walking again.

I nodded, though I didn't really know. My mom and dad happily played the corny 1950s role of doting husband and loving wife. Until my death, my family never really lived through a major crisis.

"But enough about me," she said brightly. "You haven't really told me much about you, other than you're a carpenter-slash-college student and you're a phenom on skis." The smile returned to her eyes and I could tell the conversation about her personal life was over.

"Yeah, that about sums it up, especially that part about being phenomenal."

She laughed as I winked my cheesiest wink.

"Have you considered getting an agent? Maybe taking up modeling? I heard GQ is hiring."

"I should."

"But then you'd have your public to contend with. People stopping you in the streets and at gas stations, asking to squeeze your biceps and such," she said, totally deadpan.

I flexed my muscles and kissed each of my biceps. "Yep. These babies are both a blessing and a curse."

The joke did a poor job masking the guilt building in my mind. I hated lying to her. And I knew more conversations would necessitate more lies. There was nothing I could do to prevent it other than give her up entirely. Which wasn't an option.

"So as much potential as your calendar career holds, you must have another game plan," Presley teased.

My post–high school plans were already coming together by the time of my accident. I'd been offered full-ride scholarships to the University of Colorado, UNR, and Columbia University—all schools with alpine racing teams. "I don't really know. I'm . . . what do they call it? Finding myself." Our conversation flowed naturally. I shared as much about my family as I could without giving myself away. My dad owned his own business (I neglected to mention that it was Blackwood Ski Resort) and I had two sisters and one brother (I omitted their names). I left Reese completely out of it.

I learned, among other things, that Presley loved her Aunt Lily who had just turned ninety, had a younger brother with autism (which I already knew), and that her mom was the new principal (which I also already knew). She took advanced everything in school and hoped to graduate early. Her mom never remarried or even dated for that matter, and didn't approve at all of Presley dating until college.

"So if you're mom doesn't like you dating," I said casually, "you must not have a boyfriend, then." I didn't think what she and Reese had was considered boyfriend status. It couldn't have been or she wouldn't have been with me.

"I have friends that are boys." She tried to play it cool but the squeak in her voice betrayed her. Unexpectedly, her eyes turned from teasing to tense and distant. She hugged her ribs and shivered slightly. She worked up quite a sweat, so I doubted she was cold. As I looked more closely at her, I noticed shaded crescents under her eyes.

My voice came out soft. "Did I say something wrong? I didn't mean to get too personal."

She shook her head and dropped her eyes. "No, it's not that." She squinted and her confidence seemed to dim a bit. "I barely know you and I don't want you to think I'm crazy." She laughed awkwardly.

"It's fine. You can tell me."

I could see the debate in her eyes. Finally, she said, "You know what? It's nothing. Never mind."

"It doesn't look like nothing." I took a step closer, and then realized that might not have been wise. "You have to trust somebody, right?" I choked on the irony of those words.

She exhaled and tucked a stray curl behind her ear. "It's this dream—a nightmare, really. I've been having it every night for weeks." She dared a glance at me. I nodded to reassure her. "You must have heard about that kid who drowned last year."

Alarm sounded inside of me and I closed my eyes briefly, composed my face. "Yeah."

"Well, he was my friend's twin brother."

I swallowed hard. The poisonous feeling crept from my chest and through my veins until it stung my fingertips.

She continued, her words edged with distress. "I dream about him every night. It's so real. I feel the rain, I hear the bridge creaking when the train blasts over. I've memorized the face of each of the rescuers." She closed her eyes tightly. "The body. I try to look away every time, but I can't."

I wanted to run. To get away from her words. I purposely stayed as far away from the memory of that night as I could. I *never* visited it. Her razor-sharp details sliced through me again and again. Disturbing that she shared specifics that only people present that night should know. Reese must've really opened up.

It was obvious she hadn't made the connection that I was that guy. But there was a profound ache in my chest, like something cold and jagged was buried there.

Dangerous. Wrong. She could be so close to finding out who I really was and I didn't want to think how badly that could damage her. If I had any conscience, I would turn and run. But I couldn't let her go.

Chapter Twenty

Secret Place

(PRESLEY)

I thought I might have freaked Krew out because I didn't hear from him for a week after our run. But then he'd showed up yesterday at the football field while I was running laps and invited me to hang out at his "secret place." I hoped it wasn't the trunk of his car and that there wasn't duct tape and rope in there.

Seriously though, I'm giving Krew my number today. It's happening. Who doesn't text? Krew's indifference to phone contact was just weird. I found myself checking my phone several times a day, hoping to see a missed call or text from him. But of course there never was. He'd never asked for my number. Or offered his.

I realized yesterday that every interaction we'd had was face-to-face. There was something kind of old-fashioned and charming about it, actually. Like Mr. Darcy coming to call on Elizabeth. He never sent a text.

It was killing me. I couldn't even get a Facebook or Instagram fix in between "social calls" because he didn't have accounts. I checked Twitter too, even though I didn't use it. He was like. . . Amish. I'd never even seen him in a car.

And I thought it was bizarre that he'd asked me to meet him at a mile marker. I sat in my freshly painted Romeo with his four new tires on a wide patch of shoulder, somewhere between Kings Beach and Sand Harbor. I couldn't imagine why he'd picked this place; there was nothing but pine-covered mountains across the two-lane road to my left, and a treacherous looking drop-off to the lake on my right. I reapplied vanilla lip balm for the second time because he was ten minutes late.

With zero details on this secret place, I wasn't sure how to dress. Going for something that might suit any place, I'd opted for a simple cream tunic, my crazy tribal print leggings and some strappy leather sandals. With some extra time for my hair, I'd watched a YouTube thing on how to do a messy side braid. It turned out awesome.

I fidgeted with the worn slip of paper in my hand. It was warm and wrinkled by now. Still working up the courage to find a way to give him my number, I considered just tearing it up. It wasn't like he was giving me any encouragement. How many ways had Reese found to touch me? The friendly hugs, throwing me over his shoulder, letting me win at arm wrestling. Come to think of it, Reese was touching me more than not. And Krew had rarely come closer than arm's length. But, the way he looked at me sometimes.

Like that one time.

The first time we'd met on our running trail. Before we'd said goodbye. My heart still raced when I thought of his expression. And why did I replay that moment practically every day?

Am I sweating?

"Presley?" Krew's voice floated in through my cracked window.

I jumped, and he stifled a laugh.

"What the heck were you thinking about?" he said through a wide smile.

"Nothing."

"It didn't look like nothing," he teased.

I felt my face burning. "Why do you say that?"

"Umm . . . because I called your name three times before you answered."

"Shut up!" I said. "You're lying."

"No, seriously." He looked amused. "Three times. What were you thinking about?"

I'd rather eat five pounds of toenails that admit I was daydreaming about you. I threw my keys and lip balm into my purse. "Maybe I was zoned out since someone was over ten minutes late," I chided.

"Stop whining and get out here," he said.

He led the way off the shoulder and into the trees where the ground quickly gave way to a steep, sloped path.

"Where are you taking me?" I asked.

"I told you already—it's a secret."

"FYI—I left a note for my mom that said I was at mile marker forty-two, just in case you have nefarious plans for me." I didn't tell him about the mace in my glove box.

He tossed his head back and laughed out loud.

We came to a place where the path was washed out and a small stream cut through, making muddy ribbons across the way.

My instinct was to reach for him and have him help me across, but he didn't take my hand. Instead, he turned back and looked at me for a moment. My stomach flipped. It was that look again. I wondered if he looked at other girls that way.

He scrubbed the back of his head with one hand and exhaled. His eyes kept mine and he smiled crookedly. "Sorry, it's a little tricky here—watch me."

He leapfrogged over the stream, using a rock in the middle to keep his feet dry. It was a lot harder than he made it look. I slipped off the stepping-stone and hoped he wouldn't notice the sucking sound of my foot pulling out of the mud.

"Aw, Pres. That sucks. Scrape it off on that log."

"I guess this wasn't the wisest choice of footwear."

"I disagree. You have freakishly cute feet—like kitten cute."

"Are you one of those foot fetish people?"

He cocked an eyebrow. "I never thought so, but I'm open-minded." His eyes glinted and he said, "Come on, we're almost there."

I followed him a few more yards and a weathered and overgrown staircase appeared through the trees. The wood steps clung to the side of the mountain and led steeply down to the lake. At the bottom landing, a dock stretched over the water to a secluded log boathouse.

"What's this?" I said, taking note of the playful way he was smiling.

"I've been wanting to take you here; it's one of my favorite places."

"I can see why. This is amazing."

"And secret." He winked and started down the stairs.

"Mmmhmm. The perfect lair to lure all the girls," I said, following him.

He turned to me with a look of genuine insult. "I've never taken any girl here."

I smiled. I couldn't help it.

We reached the dock and he led me around the edge of the boathouse to the side that faced the lake. The bay's door was open and an antique, wooden motorboat, glossy and lacquered hung over the water, suspended on cables from a beam.

"What a cool boat!" I stepped over and ran a hand over the bow. I turned back to him. "Is this *yours?*"

"Mine and my dad's."

"So gorgeous." I had never thought a day in my life about boats, but the old-school charm of this one called to me somehow. "Are we taking a ride?"

He shook his head. "It's not finished yet. We've been restoring it, but we still have a few things left to do before we can take it out."

"How much longer, do you think?"

His face shifted. "I don't know; we haven't been down here in months." He followed me into the shade of the structure. "Stuff gets in the way, you know?"

"Totally. I'm still digging clothes out of cardboard boxes. How long have I lived here now?"

"Well, we can't take a ride today, but do you want to look inside?"

"Yeah, of course." I swept the workspace for some sort of stool or ladder, but didn't see one among the scattered tools and extension cords.

"Just hit that switch behind you."

With the touch of a button, the boat lowered slowly into the water with a mechanical hum. I liked the sound of the water gently lapping against the sides.

"Climb on in. Watch your step, there's a little gap."

I swung a leg over the edge of the boat. "So do you I have to call you Captain?" I said, sliding down onto the leather upholstery.

"Please do," he said as he situated himself behind the wheel and panel of chrome instruments.

I took a moment to look out over the lake. One of the things that always took me by surprise was how clear the water was. And the color of the shallow parts, turquoise, almost tropical.

Krew cleared his throat and squared his shoulders to me. "So, what's the craziest thing you've ever done?"

That caught me off guard. I gave a nervous laugh. "Not wasting any time, I see." I rubbed my palms against my legs.

"I'm taking advantage of every second I have with you."

He said it casually, but a blanket of warmth came over me.

"So . . . crazy. Hmm." I scanned my memory for something that might be interesting. "I would have to say the time my best friend Ellie drove me around the block on the hood of my mom's Pontiac. My neighbor told on me and I was grounded for a week."

Krew's lips were clamped and his chin quivered with the effort of holding back a laugh. It proved too much for him and he bent over and let it out.

"Why are you laughing? That is totally dangerous!"

"How old were you when you did that?"

"Sixteen."

He laughed even harder.

"Fine then, what have you done that's so crazy?"

He tapped his chin and looked out over the water. "Hard to choose, hard to choose."

"Oh, here we go."

"I've got one," he said, laughing at himself.

Unexpectedly, I found myself wanting to lean over and kiss the corner of his perfect smile.

"Have you met Price yet?"

"The government teacher?" I said, shaking amorous thoughts from my mind.

"Yeah. Did you know he drives a moped?"

I snickered. "What? He's like six-four!"

"I know, right? I can't believe you haven't seen him yet. He's like a circus bear on a unicycle." He ran a tanned hand through his almost-black hair. "Anyway, he announces all of the home football games up in the stand." He laughed again at the memory. "One game, I stole his moped and rode it across the field at halftime."

I was expecting more than that. I gave a courtesy laugh.

"Naked." He arched a dark eyebrow.

I gasped. "No you did not!"

Grasping the wheel, he appraised me from the corner of his eye. "Just kidding. I had on a red cape and a swim team Speedo."

There was that kissable smile again. I shook it out of my mind "Still, indecent exposure. So, what happened? Were you suspended?"

He locked his elbows and dropped his chin. "Nah, just a week's detention."

"Detention. You must be some kind of golden boy."

He shrugged it off. "They just needed me eligible for alpine."

This guy was fearless. A total rebel. I couldn't imagine doing anything that daring. I chewed on my thumbnail. If he could be that bold, surely I could give him my phone number. He was into me, wasn't he? I was the only girl he'd ever brought down here, right?

I reached into my bag and took out the slip of paper with my number on it. I held it in my lap, rubbing it between my thumb and forefinger. "I know you haven't asked for it, and I hope you don't think it too forward of me . . ." I held out the slip to him. "But I'd like to have more time to talk to you between our. . . whatever these meet-ups are." I smiled shyly.

He didn't move to take it from me. His hands were still on the wheel. He dropped them to his lap. I shrunk inside and withdrew the slip, hastily returning it to my purse.

He looked at me, wavering. "Can't we just keep things the way they are?"

Rocks in my stomach. Of course. *He has a girlfriend. Obviously he wouldn't want me texting him. His girlfriend might see it. No wonder we're here at this secluded place.* When I thought of it, every place we'd ever gone had been "secret." *He can't risk being seen with me.*

I worked to smooth the humiliation from my face. "Yeah, no problem. I'm good with the way things are." I slid to the opposite end of the bench from him and climbed out of the boat. "I was only offering it to you as a friend."

He climbed out on his side and looked at me, seeming troubled. "Pres, I didn't mean it that way."

"Look, let me just be honest with you. I've had enough people jerk me around since moving here, and I'm not about let you join the list." I grabbed the edge of the boat and leaned in. "And you should be ashamed of yourself. Whoever she is deserves better than to have her boyfriend sneaking around."

A pained look tightened his face. "What are you talking about?"

"I get it, okay? You have a girlfriend. I'm not stupid."

He grabbed the boat's side as well. "Wait. You think just because I didn't take your phone number . . . I have a girlfriend?" He leaned over and rested his forehead on the backs of his hands then looked up. And laughed at me. "What must it be like to be you, Presley? You adorable, tortured little thing."

Irritation seeped through my chest, quickly followed by a second wave of humiliation. *Seriously, how many ways can I find to embarrass myself within five minutes?* "It just seemed funny that you wouldn't want to take my number, like you don't want anything that could trace you back to me." I dropped my eyes.

"Look at me. Please."

Reluctantly, I met his eyes. They were undisguised.

"I don't have a girlfriend." He straightened, and then slowly inched toward the bow of the boat, trailing his hand along the polished wood. "You want to know why I didn't take your number?"

"Yes." My voice was small. Tentatively, I made my way toward the bow, matching his steps, my fingers running over the smoothness of the vessel.

"How could a call or text message compare to this?" He took another small step forward. "To having you here, right next to me?"

My insides ignited. I looked away.

"If we were always on the phone I'd be missing too much," he mused.

I sensed his eyes on me, but I was afraid to look up.

He continued to glide forward and his voice switched from playful, to low and soft. "Nothing's better than this."

My body tensed. In a good way. This had to be it. After all this time wondering how he really felt about me, he was finally putting himself out there. At last stepping out of the friendship circle to where I'd been shamelessly standing the whole time.

We met at the tip of the bow, our fingertips resting just inches apart. Emboldened by this new Krew, I raised my eyes to his. There was no mistaking the hunger in his stare.

My voice escaped, before I could call it back. "What are you waiting for?"

Chapter Twenty-One

INTERFERENCE

(LANDON)

Violet was out, so I took advantage of her absence to spend some time at home to think. My family's muffled voices filtered from the dinner table into the living room. James looked out across the lake from the picture window, his back to me. He'd barely given me a minute to myself the last couple of days. I just wanted to be alone to figure some stuff out.

Like what to do about Presley. *She's expecting me to touch her. I know it. I'm even expecting myself to touch her. I almost did at the boathouse. It's almost like I believe I can. That was too close. What would I have done if Presley's mom hadn't called and interrupted us when she did? I have to be more careful. But I don't want to be.*

"We need to talk," James said.

His voice snipped the last threads of my thoughts about Presley. "So talk."

"It's been nearly six months."

"I know."

He evaluated me. "And now we've got *two* things holding you back." James sighed and waited patiently.

He was a good guy and I took him for granted, no doubt. I'm sure most people would've given up by now, but he still hung with me, even after all this time. I measured my tone, kept it respectful.

"I've kept my promise. I've stayed completely away from Violet, just like you asked."

"I'll give you that. But I wonder if you're any more willing to leave her than you were before?"

He was right. I wasn't remotely ready to leave Violet. Every time I considered it, it made me sick. I was still at ground zero. Nonnegotiable.

From the beginning, I'd known Violet could still sense me so I'd thought staying nearby comforted her. Though James had shown me that my presence was keeping Violet's wound open, he'd neglected to mention that simply keeping my distance would've allowed her to begin healing. I can't believe James almost had me talked into leaving.

And now there was more than Violet to consider—Presley. I knew I wasn't entitled to her, but that didn't change how badly I wanted her. And my presence didn't seem to affect her negatively. The opposite, actually.

"I'm keeping my word about Violet, but I can't leave Presley. Not yet."

"Leaving is part of the plan," James said matter-of-factly.

"You just don't get it, James," I said, exasperated. "It's not like I'm able to just turn my emotions off now that I'm dead. And Presley's proven that I can form new relationships too." I challenged him with my eyes. "It's not worth leaving."

"That doesn't change the fact that you don't belong here." James matched my gaze.

I rose from my dad's chair and started to pace. "I don't believe that. There has to be a reason I met Presley. I don't know . . . fate."

"Your fate has been set. There's no undoing it."

I could tell that James was done mincing words. He appraised me with new gravity on his face.

"The Vigilum's interest in you has increased; are you aware?"

"So?" I retorted. "They want my passage. I won't give it. End of story."

"Not necessarily."

"What? Are they going to all gang up on me? Hold me down till I say uncle?"

"That's not how Vigilum work. Their physical abilities are limited like yours." James scratched his chin. "They are adept deceivers. They don't rely on brute force."

"You've told me about them. I know what I need to know. Their schemes, whatever they may be, won't deceive me."

"Even if their plans included Presley? Or Reese? Or Violet?"

"What are you getting at, James?"

Ignoring my interruption, James probed further. "Have you not considered that those closest to you may serve as excellent leverage when it comes to obtaining your passage?"

"How could Vigilum have any effect on them? They're living." I said the words but inside a warning sounded because so far, James had always been right. I stopped fighting and sighed. The seconds on the mantle clock ticked by accusingly. "Fine, give it to me."

"Consider this. Presley can see and hear them. They know she can. Since the night they experimented with her at the biology lab . . ."

"Wait, what? They weren't there that night. And neither were you for that matter."

"Landon, I'm never far and neither are the Vigilum."

I was ashamed of myself. Concerned that Presley's mom would overhear her one-sided conversation, I'd deserted her, not knowing I had exposed her to Vigilum threat.

"What do you mean, experimented? What did they do to her?" A parade of dark possibilities marched through my mind.

"They startled her, but she wasn't physically harmed. They were merely confirming what they already suspected—Presley can see anyone who is dead."

My interactions with Presley, which started innocently and felt so simple, now blazed into dangerous complication. She didn't deserve the side effects of knowing someone like me.

My eyes searched James's. They were perceptive, but gentle. Everything he warned that could happen to Presley was systematically unfolding just as he said it would. I wanted to be alone. To think on what I had started, but there was no time to wallow in such a luxury. I had others to consider.

"What about Violet? She can't see dead people. What can they do to her?" I asked, needing the answer, not wanting it though.

"Naturally, because of the closeness of your relationship, they will view her as leverage as well. Vigilum are proficients at searching out a human's darkest tendency. How can I explain in a way you'd understand?" James grappled with his thought for a moment, then a flicker dawned in his eyes. "They find one's weakness and they feed it; they expand it and then reflect it back to the victim."

"And Violet's weakness is?"

"Undoubtedly, her grief."

That wasn't hard for me to understand. James paused and my insides reacted with fear. When James hesitated it was always bad news. "Worsening her grief is only one form of torture they're capable of."

I couldn't bring myself to imagine the other "talents" the Vigilum had. The thought of them hurting Violet in any way was agony. She'd already endured so much. A knot formed in my throat. "Are they doing it to her already? Are they worsening her pain by experimenting on her too?"

James's face was a mix of kindness and authority. "She feels their drain. It's wearing her down."

I growled and stalked across the room, pausing in the shadow just outside the firelight. "Can't they be stopped?" James always had the answers. There had to be a way—something that could be done.

"Unfortunately, they've had so much time to observe you and your family . . ." The full weight of his gaze caught me. "They know what to do now." He shook his head like a doctor whose patient had just flatlined.

"Why didn't you tell me any of this back when it mattered? I might have thought differently; I might have used my passage if I'd known."

James arched an eyebrow. "Strangely, the Vigilum weren't an issue until your interrelations began with Presley. They were present the night of your death, but when they saw that I reached you before they did, they retreated. They held a casual interest, likely because your lengthy hesitation was a novelty, but they knew their chances with you were slim. That all changed after your conversation with Presley on the trail. After that day, they sensed something different in you." James gave a half smile. "You see, it is not only the living who have weaknesses."

"Presley is not a weakness," I thoroughly lied. In truth, she was. I sighed, frustrated. "It seems like I'm damned if I do, damned if I don't."

"Trust me when I say, you're much more damned if you don't." James's gaze flickered quickly over my shoulder—almost imperceptibly. But the resulting change that came over his face caused me to turn around.

The Vigilum were outside. If I hadn't known what to look for I may not have noticed them, camouflaged in the moonlight and shadows. Much like the night at the cemetery, I saw them perched outside the windows, predator-like in the limbs of the pines. The group stirred restlessly, but Liam held still, watching me with concentration.

Skipping an explanation to James, I moved straight through the glass to confront my stalkers.

James called after me, "Landon, stop!"

I ignored him, focused only on ending this. I covered ground quickly and Liam dropped from his perch to meet me.

"Hey, River Boy," Liam said, his eyes gleaming with provocation.

"Leave them alone." I'd never wanted to kill someone until that moment.

"Simmer down, Landon. And point that finger not at me, but back at yourself. You opened the door." He took a step nearer me, purposely invading that unspoken slice of space that treaded on threatening. "You invited us in." He challenged me with an unbroken stare.

I responded with a fist to his face.

His head whipped to the side with the force of my blow. He froze there momentarily and then chuckled low in his throat. Slowly, his face turned to meet mine.

"I think we need a lesson on who's in charge here."

Like a shark preparing for attack, Liam's pale eyes lost all traces of recognition and changed into black pools. I'd had many emotions in the last six months, but raw fear was never one of them. Now it paralyzed me.

The first vision assaulted me. I was under water; the frigid current merciless in its hold. I struggled to reach the surface, but it was in vain. Panicked, I let the last air out of my lungs and watched it bubble up and disappear. The river's lethal energy roiled around me and I watched in silent dismay as my class ring was ripped from my finger. The moon glinted once against the gold before I lost sight of it. I knew the encroaching blackness signaled the end.

The next vision was a scene I'd tried never to think about, relieved I'd never actually witnessed it firsthand. The sheriff sagged as he stood at my parents' front door. His hand hesitated at the door-bell. My father opened the door before the bell rang, desperation in his every feature. I didn't hear the words that sent my hovering mother to the floor. But I heard her wails.

In the last vision I was trapped inside my corpse. I laid in an open body bag on a cold table showered in the warm tears of my family. My father stood supporting my mother and Violet and then said in a broken voice, "It's time to go my loves. It's time to go." The coroner zipped the bag, covering my chest and neck. Violet broke from my father and threw herself over me. As my dad tried to pull her away, she clawed at the bag, disturbing my stillness. The last thing I saw before the bag enclosed my face was Violet's fingers, bone white in their straining, grasping the doorjam before they finally slipped loose.

Liam's black eyes returned to their usual eerie shade. "Nice to see you again, James. You've got a stubborn one here. Looks like I won't be the only F on your report card."

"I want you all to clear out. Now," James commanded.

Liam's companions dropped one by one from the trees, clearly nervous, but Liam remained planted. "Your boy asked for this tonight. In case you didn't see, I was defending myself."

"You did much more than that," James said. "We're leaving, Landon."

I had no problem with that. We turned to go as the majority of the group retreated into the darkness.

Liam called over his shoulder, his eyes threatening, "That was just a taste, Landon. I've got plans for your girlfriend and your sister. You can count on that."

Chapter
Twenty-Two

REVELATION

(PRESLEY)

I wished Gayle would take the time to learn Chase's calming strate-
gies. It sucked being the only one who could bring him down.

When I was at the boathouse, she'd called me all frantic. She'd
locked herself in her room because she couldn't get Chase calmed
down. She had let it get so bad, he'd bitten her. When I'd gotten
home, he had been covered in his own bite marks and had split the
bridge of his nose from banging his head against her door. Poor
Chase. I hadn't been home five minutes before he was calmed.

What did she think she was going to do when I went to college?
Would I need to take him with me? I was worried he wouldn't be
able to cope at home without me. Or did she expect me to live at
home forever?

So much for the first kiss.

Also, Violet had invited me over for dinner. I was nervous. I
wondered how her family was coping with Landon's death. It wasn't
that long ago. Should I say anything? Offer my condolences? My
mind played over these things as I drove to Violet's. I drove down a
tree-lined drive and wondered if I was lost. Soaring pines, so numer-
ous and thick they formed dark green walls, lined both sides of the
rust-colored dirt road. The sun had retreated behind the western
mountains and it was nearly dark now.

Finally, I noticed tiny pinholes of light peeking through the trees
ahead and breathed a sigh of relief. The estate at the end of the drive

made me wonder, though, if I'd made a wrong turn. The sprawling cedar and stone edifice couldn't possibly be a home; it looked more like a resort or fancy lodge. Three stone chimneys jutted from the structure, and warm light cast its glow from oversized windows.

A Dodge Durango with the license plate VBLCKWD was parked near the mammoth stand-alone garage. A path of reddish stone cut its way through the thick green lawn and led to a deck made of logs that wrapped around the entire home.

I climbed the stone steps that led to imposing front doors. Before I could even ring the bell, I heard a dog barking from inside. One of the doors swung open and Violet stood in the entrance, a huge smile stretched across her face as she gripped the collar of a very fat, very excited black lab. "Rosie! Chill!" she commanded as she tried to get the dog under control. After a few moments of struggle she sighed and said, "You might as well let her love on you; she won't settle down until she's licked the majority of your body surface. Sorry."

I knelt down gladly and roughed Rosie up behind the ears, and she indeed tasted most of my face. "It's fine. I like dogs." Rosie, apparently satisfied with me in some canine way, waddled off, her claws clicking on the stone floor.

Tantalizing breakfast smells of bacon, maple syrup, and eggs wafted through the house seducing my senses and informing me that I was ravenous.

"Well, I'm glad you made it!" Violet wrapped a slender arm around me and squeezed tightly as she led me through the doorway. "I saw your headlights coming up the drive. People have a hard time sneaking up on us here."

"Yeah, I can see that. I was actually starting to freak myself out a little bit, coming up your drive."

"I know. Sorry about that. I should've warned you. Everyone thinks they're lost their first time here. Come on—my family's been dying to meet you." She grabbed my hand and pulled me into the warmth of her enormous home.

Bright flames danced in a colossal, stone fireplace that spanned the entire south wall of the living room and pictures adorned the mantle from one end to the other. Floor to ceiling, windows consumed the west wall, promising what must be a spectacular view in the daylight.

Children's laughter and squealing drifted in from the kitchen. Violet picked up on my confusion and explained, "My entire family's here for dinner tonight, including my brother's rug rats. She smiled affectionately and added, "I hope you don't mind a little chaos. My sister Becca is getting married in December and in true Blackwood fashion, we've left everything to the last minute. Now we're all in panic mode getting everything ready. Watch your step . . . we're up to our ears in wedding crap."

I nimbly navigated through boxes of champagne flutes and invitations. From the banter that drifted in from the other room, it sounded like they were discussing the seating arrangements.

"Are you crazy?" someone yelled. "We can't sit Aunt Ruth next to Maggie. You know how sensitive she is. Ruth will decimate her in five minutes." I suppressed a giggle.

A blonde toddler ran right in front of me on his way to the kitchen, bare butt jiggling as he went.

Violet rolled her eyes. "Sorry about that. He's potty training."

"No prob," I laughed. I closed my eyes and inhaled deeply. "It smells so good."

Violet nodded, a sympathetic gesture. "Well, like I said, the Blackwoods are slightly crazy. We try to have dinner together at least once a week. Last week was Italian and tonight it's 'breakfast for dinner,'" Violet finger quoted.

Several curious eyes met mine as Violet and I moseyed into the kitchen. It was nearly the size of my home's entire first floor.

"Hey everyone, this is Presley." Violet wrapped a reassuring arm around my shoulders.

A tiny woman, even shorter than me, with a heart-shaped face and brilliant sapphire eyes wiped her hands on her red checkered apron. "Hi sweetie; so nice to finally meet you." She grabbed my hands in her own and gave them a tight squeeze. "I'm Afton, but everyone around here just calls me 'mom.' And this handsome guy is the love of my life, Frank." She reached up on tiptoes and kissed his cheek. "And this is Becca and her fiancé, Ben. And this is my brave policeman Eric and his wife Amber, and their beautiful little ballerina Jemma, who just turned three—didn't you big girl . . . and Princess Savannah who just started first grade, and heavens, where's the baby?"

A loud crash made everyone jump as the tiny streaker peeked around from a freshly-tipped trash can.

"Oh," Afton breathed with exaggerated relief. "There he is." She scooped him up and repeatedly kissed every inch of his plump face. "And this little troublemaker is Jackson, the newest addition to our family."

"So how's the city girl enjoying Truckee so far?" Frank asked on hands and knees, as he threw piles of trash back into the can.

"I can't believe how cold it gets at night. We're using our heater already."

Laughter erupted all around. "I'm guessing you don't know we use our heaters year round in Truckee." Frank made a face as he pinched dripping bacon packages between his fingers. "Temperatures go below freezing every month of the year here. Warms up in the day quite nice but don't be surprised to see a thirty-two degree night in July."

"I'm not sure it *ever* gets that low in Vegas."

"Aside from the weather, you like the town okay?"

"I love it," I said as convincingly as I could. Certain they would not be interested in hearing about the mean pranks and new hottie in my life, I stuck to topics I was sure they would embrace. "And I *love* Lake Tahoe. I just had my first beach trip a couple of days ago. Kings Beach."

I instantly regretted saying it. Violet's eyes darted in my direction and looked double their normal size.

"Really?" Afton quizzed. "Did you go with friends?" She shot a glance at Vi.

"No, just me." A twinge of guilt thrummed through my veins.

"Hmm." Afton's gaze faded somewhere far away. "That was always Landon's favorite beach."

"I'll say," Frank said in an obvious attempt to be lighthearted. "Boy shoulda just set up a tent there during the summer if you ask me."

"Well, are we ready to eat or what?" Violet was suddenly moving in super speed carrying stacks of dishes from the counter to the large knotty pine table in the adjoining dining room.

Three pancakes, two fried eggs, four pieces of bacon, and a large glass of orange juice later, I felt welcome, happy, and relaxed. The Blackwood family did their best to politely interrogate me in between cleaning up spilled orange juice and cutting baby-sized bites of pancakes. What were my hobbies? Where did I plan on attending college? How was my brother adjusting? Did I leave a boyfriend behind? How had Gayle survived the first month as Truckee High's new principal?

"Okay, okay guys," Violet held both hands in the air, "enough questions for tonight. We'll scare her off and she'll never want to come over again."

I smiled. "No, no I don't mind at all."

Not accustomed to being doted on, I actually enjoyed the attention. "And thank you so much for dinner," I remembered to add last minute.

"Vi—will you grab Jackson's binkie from my diaper bag, please?" Amber had her hands busy with the now-fussy toddler. "It's just on the sofa in the living room there."

"Sure." Violet disappeared into the living room.

Then Afton leaned in, speaking softly. "Sweetie, I can't tell you how happy we are that you and Violet have found each other." She scooted her chair in closer and clasped both of her hands around mine, a gesture that seemed commonplace for her. "We've not seen her this happy since, well. . . you must have heard by now. . . "

"Yes. Reese told me a little bit." I squeezed Afton's hands now. "And I'm so, so sorry for your loss."

Her eyes shone. "Yes, well. I'm just very grateful now that Violet has you. I think you are just what the doctor ordered."

"I think Landon would have liked you too." Frank cleared the instability from his voice. "Think he would have liked your spunk." He nodded.

I took a brief moment to glance at everyone seated. Their eyes were on me and I felt my cheeks suddenly turn warm. "Well, I'm sorry that I didn't have the chance to get to know him."

"What's going on?" Violet had returned from her task and looked at all of us with a hint of suspicion. She stood in the archway between the dining and living rooms with a bright orange pacifier in one hand, the other on her hip.

Afton released my hands quickly and busied herself clearing the table. "Nothing, dear. Just enjoying Presley." She smiled a knowing smile in my direction. An awkward silence hung in the room.

"You want to see my room?" Violet handed the pacifier to Amber, and shot a reproving glare at everyone else.

"Okay—sure." I felt slightly uncomfortable and partly responsible for the tension. "Thanks again for dinner, Mrs. Blackwood; it was delicious."

"Just call me Afton, sweetie—no formalities allowed in this household."

I followed Violet from the kitchen and said, "You have an amazing family."

"Yeah, they're a little intense at times, but I love 'em," Violet said, her tight expression subsiding. She led me through the warm and relaxing living room toward a large wooden staircase.

It was very apparent, I thought, as we reached the bottom of the twisting staircase, how hard the Blackwood family was trying to live and enjoy life despite their tragedy. I couldn't help but feel a tad guilty for the self-pity I'd indulged in since my move to Truckee. Sure, mean girls had egged my truck and slashed my tires. And sure, I'd been yanked from all of my friends during my senior year. But those things seemed trivial at best compared to the Blackwood's last several months.

A thick, polished banister flanked one side of the staircase and provided protection from the huge drop to the lower level. Halfway up the stairs, hanging at the landing, were four portraits of Afton dressed in white. In each one, she cradled one of her four infant children. Afton appeared no older than Violet in the first two photos, but resembled herself more in the last two. But in every photo, the love she had for her babies was beautifully evident.

"My mom had her first two pretty early," Violet seemed obligated to explain. "She was only married like three months before she got pregnant. I can't imagine that."

"Those are awesome pictures though," I sighed. "I bet those would be the first thing your mom would grab in a fire."

"Yeah—she's a big picture person." Violet motioned upstairs. "You'll see what I mean."

As we ascended the last half of the staircase, new pictures appeared every couple of feet. The school portraits hung in neat groupings of four and showed the Blackwood siblings at different ages.

"Here's first grade," Violet moaned. "I can't believe how hideous I look here."

Behind the glass sat a bright-eyed girl with a large smile, teeth too big for her tiny face. Dark brown bangs were cut somewhat crookedly across her forehead. Pink glasses rested on a petite freckled nose.

"Aww, I think you're cute," I countered.

Violet muttered, "Why my mom had to trim my bangs the morning of picture day every single year, I'll never know."

Next to the awkward first grade girl, hung an equally ungainly boy. Instead of two large front teeth, his smile revealed one missing and one barely emerging tooth.

"Landon doesn't look much better though, does he?" Violet giggled.

"I think you're both adorable," I insisted. "You should see my first grade pictures."

I wondered if Violet would share more information about Landon, but my musing was cut short.

"I'm sure by now you've heard the details about my brother." Violet's delicate face was solemn now.

I hesitated for a moment, and then decided it was best to be honest. "Yes. Reese told me a little bit that night in Reno."

Violet cleared her throat. "Good. Then there's less I have to explain." She pursed her lips and turned back to study the young boy on the wall. "It never gets easy—even after five months, it's really not one bit easier."

"I'm sorry." My hand rested gently on Violet's shoulder. "I can't imagine losing my brother." If Landon were anything to her like Chase was to me, it would be like losing half of my life.

Violet bit her lip and took a deep breath. I guessed how hard this must be for her. According to Reese, Violet never spoke of Landon's death, yet here she was opening up to me. I felt humbled that Violet chose me as a confidant, and a sober responsibility to be the best and most loyal friend that she had ever known.

"So you know he drowned, then." Violet continued to stare at the boy on the wall.

"Yes."

How could I forget that part? Mysteriously, my nightmares reminded me often. I shuddered at the images of death. His white hands, the matted hair. I'd never seen his face in my nightmares. And until this point, I'd still never seen Landon's face, except for these childhood pictures that now made him more real to me than before. If my guess was right, at the top of the stairs, I would finally have a face to attach to the boy in my nightmare. I dreaded it.

"I heard my dad, you know," Violet said through a sideways glance.

I remained silent.

"I heard what he said to you while everyone thought I wasn't listening."

I looked down, wondering why I suddenly felt so guilty.

"I agree with him." A small smile found its way to Violet's lips. "Landon would have liked you." She shifted her eyes from the picture and met mine. "Just as much as I do, I think."

122

I broke the silence. "Thank you."

"Shall we?" Violet motioned to the top of the stairs.

My feet were heavy.

Violet was definitely recognizable by the third grade portrait, and unexplainably, Landon seemed recognizable too, and I couldn't quite place why his dark blue eyes stared in a familiar way.

Fourth, fifth, sixth, and seventh grades passed with Violet looking more like herself every year. The young boy evolved too from the gawky toothless seven-year-old to a handsome brace-faced eighth grader.

At tenth grade, I stopped short. I seized the pine railing for support and swallowed hard. Staring behind the glass was the same handsome boy with black hair, but it was no longer unruly and flipped up around his ears. His boyish face had evolved from round and soft around the edges, into a young man's face with a more pronounced jaw and sharp angled features. Now his hair was cropped neatly above his ears and his confident expression was one I knew well. This was not Landon Blackwood. This was Krew. Krew from the school parking lot . . . Krew from Kings Beach. My running partner whose company I couldn't go a day without craving.

Was this some kind of cruel and sick joke? Some kind of twisted new-girl hazing? Who would go to such lengths to play that kind of prank on me? No, it couldn't be. Her parents spoke of Landon's death. He was dead. He had to be. I could see the pain in Frank and Afton's eyes. And Violet's. So if it wasn't a joke, then what was it? Could it be an unbelievable coincidence? Could someone really resemble another person that closely? I scrutinized his portrait; he was younger than Krew, but the resemblance was unmistakable. The colors and sounds of the house swam around me as a sickening wave thrust up my throat.

Violet then noticed that she had left me behind. She threw a quick glance over her shoulder, "Coming?"

I clenched the railing and willed myself to take one step after the other. Landon's eleventh grade picture was another devastating blow. Another year older, he looked even more like the Krew I knew.

Then I saw it. On a nail next to his picture, hung the woven leather bracelet. The same bracelet Krew wore unfailingly.

I struggled to sound only slightly curious, and asked, "So, what's this bracelet?"

Violet lifted it from the nail where it hung. "A gift." She smiled fondly as she turned the bracelet in her fingers. "I made this for him at a leadership camp a couple of years ago. And for some reason, he loved it. He wore it everywhere—even to prom. When he passed away . . . well my mom just thought it would be nice to keep it. So we," Violet paused. "took it from his wrist and hung it here."

She glanced from the bracelet to my face. Suddenly urgent concern replaced her reminiscing expression.

"What's the matter, Presley? You don't look well."

A heartbreaking disillusionment suffocated me. Small details came together. How I never saw Krew eat. How no matter how much I wanted him to touch me, he never did. That night in the biology lab, maybe he couldn't open the doors because . . . he couldn't touch them. I fought to deny the facts that continued to surface. Violet gawked at me.

"I'm sorry," I covered. "It's just seeing his face." I gently touched the glass at Landon's smiling lips. Lips I'd hoped would kiss me any day.

As insane as it sounded, I couldn't come up with any explanation other than he must really be dead. I fought for an out, for any other shred of meaning or evidence to the contrary, but all of the proof before me only confirmed my worst fear. A wide chasm of sadness opened me up. "Reese told me about him. But being here with you, talking about him," my voice caught in my throat as I held back tears. "It just makes him more real to me."

The twisted irony of it all.

Violet stood in silence for several seconds, absorbing my comment, and I was grateful to not have to talk for a moment. Though questions raged in my head, I fought to keep them contained, at least for now. But I did allow myself one indulgence as I studied the initials faintly stamped on the leather bracelet. Initials I hadn't noticed before—LKB. I was sure I already knew the answer but I had to ask.

"Do you mind telling me what the K stands for?"

Violet grinned, painfully, as she hung the bracelet back on its nail. "It was kind of an inside joke actually. Landon had this middle name that he didn't really like. My crazy dad named him after a snowboarding brand. He'd never tell it to anyone. I knew if I put it on his bracelet, people would constantly ask him about it.

I just needed Violet to say it. Her eyes met mine. They were brimming with emotion.

"The K stands for Krew," she said.

Chapter Twenty-Three

SPILLED BEANS

(LANDON)

I was confused when James insisted we pay a visit to my house. He'd spent so much energy trying to convince me to steer clear of Violet.

We walked up my long driveway in silence. I'd tried several times to get James to tell me why we had to come here, but he just said that I needed to see for myself. The lights from our porch pierced the trees at last.

My insides turned to lead when I saw Presley's Jeep in our drive. Because Violet had been so closed off for the past few months, even to friends she'd had for years, I never imagined her inviting Presley here.

James and I quickly slid behind a large tree as Presley exploded out the front doors and to her Jeep. Violet, who had quickly followed her, now stood confused in the frame of the front door, her slender body casting a willowy shadow across the porch.

Presley fumbled with her keys, finally opening the driver side door. She started her Jeep and rolled down the passenger window calling out to Violet, "I'm sorry," she choked. "I'll call you. I promise." Presley sped down our driveway toward the highway.

This is bad.

I dared a glance at James.

"Did you know she was here?" I said accusingly.

"Yes," James stated matter-of-factly. "Why are you surprised? You know that Violet's taken a strong liking to Presley and this is just the natural course of friendship . . ."

"Yes, everyone's taken a strong liking to Presley it seems. That's the problem." I left James in the drive, climbed the porch steps and walked straight through the front door.

The house was quiet except for some faint voices coming from the kitchen. Violet sat at the table, wedged between my mom and dad. Fidgeting with the tab on his soda can with one hand, Dad rubbed Vi's back with the other. Steam swirled from the mug that Mom held and she took nervous, frequent sips. Violet's head rested face down on her folded arms, which lay on the table. She was mumbling something but I couldn't hear. I moved closer. I had to know what had happened with Presley.

"What happened, Vi? What did you tell her?"

Probably sensing me, Violet lifted her head and looked in my direction, straight through me.

"Now tell me again, sweetie. What exactly happened?" Afton encouraged.

"She freaked out when she saw his picture. That's it. I already told you."

I closed my eyes and exhaled. The pictures. Of course. How could I have not thought of that?

"Describe 'freaked out' for me," Afton prodded.

Violet rolled her eyes. "She totally tried to hide it, actually, but I could tell something was bothering her. She was laughing and joking around when we started up the stairs. I showed her all our school pictures. And it just seemed like with every new picture she got . . . I don't know . . . nervous, somehow. By the time we got to the top of the stairs, she looked like she was going to puke.

"She saw Landon's junior picture, she touched his face and she looked like she was going to cry."

"Sweetie this has been so hard for everyone," Afton reassured. She gently stroked Violet's jet-black mane. "Presley really likes you. I know that she never met Landon, but this is so recent, I bet she's probably just absorbing some of your pain. She seems like a very intuitive and sensitive girl."

"You might be right. I don't know. But the weirdest thing was when I told her about the bracelet I'd made for him. I told her the K stood for Krew and I swear her face turned as white as snow. I'm not kidding. She had zero color left, and was gripping the banister so hard her knuckles turned white."

"Why, Violet? Why did you have to show her the pictures?" I moaned.

Violet looked again in my direction, and guilt tore at my chest.

"I'm sorry Violet. I know it's not your fault. I know, I know," I apologized as I turned on my heel and tore through the walls heading for the door.

I need to get to her house. I need to go now.

Outside, James stood still, pale as ocean sand, shining under the full moon's glow. "She's at the cemetery."

"What?" I said, even though I'd heard his every word.

"She needs to see your grave to reconcile this in her mind. I'd tell you not to go if I thought you'd listen, but I know you better than that, by now." James exhaled and looked up at the moon. "Just imagine how traumatic tonight was for Presley. Please be cautious and sensitive. Undoubtedly, she won't think of you the same." His eyes bored into mine. "Do nothing that will cause her more damage tonight."

"I won't." I stepped past James, but he grabbed my arm and held it tight like a vice.

"I'm serious about this. I will be in your head. Do not traumatize her any further. If she asks you to leave, do it."

"I promise."

Chapter Twenty-Four

WRITTEN IN STONE

(LANDON)

I avoided this place at all costs. Nothing was ever gained from coming here. But tonight—there was no getting away from the arched iron gate of the Truckee Cemetery. On the day of my funeral, I'd stood with James near the mausoleum, under the shelter of an enormous pine. From a distance, I'd watched as my family's gray Suburban had slowly followed the black hearse through the grounds and toward our family plot. I remember I was grateful for the rain that day, as the blooms of umbrellas hid the mourning faces of my loved ones who struggled through the graveside service.

I tried, but could not forget, that when the service ended and everyone had gone, Violet stayed. She let her umbrella fall to her side and allowed the pounding rain to stream over her face, camouflaging her tears. After an hour of that, it was clear she had no intention of leaving my grave. The gravediggers lingered, unsure of what to do. They didn't dare lower my casket into the ground while she watched. At long last, my father and Reese appeared at her side, gently lifting her arms over their necks and supporting her failed legs back to the car.

No, the cemetery was not my favorite place. I steered clear of the pea-gravel road my body had last traveled inside the hearse, and instead wove through the gravestones of the other dead. I'd used to love to explore this historic place as a kid—marveled at the ancient resting places of pioneers, children, and soldiers. I used to make a game of trying to find the oldest headstone, never imagining that my name too, would soon be etched in stone. As I crested a slope, I found Presley standing at the Blackwood family plot, safeguarded as it seemed, by the large slate angel with a broken wing.

The moon shined full and a pale glow emanated from the sculpture, causing her serene face to appear even more peaceful. In shocking contrast, Presley's face was harrowed. She stood at my grave and scrutinized the polished granite. I hated to read the inscription, because now I read it through her eyes, knowing what those words meant. How they proved what I really was.

LANDON KREW BLACKWOOD
BELOVED SON, BROTHER, UNCLE, AND FRIEND
UNTIL WE MEET AGAIN.

Presley did not detect my silent approach. I painfully watched her for a moment as she sunk to her knees, and hesitantly reached out to finger the crumbling flowers left there.

"Presley," I said, softly.

She lost her balance and struggled to get to her feet. Her breath came in gasps.

"Get away from me." She stumbled backward until she was pressed against the angel, looking terribly small and afraid.

I did not expect this reaction from her. I hated to admit that James was right about how she would feel, but hoped he wasn't right about everything.

I braved a step forward and reached for her. She looked about to scream; her mouth gaped and her eyes flashed pure, unadulterated terror. Her face shocked me and for the first time, I comprehended in full, my death.

"How is this happening? How are you still here?" Presley asked through trembling lips.

"You don't have to be afraid," I said. "Give me a chance to explain."

"No! Why would you do this to me?" Tears freely spilled down her cheeks.

I contemplated her question. What *had* I done to her? My explanation tumbled out unorganized and desperate. "I never meant to upset you. I never meant for you to know or to find out or . . ."

"I don't understand what is happening." Presley hugged her ribs and began to rock.

"I just . . . when you saw me for the first time in the parking lot I had to know why . . . I swear I didn't mean for you to find out or to scare you . . ." In light of her state of mind, every word I said only sounded deplorable.

Presley's voice was high and tight, "How can you say you never meant for me to find out? How did you plan on hiding that? Why *would* you?"

I knew exactly why. I was selfish. Despite James's continual warnings about what could happen to Presley, I ignored him. And for what? Mere curiosity? No, it was more than that.

She made me feel like there was a reason I should stay. But still, it was selfish. Seeing her face, terrified, straining against the oncoming hysteria, I knew that now. I had done the wrong thing. I had tortured Violet with my presence without even knowing it and now I'd caused pain to another, so needlessly.

Yet, my feet remained planted.

So why couldn't I just walk away? Knowing all I had done, I still couldn't walk away. And I hated myself for it.

"Presley, please don't be scared of me," I pleaded. "I would never hurt you. Never."

"I *am* scared of you, Krew."

We stood appraising each other, not sure what was left to be said. I offered the only thing I could think of.

"You don't have to call me Krew anymore. You can call me Landon."

Presley's eyes were guarded. I was desperate to connect with her.

"Please don't be scared. I can't take it if you are scared of me," I said.

Her voice changed. Its tone—airy and detached, unsettled me. "I don't care what you can and cannot take." The fear once on her face had morphed into something else.

I had to fix what I had done. "Presley, please, just tell me what to do. I swear to you I will do *whatever* you ask of me. I swear it." I gambled and took another step toward her knowing I could cause her to shatter. But she didn't. In fact, she stood taller and fixed her determined eyes in a deadlock with mine—her voice, now smooth and decided.

"You want to know what you can do? I'll tell you. Stay away from me."

Chapter Twenty-Five

Run and Hide

(Presley)

I must've looked as bad as I felt, because Gayle didn't give me any crap when I told her I wasn't going to school and I wouldn't be helping with Chase later in the day. I think she was in shock because I've never stood up to her like that.

Processing the reality of my situation made my brain feel like scrambled eggs. I'd always hoped there was life after death, but the circumstances in which I gained that proof gave me no comfort. How could the dead simply walk among the living?

I had never imagined I would be heavily interested in any one person while in Truckee. My plan was to endure my senior year then get out. I certainly never imagined I'd fall for a walking, talking, completely beautiful dead person.

And how was I supposed to face Violet? And Reese? How could I even be in the same room with them? Was I supposed to just put on some stoic poker face? With everything I knew, it felt like a betrayal. And speaking of betrayal, how could Landon put me in this position? Did he not think about how hard this would be for me? Did he really think I'd never find out? Was I supposed to keep this a secret from his family? They had the right to know, but telling them would have just landed me in a mental ward.

I had to give him a little bit of credit, though. He never once asked me to contact his family for him. And if I were in his shoes, I'm not sure I would have done the same.

I knew a high school diploma was important. I knew Chase would need me.

But I was never coming out of my room again.

Chapter Twenty-Six

ALONE

(REESE)

After Presley missed three days of school, I began to worry. She hadn't answered any calls or texts and I started to wonder if it was something more than the flu. She'd been juggling Chase and homework, drama at school, and though I couldn't put my finger on the cause, she'd seemed a little aloof and distracted before she went MIA. I psyched myself up and dialed her home number, hoping to reach Dr. Hale. Surprisingly, she picked up on the first ring.

"Dr. Hale, sorry to bother you. It's Reese Blackwood."

"Yes?"

"I've been trying to get a hold of Presley and she hasn't answered in a few days. I'm just calling to check on her."

"Yes. Well, it's just that Presley. . . she's been—unavailable."

"What do you mean?"

Dr. Hale waited a moment before she continued. "She came home the other night very upset. She wouldn't tell me why. She hasn't left her room."

"Really."

"Do you know of anything that's happened that I should be aware of?" I thought I detected a slight note of accusation in her tone, but ignored it.

"I honestly have no idea. Can I talk to her?"

"I'm with her now. Hold on."

I could hear Dr. Hale now, addressing Presley in a tender voice.

"Presley, hon. Reese is on the phone. He's been worried about you. Will you talk to him?"

I listened hard, hoping to hear Presley say "yes."

"Tell him to come. I want him here," she said, instead.

My chest swelled involuntarily. Presley was *asking* for me.

"I'm coming." I said, not waiting for details, and hung up the phone.

When I pulled up to the Hale's around 10 p.m., the house showed little sign of life inside other than a small lamp in the entry-way window. The wind rattled through the tree limbs as I waited. Dr. Hale quickly answered my knock. Chase, who was whining and biting his forearm, tugged at her.

"No, Chase. We aren't going upstairs. Presley needs to rest."

Dr. Hale looked tired. Instead of her normally coiffed principal hairdo, she wore a ratty ponytail. "Come on in," she said wearily.

Presley's door was slightly ajar. The only light coming from her room was the flickering blue glow of her T.V. I quietly pushed her door wider. She was lying down, curled in a tangle of blankets. She didn't stir in the least when I entered the room.

I carefully sat at the edge of her bed and placed an unsure hand on the small of her back.

"Reese," was all she said.

I lay down behind Presley and placed a protective arm around her, gently caressing her hair away from her face in a slow rhythm. Only then did she allow a great sob to escape, and I felt the hot tears land in the crook of my arm where her head was supported. I lay behind her like that for a while, not one word exchanged. Only the sound of Presley's soft breath interrupted by the hiccups of crying.

At last she was cried out, and I was surprised when she rolled over and faced me. Her face was blotchy and pink, and the lids of her eyes swollen from crying. I waited for her to say something. She didn't, but looked straight into my eyes with an expression that I couldn't discern.

"You don't have to say anything, Pres," I softly assured. "I don't need to know. I just want you to know that I'm here."

"Look at you," Presley whispered. "You are here."

I felt the blood quicken in my body as she extended her small pale hand and cradled one side of my face and closed my eyes to hide the leaping desire that erupted inside of me. I suppressed it and reminded myself that wasn't why I was here.

She continued, "You are here. All of you . . . here for me." She softly stroked from my face down to my neck. I felt her melt into my embrace.

I rested my chin on the top of her head, and slid my hand up under her nest of curls to support the back of her thin neck. I loved the comfort I provided for her but it took all of my will to maintain that position without searching out her lips. Presley finally looked up at me. She was beautiful. Not the beauty I was used to, but the clean, pure beauty guys forsake other girls for.

After Presley glanced twice at my lips, I knew what she wanted from me. I breathed her in and she closed her eyes. Taking advantage of that brief beat of time, I took one last look at her before I pressed my lips against hers.

I couldn't help but compare her kiss to others I'd had. She was tender and sweet and though her mouth was the absolute definition of bliss, I didn't want to spoil it by being too eager.

The kiss lasted longer than I'd hoped. With pleasure, I reached to cradle her jaw in my hand and as I did so, I felt them. Tears. I immediately pulled away and searched Presley's face. Her eyes seemed to be apologizing.

"What's wrong?" I probed. "Did I do something wrong?"

Presley sat up and grabbed at her hair, gathering it all to the top of her head. Her eyes held an expression I couldn't decipher. Was it regret? Fear?

"No. It's not you. You didn't do anything wrong. I just . . ."

"Did I read you wrong? I'm sorry Pres, I thought you wanted me to kiss you," I said.

"No. I mean yes! Yes, I wanted you to kiss me. No you didn't read me wrong." She looked around for someone or something to save her from the conversation.

Embarrassment pricked at me. It wasn't a feeling I was used to.

Presley tried to explain, "It isn't anything you have done." She pondered for a moment and an icy look veiled her face. "It isn't anything *I've* done either, for that matter." She let all of her hair go and it fell around her shoulders in tangled brown curls.

I finally understood. If the problem wasn't with something she had done or anything I had done—it was *someone else*. A brick wall stood between the idea that formed in my head and the ability to express it. Was it pride or was I just scared to hear the answer? I steeled myself.

"So that's it then? There's someone else?" I hoped she would look surprised or shocked by the accusation, but she didn't.

Her eyes pleaded with me. "I don't know."

I would have gladly accepted a "no." With difficulty, I may have been able to process a "yes." But an "I don't know" was unacceptable. A black vein of anger seethed through me, exposing itself in my voice. "What do you mean you don't know? There is or there isn't, Presley."

She looked away.

"Okay. You not answering me obviously means yes." I turned my head to the side and bit the inside of my cheek. "You should have said something. I feel like an idiot."

"Reese . . ."

Three small knocks sounded on the door. Gayle pressed her face into the room. I promptly sat up in the bed next to Presley. We scooted apart. Gayle didn't seem to notice.

She smiled and said, "I made soup."

Presley swallowed and rubbed her temples, avoiding Gayle's eyes. "Mom, it's late."

"I know," Gayle countered, "but you still haven't eaten anything. And it's good to see you up and talking and I thought . . ."

Presley sighed, too loudly.

"Come down and help me. I've got a tray ready. And some for Reese if he'd like." Gayle's face looked eager. "Get up," she added, "it will be good for you."

I looked straight at the floor as Presley got up and left the room, the muscles in my jaw flexing and working. A hunger for answers overtook me. It was unlike me to feel so desperate. I guessed it was because I'd never been rejected. Unprepared for this slap in the face.

Immediately I stood up from the bed and looked around her room. There were pictures wedged in the frame of Presley's mirror. One photo showed a group of four girls holding hands as they jumped into a pool on a sunny day. Another of Presley with her arm around an elderly woman with cropped white hair. A ticket to a movie premiere, a dried rose hung from a ribbon . . . all pieces of her life, but nothing to give me even a small clue of whom I was up against. In an action I wasn't proud of, I even hastily dug through a drawer looking for a note or letter. Nothing. I thought about my own life and how I interacted with girls.

Her phone.

I heard Gayle and Presley trying to quietly argue downstairs. On my phone, I quickly dialed Presley's number. I listened for the ringer hoping it wouldn't draw Presley upstairs. A soft vibration sounded from the floor. I found her phone inside the pocket of her jeans. My own face looked up at me from the screen. Presley had taken that picture of me while I sat in the secretary's office awaiting my fate after some shenanigan I had pulled with Garett. I remembered Presley saying "Say 'guilty'!" as she took the photo.

I felt a little guilty now as I searched her call history. Calls coming and going from Violet, Sam, myself, her mother. There was little to give me a clue as to who was coming between Presley and me. Again, I was surprised at the bitter disappointment and anger that boiled inside me. In a last attempt to discover someone, anyone, I skipped to the photo section of her phone. It wasn't the first picture, but more toward the middle of the cache, that I saw a face that unsettled me.

Landon.

I knew that picture all too well. It was the same as the glossy 8x10 my aunt and uncle had framed and displayed on the top of Landon's casket. Why Presley had this on her phone was a mystery, and the pain of seeing that face was enough to make me want to run from the room.

Something wasn't right.

Chapter Twenty-Seven

POISONED

(PRESLEY)

Reese left hastily, and after he was gone, I spent more of that night awake than asleep. I'd just hurt and alienated one of the few people I could depend on. But processing the reality of my situation kept me from giving Reese what he wanted. And maybe even what I wanted.

But things were so messed up right now. How could the dead simply walk among the living?

As mind-boggling as that was, I also had a simple, earthly problem to contemplate. One girl, one heart—two guys. And who would believe that one of those guys was a ghost?

I lay in my bed, not at all surprised at the hint of sunlight beginning to leak through the cracks of the curtains. I couldn't spend another day in this room. The air was stale. My clothes were rumpled and needing a wash. *Even girls who have learned mind-blowing secrets of the universe must bathe and brush their teeth*, I thought.

Later, looking at my reflection, a girl with wet hair, clean clothes, and a touch of makeup, I felt more put together.

On my drive to school, I passed my and Landon's trail along the river. We'd run almost every day since that first time. We'd spent so many happy hours there. I imagined him next to me, smiling easily, his dark hair shining in the sun. So quick to tease me and make me laugh. His bright eyes were all I could think of. It was too easy to think of him that way. But now I knew that was only half of him.

His other half was pieced together, to my horror, over the last three nights.

Landon was not only the recent happy obsession of my life, he was the boy pulled from the river.

It took my breath away to think of it. He was an Everest in front of me. Impossible to ignore, hopelessly present and looming.

How was I supposed to go to school and take notes, or eat a sandwich? How was I to act or look normal enough to simply talk to people? Faking normalcy all day at Truckee High was the last thing I wanted to do, but where else could I go?

I slowed my pace as I neared the front doors of the school, half expecting to see Violet waiting for me. She'd blown up my phone with texts all morning. I hoped she'd buy my food poisoning story. Reese ascended the steps, his dark hair a contrast to the bright red and white of his letterman jacket. Around him walked a group of people I hadn't met. It seemed weird that I'd never seen this group around. The school wasn't *that* big. Reese seemed to always travel with an entourage, though. He got along with everyone. He was magnetic.

Today's crowd was a bit sullen. Five people hovered around him, all dressed in dark clothes. Goths? Not Reese's usual crowd. The tallest boy's gait made me uneasy and I wondered why he followed so closely behind Reese.

A touch on my back startled me. A quick gasp escaped my mouth at the same moment Sam greeted me.

"Hey, stranger!" Sam's eyes were warm chocolate. "Where in the world have you been? Girl, you look tired! What did you catch?"

I wished it were all as simple as a flu bug. I searched for an explanation. "Oh . . . I've been sick," I lied, clearing my throat for effect. "It was bad. I'll tell you one thing, I'll never eat seafood again." I appraised Sam's expression, hoping I had given a believable story.

The friendly arm around my shoulder proved my story had worked. Sam had an amazing ability to make me feel like I was four years old, sitting on my grandma's lap with a cookie in my hand.

"Ugh, that's the worst! Don't worry about a thing; Violet and I can get you all caught up." Sam flashed an uneasy look. "I'm not going to lie, Price is on one this week and he dumped a mountain of work on us. But don't fret. We got this."

I wished I could take that advice.

There was no way Sam could have known that Reese was the last person I wanted to speak with that day. So when she yelled for him to wait up, I tried to hide the cringe that rippled through my body. Sam grabbed my arm and jogged to Reese's side as we all were about to enter Price's government class.

"What up, Sammy?" Reese greeted Sam with a broad smile. I couldn't help but notice the ruddy stain that appeared on Sam's cheeks and the light that suddenly filled her eyes. Why hadn't I noticed her reactions around Reese before?

Sam beamed. "Nothin', just psychin' myself up for Government à la Price. You know, livin' the dream. Oh, and reassuring Presley here that though she's been MIA for three days she will indeed graduate with the help of Violet and my excellent self."

I forced myself to look at Reese. I needn't have bothered, because he completely ignored me. Instead he put a muscular arm around Sam.

"You're so good," Reese cooed. He led her into the door of the classroom, leaving me to stand alone in the hall. Sam turned her head back around and gawked at me with wide, excited eyes.

Focusing on school was hard enough in light of the events of the last three days. But Reese's new behavior added an extra sardine to the sundae. At lunchtime, I sat with Sam and Violet and tried not to notice Reese too much as he and his friends watched a gaggle of freshmen girls who coasted past their table.

After school, I stood in front of my locker and stared at the books inside. I had several homework assignments, not including the make-up work from my absences. Organizing my thoughts though was like trying to build a house of cards on a windy day. Luckily, Sam had the locker next to me and in her typical selfless manner, began to narrate all of the books I would need for my work. I turned to her, grateful.

"Sam, I don't deserve you. I'm a mess."

"Everybody's a mess sometimes, Pres," Sam reasoned.

"I'll say," Reese seemed to appear from nowhere and interrupted the conversation. "You look awful today. You should go home and rest."

He looked at me coolly, then turned to Sam and switched on his "Reese-ness." Now that I knew, I could easily see the signs that Sam was hopelessly infatuated. The tips of her ears were red, she giggled too much, her fingers nervously twisted a strand of hair, and she had a hard time making eye contact with him for more than a few seconds. I cringed, hoping I hadn't ever acted that way around him. Then a tiny knife of humiliation twisted in my gut because that was probably exactly how I'd acted. It was beneath Reese to play Sam like that, though.

I knew he wasn't really interested in her. Plainly, he was trying to get under my skin. It was working all right, but not in the way he hoped. I wasn't jealous; I was angry at how carelessly he manipulated the kindest people I'd met here. It was my turn to manipulate Sam, but for her own good.

"Um, Sam?" I interrupted.

Immediately, Sam turned to me, concern already growing on her face.

"I'm so sorry," I said. "But I'm feeling really sick again and I just realized that I didn't talk to Mrs. Freeman about what she wants me to do about the missed lab." I hated to do it; I was perfectly capable of taking care of the issue with my teacher, but I knew Sam wouldn't refuse me the favor of running down the hall to get my assignment. "I feel bad asking; you've already helped me so much, I'm just all of a sudden so nauseated." I willed my face to appear green.

Sam gripped both of my arms. "Oh! No, no, no. Don't even worry about it. I'll be right back. You should sit down. Reese, take her somewhere to rest for a sec until I get back."

Reese dissected me with his eyes as Sam jogged down the hall.

"You are a terrible liar." He smiled, but it didn't reach his eyes.

"Reese . . ."

"Or wait! I shouldn't say that, I guess. You fooled me easily enough last night," he interrupted.

"I didn't fool you or lie to you."

"Really? That's interesting. I'd be curious to see what you call it." His eyes narrowed and I sensed the poison in his voice. I tried to tell myself he was just embarrassed, his pride hurt. I looked for the pain in his face, something I could address rationally, but his eyes were black and hard.

"What is the matter with you, Reese? I feel like you are dishing out way more than I deserve." I looked around to make sure Sam wasn't coming back already and lowered my voice to a stern whisper. "I'm sorry, okay? I shouldn't have let the other night happen when things are so . . ." I struggled for the word that would describe what was actually happening, but nothing came.

Reese spat out a mirthless laugh. "You are a piece of work."

"Let me finish! Dang, if you could for one second let your enormous ego take a back seat and actually think about anyone but yourself."

Reese thundered back, "My ego? You are the one lining them up and knocking them down. Look at you keeping your options open, lots of irons in the fire, eh? Taking your sweet time deciding who it's going to be. Who would be the best arm candy for Presley Hale? Scratch me off the list; I'm not waiting around for you to figure out the rules to your game. I'm over it."

There was, I hated to admit, a small sliver of truth to what he said, but the intent was way off. After all, I did allow myself to feel for two people at once, but I was seventeen freaking years old! It wasn't like I had planned on any of this. I didn't mean to hurt Reese. He was wrong about my motives and it was maddening that he wouldn't get that through his fat head.

Reese was breathing hard and I could see his hand trembling at his side, the tendons tight. "It's like I don't even know who you are, Reese. I don't know . . ." I paused, looking him up and down, "this."

145

Reese took a step closer to me, his familiar sweet breath now washing over my face, only now it brought a slight ripple of fear over me instead of pleasure.

"You're right. You don't know me. You never will. You have yourself to thank for that."

Suddenly, Reese's face turned soft, almost affectionate, and for a moment I thought it had all been a bad joke and it was over. That is, until I heard Sam approaching behind me, and then I knew Reese was just acting. His eyes remained hard, but his features lifted. He stepped to the side to make room for Sam to speak with me.

While Sam filled me in on my biology make-up work, Reese watched, his back leaning against the red painted locker. I thanked Sam with a hug and a promise to take her out for all of her help. Reese rolled his eyes.

He straightened himself and approached Sam. "Can I talk to you for a second?"

Sam's face wore an apology. I slung my backpack over one shoulder and prepared to leave, even though I didn't want to. Reese was not in a good place emotionally and what he wanted with Sam couldn't be anything good. I felt the wrongness thicken in the air as I watched Reese hook a finger through Sam's belt loop and pull her a little way down the hall. Sam quivered with nervous excitement.

I couldn't bring myself to move, but watched with a sick feeling as Reese leaned into Sam, all sweetness and smiles. He spoke to her while she nodded. Reese reached forward and gently rubbed her elbow, slowly tracing his way up the back of her arm. I observed in disbelief as his strong arm wrapped around her waist and he led her from the building, pausing briefly to look over his shoulder at me.

Seemingly from nowhere, the morose knot of people that had loomed around Reese earlier that morning, drifted into the hall like mist. The tall boy that set me so on edge before walked with an even hungrier stride, his companions filing in behind him. They followed Reese and Sam down the hall, completely blocking my friends from view.

Left foot, right foot. Find the door to get out of here. A cool blast of air lifted the hair from my neck and I felt the sweat that had erupted on my skin turn cold. Outside, the parking lot was all but empty. Before I even reached my Jeep though, I saw Landon emerge from the trees with an older man. He was the guy I saw Landon argue with that first day in the school parking lot. Looking younger than I remembered, he had thick sandy hair combed loosely to the side, serious eyes, and stubble on his face. He was dressed in a tan button-down shirt, jeans, and a heavy looking pair of brown scuffed boots. His presence added to the confusion and trepidation I had at seeing Landon again after all I had learned.

Heartbreakingly, Landon looked as beautiful as ever. In a train of thought way out of left field, I marveled that he'd worn a different outfit every time I'd seen him. *Dead people change clothes?* So today, in his ghost life he was in the mood for a pair of dark washed jeans and a snug striped thermal? Top two buttons left undone? Did he have to sit down to put on his socks? The absurdity of it all was too much. The question that weighed most heavily on my mind though, was who was this man that hung around the dead guy?

I felt bold. "What are you doing here?"

"I had to talk to you," Landon said.

"Who's this?" I snapped, gesturing to Landon's companion.

Landon tore his eyes away from me to look at his friend.

"This is James."

"He dead too?" I felt on the verge of laughing. Or was it crying?

The man answered for himself. "Yes, Presley. I'm dead too. I'm here to help Landon through this transition. A guide, you could say."

I let that sink in. "Apparently I have a special knack for seeing dead people, then?" I asked.

"Apparently," was all James said.

I shook my head.

"Why?" I asked.

"We're not exactly sure," Landon offered, warily. "James has some guesses, but . . ."

"You know what? I'm in no mood to wade through a minefield of hypotheticals. I need answers." I sighed, exasperated. "Scratch that. I don't want your answers. I don't want anything. From either of you."

Landon's face was plainly crestfallen.

James cut in, "I can respect your desire to leave this all behind, but I must implore you to be patient a few moments more. For your own safety."

"My safety? What's that supposed to mean?"

"I'll get to that, I promise," James said. "That's why we're here, but first things first. Did you happen to notice Reese's new friends today?"

An image of the somber group that followed Reese drifted darkly through my mind. "Yes, I did." I felt again the unexpected recoiling I'd experienced the first time I saw them. "What's wrong with those guys, anyway?"

James and Landon looked at each other.

"What do you mean?" Landon asked, worried.

"I don't know, I just got a bad vibe from them. Reese seemed uneasy around them too, like there's something different about him. In a bad way. And the way he manipulated Sam today was disgusting. He isn't himself."

Landon addressed James. "What are they doing to him?"

"What are you talking about? Do you mean those guys who were with Reese today?" I asked.

"Vigilum," James said.

"Vigilum," I repeated. The word tasted sour on my tongue, like I wanted to spit it out. I looked at Landon for clarification.

He sighed. "Look, Presley, I won't be able to explain everything perfectly. I know this is all hard to believe and so new, but because this could be harmful to Reese, I have to talk to you about this." His eyes asked for permission to continue.

I nodded, reluctantly.

He continued, "The Vigilum are dead like me. But they are different because they already gave up something called passage."

"Passage."

"Yeah. It's like their ticket to the next life."

He gauged if I was following him or not. I guess I looked okay, because he continued on, gesturing with his hands.

"Because they stayed behind they are trapped here. They want to move on, but they can't. That's why they do what they do. It's all because they want another passage—or in other words, another chance to leave."

I considered his words. "So what's that have to do with Reese? Why are they involved with him? Can he offer them his passage if he hasn't even died yet?"

James explained, "No, but both you and Reese are a means to an end in their quest for *Landon's* passage."

I couldn't understand what he was trying to tell me.

"I get that Landon obviously hasn't used his passage because he's still here. But I still don't understand how that involves me or Reese."

"I would have thought it was obvious," James said candidly. "Reese is in love with you."

I opened my mouth to protest, but Landon cut me off.

"Don't you think 'love' is a bit of an exaggeration?" he said to James. "Reese always has girls lined up."

"No. I don't," James answered. "Make no mistake. Reese loves Presley."

"James—" Landon scoffed.

"Think about it, Landon. The Vigilum have been watching you. Watching you with Presley. Because of her ability to see you and because of the relationship you have been building, she has become your biggest reason to stay. And your deciding to stay is exactly what they want. If you stay for Presley and forfeit your passage, one of them can take it and go."

Bitterness tinged Landon's voice. "So if she chooses Reese, there would be no reason for me to stay, and my passage would no longer up for grabs."

The words pulled at my heart. No matter how twisted this situation was, and no matter how mad I was at him for lying to me, I knew saying goodbye wouldn't be easy.

James addressed Landon and clarified. "Reese is the key. In numbers, the Vigilum have a strong influence and if they can affect him enough, in other words if they can cause him to ruin his chances with Presley, the odds improve that you two will stay together. And you will likely give your passage to one of them without a fight."

"But Reese can't even see them, can he? How can they affect him?" I grasped.

James nodded. "True, he can't see them. But he can feel them. Vigilum prey on the weaknesses of people—exacerbating their worst tendencies. Reese is vulnerable right now. He desperately wants you, but senses your heart is divided. That intensifies his deepest insecurities. Even before you came to Truckee, Reese didn't like to lose. He knows you're slipping through his fingers, and with Vigilum influence, he's become quite extreme in his behavior."

Landon fumed at me. I felt awkward, yet obligated to explain myself. "Landon, it's not like that with Reese and me."

His jaw flexed. "Have you kissed him?"

"Excuse me?"

"You heard me."

Thankfully, James intervened before I had to incriminate myself or tell a bald-faced lie.

"That's not why we're here, Landon," James reminded.

Landon rolled his eyes, but then collected himself and gave his attention back to James.

"There's one more thing, Presley," James continued.

Somehow I sensed I wouldn't like this information.

"The Vigilum have been shadowing you. Watching you."

A chill crawled down my back as I thought that over for a moment. Horrifyingly, it all made sense. The uneasy feelings I'd had on my runs, the times I thought I was crazy when I thought I saw a glimpse of people watching me, the whispers. The nightmares. I didn't imagine any of it.

James continued carefully and confirmed my thoughts. "I've seen them at the school. They wait in the trees when you pass by on your runs. I've even witnessed them on several occasions outside your home, studying you. Your ability to see the dead has them curious."

Sinister dead people have been stalking me. I peered past James and Landon into the forest expecting they may be watching me now. Was there a movement among the pines? I couldn't trust myself to be sure.

"I know what they want with Reese," James said. "But what concerns me, is what it is they want with you."

Chapter Twenty-Eight

GUARDED

(PRESLEY)

I knew I should try to sleep. I couldn't bring myself to lie down though. I'd been trying and trying to rub everything smooth again. To shake out the sheet of my confusion and will it to lay flat. But it wouldn't. My mind felt twisted, a mess beyond setting right. Too many questions. Why could I see Landon and James and the Vigilum? What would happen to Reese if the Vigilum kept at him? What was their endgame with me? Should I tell Violet about Landon? Most importantly, what to do about Landon and me? Over and over like a rolling stone, these questions tumbled around my head.

Learning how to live in a constant state of fear was hard. I couldn't tell anyone about the Vigilum. Not my mom, not Violet, and for sure not Reese. I couldn't protect myself in any way. I had to rely only on Landon and James.

Landon. He had to be somewhere nearby. I felt a tiny thaw in my chest at the memory of his face. He'd pledged himself to me and my safety.

I marched to my window, tore the curtains open and thrust up the pane. He was there, standing on the lawn below, facing the darkness that crept in from the surrounding forest. He turned his face up to mine.

"Get in here," I said, defeated.

The apprehension erased itself from his features and a hint of a grin appeared on his lips. I turned from the window, took two steps into my room, and then felt him. He was already there.

On my own, I'd figured a few things out concerning spirits. They were often felt before they were seen or heard. From behind, his presence felt warm; it enveloped me and I was suddenly very, very tired. I relished the moment—a welcome relief. I kept my back to him and left him by the window, less than an arm's reach away.

"I don't know why I want you here, but I do. Just be here." The words came out of me like a prayer.

"I won't leave you."

—

I woke up while it was still dark. Disorientation melted away into my living nightmare. Death, danger. I clutched my blankets to my chest as the fear crawled through me.

"It's okay," he said. "I'm still here."

Landon sat in my window sill. His silhouette beautiful and reassuring against the moon. He cast no shadow onto my floor.

"You can sleep." He stood up and walked a few paces to my bedside. "Please Presley, you need it."

I sat up in bed, gathered my knees against me, and rested my chin in their nest. Landon sat next to me on the edge of my bed, disturbing nothing. A ghost.

"What's it like?" I asked.

He looked at me, then dropped his eyes into his lap.

"What's it like being dead?" I continued, my voice catching on the last word.

His thumb made small circles on my sheets. "What's it feel like? What exactly do you want to know?"

I pondered the question. "I mean, what do you do all day? How do you feel about being here when nobody knows you are? Everything."

He studied me for a long time. I regretted asking so many questions. I wasn't even sure I wanted the answers now.

"Well," he began, "I guess I can start from the beginning. At first, it was the worst thing imaginable. I saw my family grieve for me." He swallowed hard.

Landon recalled the night he'd died. How James had sat with him near the water's edge for hours, talking with him until James was sure Landon understood he was really gone. Against James's advice, he'd returned to his home—his driveway packed with the cars of family and friends—mourners.

"I tried to touch them, to talk to them, to comfort them. But, of course they couldn't see me or hear me. I'd never seen Violet like that. My parents were upset to be sure, but Violet. She broke my heart. I couldn't leave them. James was upset with me, but I could not leave them like that."

I started to see a side of him I hadn't considered. I'd been thinking for days how selfish he was to put me in the predicament of dealing with this secret. Of warping my mind with things humans can't understand. I realized now that there were many reasons why he stayed that had nothing to do with me.

"After a while I guess I kind of got into a routine," Landon continued. "James would sit with me every day and try to convince me to leave my family and move on. But every day I fought him and stayed with them. I stayed by them at home. Just watched them eat, watched them sleep. Watched Violet hide in her room and cry when everyone thought she was doing so much better. Sometimes I would go to school and see my friends. That was hard. Seeing all that I was missing, you know?"

"I can't imagine."

"It was so unexpected. I woke up that morning taking for granted that I had my entire life ahead of me. It all happened so fast though, and I didn't have time to say goodbye to any of my family."

I nodded.

"Eventually, James got through to me. He helped me see that as long as I stayed, Violet would never get better. Even though I had died, our connection hadn't and it was just keeping her wound open. So really, my staying served no purpose."

"But you did stay. I don't understand," I said.

"I wasn't going to stay, Presley," Landon said with a bit of defensiveness in his voice. "I'd finally made up my mind to leave. After saying final goodbyes to my family, I stopped by the school with James to do the same with my friends. We waited out in the parking lot for all of them to come out so I could see them one last time . . ."

I knew the end to this story. It's where my story began. *Oh, Landon.*

"Then you saw me," I said.

He laughed. A humorless laugh. "No, Presley. Then *you* saw *me.*"

Of course. Of course he would approach me. A living person could see him after months of isolation. Of course he would have done what he did. It all made sense now. His urgency to get to me. His argument with James.

"This whole time I've been bitter toward you for putting this on me. But after hearing your whole story, I might have done the same thing," I said.

"No, don't sugarcoat it, Pres. It was still a horrible thing to do. You don't understand how incredibly curious I was, to know how you could see me. I felt like I'd die all over again if I didn't get to you. But it was still a selfish move. One I'm paying for now. One you're paying for even more."

I couldn't place the reason why, but I felt like a balloon in my heart was slowly deflating. I looked at him, so handsome. I could study every detail of his face and never tire of it. His jaw, strong and set in frustration, but his mouth soft and luring.

Landon instantly saw my countenance fall. "Presley, I'm so sorry. There is no way I can . . ."

"No. It's okay . . ."

"It's not okay. I shouldn't have approached you and got you involved in this. Now you're in danger and I've overwhelmed every last bit of sanity you have with my freak show of a situation—"

"Stop! Landon! I'll be okay." I hesitated, avoiding his gaze. Timidly, I continued, "This situation is overwhelming, yes." I exhaled slowly. "But that's not what's bothering me."

I regretted the words as soon as they came out.

Landon's brow shot up. Genuine surprise. He sat back and appraised me.

"What is then?"

I wanted to fold up. Draw a curtain around me. The silence in the room was humiliating. I had to answer him.

"I guess I just get it now," I breathed. "I understand what you wanted from me."

"And?" He looked confused.

I counted the beats of my heart. They told me to stay quiet, but I owed him my honesty. "And I see now that it was something different than what I wanted from you." The steady beats pumped through my body, expanding and swelling, then caused a single tear to spill from me. No room inside for all of this feeling. All of this embarrassment. All of this love.

His voice dropped to a whisper. "What did you want from me?"

I gazed into his eyes. So easy to look in those eyes, but so hard. I searched them, hoping to find a safe place to launch my vessel. "You. I just wanted you."

He sat perfectly still, his lips pursed tightly.

I continued, my heart tossing wildly in a sea of uncertainty, "And I see now that you were with me more out of curiosity than anything else and . . ."

"Whoa!" he said. He leaned into me, his face inches from my own. "You think that? You think I was always around you because I was just curious?" His brow pulled into concern.

"You said it yourself. You said you were curious as to why I could see you."

He shook his head and stood up from the bed, pacing.

"Presley. Okay. Yes, I was curious. You shocked me. That is the reason I came to you at first. I admit that."

"It's fine, Landon. I get it. You don't have to explain."

"Listen to me." He slowed his pacing and knelt softly before me, his eyes thoughtful and concerned. "Where do I start? The more time I spent with you, the less curious I became about why you could see me. I just wanted to be with you. You surprised me. Your compassion for Violet. It's so easy for me to see why she trusts you and loves you. Your loyalty, your strength. Seriously—the day you took Megan down to defend your brother. . . "

"You saw that?"

He looked ashamed now. "Presley, I don't want to sound like a creeper, but I've pretty much seen everything since that day in the parking lot."

His eyes met mine and his face smoothed as he spoke. "After spending all this time with you, I feel more for you than I've ever felt for anyone. It has nothing to do with the craziness of you being able to see me." He hesitated and then seemed to push it away. "Dead or alive, I'd follow you."

My emotions betrayed me as two, three, four tears spilled over.

Landon closed his eyes. "I wish I could wipe those away for you. You don't even know."

The tears reached my smile.

Chapter
Twenty-Nine

FADING

(PRESLEY)

Mr. Price leaned over my desk and tapped a curved finger on the government test in front of me. "Checks and balances." *Tap. Tap.*

I winced at the big red F minus scrawled in the top corner. I didn't even know there were F minuses.

He glowered at me. "Miss Hale, I'm afraid it's summer school for you." He tapped question number two this time. "Twenty-seven amendments. Twenty." *Tap.* "Seven."

I woke up and read the clock. 2:14 a.m. I rubbed sleep from my eyes and turned on the punishing light on my nightstand. *Tap. Tap.* Unsure of where that tapping sound was coming from, I scanned my room. Landon stood at the window, looking out.

"It's Violet." He said, his face screwed up, perplexed. "She's throwing pebbles."

I crawled out of bed and met him at the window. "Why would she be here?"

"I'm not sure." He paused and looked down at his sister, his mouth in a grim line. "I'd better go, though." Landon had stayed with me the last five nights. I'd hoped he was only being overprotective, but we both knew the Vigilum were likely always nearby. He seemed to sense my uneasiness.

"I won't be far," he assured.

My phone vibrated on my bedside table. Violet had tried repeatedly to text me.

Are you up?

Can I come over?

Ok. I'm coming over.

I'm outside.

Please wake up! It's freezing. I don't have a coat!

Please, Presley. Wake up.

There were more messages, but I felt bad making her wait, so I tossed my phone onto my bed and threw one more nervous glance at Landon as he slipped from my room.

—

Violet's shivering had finally subsided and she sat wrapped up in my comforter at the foot of my bed. We sat cross-legged, knees to knees. I could tell she had been crying for a while. I laid my hand over hers.

"Tell me what's going on."

Violet didn't look at me, but stared over my shoulder. "I'm forgetting."

"What do you mean?"

"I feel like I'm forgetting my brother," she said, her voice distant.

"No, Vi. Of course you're not." Again, I felt the choking guilt of having free access to the one thing that Violet missed the most.

She met my eyes. "That day we ditched and went to Kings Beach. Landon's beach. That was our place. But I let myself have fun that day without him. How could I?"

"That's a good thing."

"I don't think so. He used to be in my thoughts every minute. And now I find myself going an hour, maybe two, not thinking of him at all."

"Why is allowing yourself a little happiness bad?"

"Because I'm *forgetting*." Her voice broke.

"He's your twin; you are never going to forget."

"Exactly. He was my twin and I have to pull up videos to remember how his laugh sounded."

His voice gets husky when he laughs, I thought.

"Which side his dimple was on when he smiled. The exact shade of his hair." She pressed her face into her hands, then roughly pulled her fingers through her hair. "It's getting blurred."

Dimple on the left. Hair—the color of coffee without cream.

My eyes dropped to my hands in my lap. "I know it's not the same, and I'm not trying to marginalize your pain, but sometimes when I look at Chase, I feel like I've lost a brother too. I've thought of that day at Kings Beach also. Where was Chase? While we were ditching school, he was in a special-ed classroom. If he didn't have autism, I would have brought him with us. Who am I to be making new friends and being all spontaneous when both of those things are so hard for him?"

I risked a glance and looked at her carefully. Her eyes were locked on mine and filling with tears, but I felt safe to continue. "I just want you to know that I understand how it feels to have things not turn out the way you'd hoped. What it's like to be alone."

Violet nodded. "There's just no escaping it. I can't run fast enough. It doesn't matter how many things I fill my life with; how I try to distract myself. The pain is always there. It will always be there."

I squeezed her hands.

She continued. "I'm just so scared I'm losing that connection we had. I'm telling you, Presley . . . it was like, paranormal." She smiled ruefully. "There was this one time I was at leadership camp in Sacramento. I got totally sick in the middle of the night. I thought it was just food poisoning. Then it got so bad that I couldn't get off the bathroom floor to ask for help. Somehow, from a hundred miles away, Landon *knew* I was in trouble. He called and woke up my camp counselor to make her check on me." Her eyes rounded. "My appendix ruptured and the surgeon said I would've been dead by morning."

"That's incredible," I said.

"Exactly. Who has that? It was something unexplainable. And after he died, I could still feel him. That probably sounds crazy, but I swear I could sense him. And it's fading. And I will never get it back."

I could've fixed it in one sentence and just told her that Landon was standing outside right now. But that wasn't my place. And who knew? It might make things worse.

I chose my words carefully. "I think I've learned enough about Landon to know that he'd want you to be happy. That he would be glad that things are getting a little easier for you. You're not betraying him."

Violet leaned forward and threw her arms around me. Her chin rested on my shoulder. "Can I just stay here tonight?"

"Of course you can."

Long after Violet's breaths grew slow and rhythmic, I lay there wondering how I'd landed here and how long I could keep this up.

Chapter Thirty

THREE BLACKWOODS

(PRESLEY)

The early snow storm had melted off, but things were still wet and frigid outside. The ground looked like a chocolate macadamia nut cookie; mostly mud, but patches of snow here and there. Violet had talked me into working the concession stand for the homecoming football game, which also fell on Halloween. She was dressed as a cat in black leggings, black Uggs, a long-sleeved black T-shirt, and a pin-on furry tail. She had painted on a cute pink nose, carefully outlined in black, and a few thin whiskers. Her dark hair was pulled up in two high buns that looked like kitty ears.

Chase was my sidekick, dressed in a big yellow banana suit he had from last year. Gayle was sick, so she opted to stay home in bed. I knew she must have been pretty bad, because as the principal, she always felt obligated to attend big events like a homecoming game.

I felt a little like a jerk, because I loved Chase and knew he needed to get out of the house and experience things as much as anyone else, but part of me just wanted to do homecoming without having to watch him. I made the best of the situation though, and decided to dress in a fruit-themed costume along with him. The dollar store had cheap balloons and I bought every bag of purple they had. I ordered green tights and a leotard online, so pinning a bunch of inflated balloons on made the perfect grape costume. As I maneuvered around the cramped concession stand though, I started to rethink my cleverness.

POP! "Dang! That's the third one," I said as I plucked another floppy balloon off of my hip and tossed it in the trash. An inflatable outfit didn't mix well with scalding hot Crock-Pots of nacho cheese, a giant walking banana, and ten square-feet of floor space.

Violet, busy shoving crinkled bills into the cash register, glanced at me over her shoulder. "Do you want me to handle the food and you take orders?"

"That's okay, I'll just be more careful." I tried to imagine myself running the counter as efficiently as Violet did and it made me laugh.

"No, no Chase," I said. He kept sticking plastic forks into the melted cheese and stretching his arm up high so he could watch the cascading yellow stream down. It was a new way for him to pour. He loved pouring anything. Water, soda, sand, and now nacho cheese. I sat him down in a folding chair and pulled a third ice cream bar out of the freezer. "Here, buddy. You want some ice cream?" I made another mental tally of how much money I would owe the snack bar by the end of the game.

"Three nachos! Two plain and one with extra jalapeño!" Violet belted out.

The jalapeño jar was getting low, mostly juice and seeds, so I jogged over to the stock cabinet to fish out another jar. The lid was tight and I hunched over using all of my strength to loosen it.

"Oh no! Presley help!" Violet screeched.

I whipped around and saw Chase tipping a Crock-Pot up on one end. He watched with glee as the gloppy cheese flowed over the ice cream bar he held under its stream. A creeping cheesy puddle spread out on the ground at his feet, finally reaching the tips of his tennis shoes.

"Chase! No!" I slammed the jar down on the counter, grabbed a stack of napkins and crouched down to absorb as much mess as I could before Chase tracked it all over.

"How long is this going to take? I've been standing in line for fifteen minutes." A big-bellied guy with a mustache that very much reminded me of a walrus leaned into the window, his sausage-like fingers curled over the sill.

Violet snatched the unopened jar of jalapeños and handed it to him. "Here. Open these. That will move things along." He looked at her, then at the jar. Shrugging, he twisted the lid off with a sucking pop.

There weren't any more napkins and I still had a ton of cheese to get off of the floor and Chase's shoes. "I need something else to clean this."

Already picking up my slack, Violet topped a steaming tray of nachos with an extra spoonful of jalapeños. "The restrooms should have some paper towels. I'd check the men's first. They wash their hands less than women do." She smiled a saccharine smile at walrus guy and handed him the food. He glared and walked away. "Enjoy!" Violet turned back to me. "Run and grab some. I've got Chase."

"Are you sure?" I glanced at Chase, who had fished my phone out of my purse and was watching YouTube.

"Yes, go. I've got this." She turned back to the growing line outside. "Who's next?"

I'd just left the men's restroom with a handful of wet paper towels. A biting wind blew through my clothing, giving me another reason to regret my costume choice. My leotard and thirty-four balloons did little to insulate me against the rapidly dropping temperatures. To make matters worse, the cold air caused my balloons to shrivel and I looked more like a bunch of raisins that a cluster of grapes.

"Let me guess . . .there's a constipation epidemic in Truckee and Super Prune is on her way to save the day."

Landon's voice startled me and the paper towels fell to the ground in a wet splat. Before I had a chance to respond, he added, "But where's your cape?"

I laughed in spite of myself. "It actually looked way better when I first made it."

He covered his mouth and shook against the ongoing fits of laughter. "I wouldn't change a thing."

I was so glad to see him that I ignored my shivering.

"Follow me," he said.

I didn't know where he was taking me and I knew I needed to get back to Violet, but I promised myself I'd just be a minute.

The band's equipment trailer was surprisingly warm from the metal walls, which must have soaked up some afternoon sun. Empty instrument cases were stacked neatly against the edges and extra scarlet uniforms hung in a row in the back. A narrow shaft of bright field lights shone through a small window creating a dim, but inviting ambience.

"I didn't expect to see you here tonight," I said, pleasure bubbling inside me.

"Well, I missed you." His eyes sparkled irresistibly.

I grinned, and my first instinct was to hug him. But, frustratingly, I had to find another way to show my affection. It felt impossible, so I reverted to sarcasm to diffuse the awkwardness. "I don't blame you." I gestured to my Super Prune costume and struck a pose. He whistled obligingly.

"So, who's winning out there?" he asked.

"Haven't you been watching?"

"Oh, I've been watching."

"So, you know that Reese has scored three touchdowns, then."

He smirked deliciously. "I didn't mean I was watching the game."

My heart hammered and I reveled in knowing that he was that interested in me.

"This is so not fair," I pouted. "If I could be some invisible creeper, I'd watch your every move too."

"I'm flattered," he smiled. "But all you would see is me watching you. Then we'd be locked in the world's longest staring contest. So I guess it's best that I'm the only invisible creeper around here."

"Whatever you say, Creepy." I laughed. He laughed too, but I could tell if he could have touched me, he would have. I wished I could have touched him too. His eyes mirrored the intensity I felt. And then we both sighed.

"So, are you going to the dance?" he asked. "I bet you've got some moves."

"Ha! I don't think so. No moves here." The dance seemed so stupid compared to standing there, looking at him. "How about we just hang out after the game?"

"Presley—it's Halloween *and* homecoming. It's like Halley's Comet or something. Only happens once every hundred years. You can't miss it." He was persuasive.

"How about this?" I raised an eyebrow, ready to bargain. "I'll go if you go."

"Oh that'll be fun for you," he teased.

"It *would*."

"I'm not doing that to you. An isolated running trail or your bedroom is one thing. A crowded dance floor filled with friends you should be hanging out with is another. You know I love to be with you, but that kind of situation just doesn't make sense." Then Landon's face changed to a serious but tender expression. "You should go. Really."

"I just want to be with you," I said lightly.

"I know. And I want to be with you too. But you're a senior. This is kind of a rite of passage."

"I don't care about that stuff," I huffed.

"Well, you should care. It only happens once and you can't get it back." I detected a note of regret in his voice.

"It wouldn't be what you think anyway. I won't be partying and mingling. My mom is sick so I'll have Chase tonight." A jolt of adrenaline jogged my memory. "Oh crap! I've got Chase. Violet's going to kill me!"

"Oh, she'll live," he dismissed with a wave of his hand. "A little nacho cheese never hurt anyone."

"Yeah, but wrangling him and serving a mile-long line is enough to crack even her." I headed toward the door.

Landon playfully positioned himself in front of the exit. "Promise you'll go to the dance and I'll let you by." His eyes were warm and insistent. "It would be good for Violet."

His point hit the mark. Violet needed any form of unwinding possible.

"Fine. I promise, but let me go before I lose my last friend in this town." I tried not to imagine the many snack shack shenanigans Violet might have endured. How long *had* I been gone? My question was immediately answered when I heard the band strike up Truckee's victory march and the crowd erupt. Game over.

"Have fun tonight." His eyes were kind, but lacked their usual playful spark.

"I wish you could be there," I said, dispirited.

"Me too."

—

The concession stand window was closed, the door locked. Guilt seeped through me. I scanned the milling crowd for Violet and Chase and found them seated together in the front row of the bleachers, huddled under a blanket. Chase was now nacho-cheese-free, and playing a game on Vi's phone. Violet, unsurprisingly, looked composed on the outside, but I knew her well enough to know that she was adept at hiding the most intense emotions. I reluctantly approached them.

"You ditched me," Violet said matter-of-factly.

I sat down next to her, knowing I deserved that. "I know, I'm sorry," I grasped. And then I lied. "My mom called and . . ."

"I'm aware. Chase had your phone, remember? I answered it."

I never was a great liar. I was always forgetting small details that gave me away. Like leaving my phone behind with the person I just lied to. *Stupid.*

"She's feeling better, by the way." Her eyes were cool. "What's up with you lately?"

"What do you mean?" But I knew exactly what she meant. I spent most of my free time with Landon, running in the mornings and holed up with him in my room at night. He was absent during the day, adamant on giving me space. But he consumed my thoughts, and I could see how I might appear distant or distracted to Violet.

"It seems like you're pulling away from me." Violet's voice was bruised. "I know I come with baggage, Presley. It can't be easy sharing my issues. I'm trying my best to be here, be present, but there's no instruction manual on how to move forward when you've lost half of your life."

I tried to interject, but Violet cut me off.

"And, I'm sorry that I'm not a normal friend to you."

"You're normal, Vi . . ."

"Let me finish." Her face pinched and she seemed to search for the right words. Her voice came out cracked and weak. "Grief is with me all of the time. Do you get that? There's no relief. I'm sure that's not exactly fun for you. So I get it if you feel the need to pull back. You don't have to lie to me and you certainly don't have to shoulder this with me. You didn't even know Landon."

That was a knife to my heart. The need I felt to tell Violet that I *did* know Landon was crushing. If she could only know that the person she loved and missed was the same person I'd spoken to only minutes before. And that I loved him too.

The situation was so twisted. Even I couldn't justify my relationship with Landon and how it caused every interaction with Violet, and everyone else for that matter, to be a lie.

I scrambled to make some kind of repair. Stop the hemorrhage before our friendship bled out entirely. "You are the best friend I have here. I didn't know Landon, but that doesn't mean I don't hurt for you. I'm sorry I've been aloof." I picked from the many reasons for my behavior and found a couple that applied and weren't a lie. I hoped they would be enough.

"Vi, my mom is always working and I'm always taking care of Chase. I'm tired." Truthfully, it was exhausting caring for Chase. Adding to that, there was the strain of making sure my life with Landon never crossed into my life with Violet. Every word I said to her had to be carefully monitored to make no mention of Landon. The excuses I made when Violet wanted to hang out with me when I was with Landon were lies. I constantly fabricated stories of where I was or what I was doing when I was actually with Landon.

My life before Landon, though less thrilling, was also less burdensome. I never knew the toll lying would take.

Violet's face softened. "I can see that." She laughed quietly. "I just spent the last thirty minutes with Chase, and I can see everything it takes to keep him out of trouble. You deserve to be tired."

As if on cue, Chase jumped up and bolted over to a man holding a soda. He snatched it from him and took a long swig, replaced the cup in the stranger's hand and then dashed toward the parking lot, which gratefully put an abrupt end to our conversation.

—

At the gym, Violet and I stood at the counter of the ladies' room while Chase, still dressed in a banana suit, rocked back and forth to the thud of bass vibrating through the wall. I was glad she wanted to go to the dance and that I didn't have to convince her "it would be good for her." Violet worked magic on my hair, fluffing and tugging it into an adorable top knot as I replaced pruny balloons with newly inflated ones. She convinced me that nighttime events called for vamped-up makeup. I held still as she brushed my lids with smoky coats of shadow and lined my eyes in cat-like strokes. Though, entirely unlike my basic mascara and lip-gloss routine, I had to admit Violet's results were surprisingly striking. I barely recognized my reflection.

Violet had already changed out of her cat costume and dumfounded me with her Medusa one. Her olive skin glowed next to the white toga and her wasp-like waist looked amazing belted in a shiny gold rope. Several green, fake plastic snakes wove their way through her hair which had been curled and pinned into a glamorous arrangement atop her head. Her ability to merge supermodel with evil was impressive.

Violet appraised both of our reflections and seemed pleased with my makeover. Then she examined my costume more closely, parting the balloons and wondering aloud, "How are these things attached, anyway?"

"With safety pins," I answered, a little exasperated. "Didn't you just see me . . ."

"Perfect," she said, while removing a balloon with its pin from my shoulder. She threw the balloon behind her and used the safety pin to pop the balloon on my other shoulder.

169

"Violet!" I protested. "I just spent like twenty minutes fixing this . . ."

"This what?" she laughed. "I'm not letting you attend the homecoming dance dressed as fruit. No offense, Chase." Chase walked over to a sink, turned on the faucet, and busied himself playing with the stream of water.

Violet continued to pop my costume. "Stop," I complained. "I'm not going out there in a leotard."

"Well it would be better than this," she giggled. "Seriously— grapes were fine for the snack shack," she smiled impishly and the mischief in her eyes made her resemble Landon, or Reese, or both. "Not to worry," she continued, spiritedly. "When you told me you were going as grapes, I made arrangements."

She made fast work of the remaining balloons, then turned to her duffle bag on the counter. I stood in my leotard feeling nearly naked. "This," she gushed, as she pulled something from the bag, "is more fitting for tonight."

The floor length gown was jet black. Long fitted sleeves to the wrist, with a full skirt entirely covered in sleek black feathers. It was breathtaking.

"The Black Swan. My sister still had it from a modeling shoot. It's going to look amazing with your hair and makeup."

I glanced at myself in the mirror again, the dark eyeliner and up-do making so much more sense. A little thrill of excitement winged through my stomach. "It's so pretty, Vi!" I bit my lip attempting to hold back the wide smile that was trying to stretch across my face. "Help me into it?"

Once in the gown, I turned slowly in front of the mirror. The back was open and low. Violet appraised her handiwork appreciatively. Her painted lips smiled, and then she patted an escaping snake back into place.

I wished more than ever that Landon would be at that dance.

Chase came over and tugged on Violet, leading her out the door and toward the gym. After thinking it through, I realized it wouldn't be too hard to engage him for the night, since dancing to loud music was one of his favorite activities. I grabbed one of his hands, and Violet the other, and we pulled him onto the floor. Happily stimulated by the fog machine and the sporadic flash of strobe lights, Chase wasted no time getting his groove on in his banana suit. Before long, several of our friends including Garett and Kade, dressed in nearly identical red and green as Mario and Luigi, joined us on the floor chanting, "Go Chase! Go Chase!" I was glad I had come to the dance after all.

After several dances, Chase pointed to the punch bowl and dragged me by the hand in that direction. Garett intervened, offering to take him. We decided to all go together, as Violet and I needed a breather as well. As the group dispersed and headed that way, Reese appeared before me dressed in a simple pair of dark jeans and a fitted grey T-shirt.

His voice was low. "Dance with me." It wasn't a question. There was a weight in his gaze, but he handled me tenderly. Grasping my hand, he led me back toward the dance floor as a popular slow song replaced the heightened energy in the room with a romantic tranquility.

He stopped near a less populated corner and held me at arm's length as he regarded my costume. "I recognize that dress. But it looks better on you than it did on Becca."

Blood rushed my cheeks, and I suddenly felt a little shy under his scrutiny.

Pulling me to him, he looked down at me and raised one mischievous eyebrow. His hand was warm and electric on the bare skin of my back.

"So where'd you run off to?" he asked.

"When?" I stalled.

"During the game, when you left Violet hanging?"

"Oh, that." A small wave of guilt rose, and then retreated. "I had to get some stuff to clean Chase up. He made a big mess in the snack bar," I half-lied.

"Hmm." His eyes were dark, but inviting.

A couple minutes passed and one slow song faded into another.

"So what have you been up to?" I asked casually.

"Missing you," he said pulling me slightly closer.

And if I was honest with myself, I'd been missing him too. "Reese—"

"Just hear me out," an earnestness in his voice. "I thought things were good between us. I was happy, you seemed happy and then something changed. You did a one-eighty on me. Look, whatever you're hung up on, we can work through it. It's time to move on with what's in front of you." His eyes searched mine for a reaction.

"You make it all sound so simple."

"It is simple. I want you." He shrugged his shoulders and smiled the most dazzling crooked smile. It was like he didn't even have to try. "That's all there is to it."

I bowed my head, resting it on his chest. The familiar smell of his cologne brought back a wash of happy memories. The comfort and protection he freely offered me from the moment we met. The warmth of his body next to mine as we sat at the river's edge.

Being with Reese was so easy.

"Say something," he said, his voice rough.

I lifted my eyes to his and wondered how I could feel such powerful feelings for two separate people.

"I want to be the one for you. I can tell you feel something for me. Will you let me try?"

The word "yes" floated on my tongue.

Then I caught a glimpse of Sam on the fringe of the dance floor, her eyes keenly fixed on Reese and me. She stood, arms crossed, resentment painted on her face. Shame welled up in me.

"What do you want me to say? You're dating one of my best friends. Have you thought about how she would feel if she knew what you're telling me?" I motioned with my head to where she stood.

Reese looked over his shoulder and gave her only half a glance. "It's not serious," he shrugged.

"Is that how Sam feels? You guys are together every day, holding hands in the hall. Don't think I haven't seen you kissing her around school. If that's not serious to you, then what is?"

"Were you jealous when you saw me kiss her?" He smiled, delighting in my discomfort. He didn't realize my discomfort wasn't solely about jealousy.

"Reese! This isn't a joke. She's a person with feelings. Not an object to be toyed with."

"I'm not toying with anyone," he said through his teeth, his face clouded with ire. "I told you it's not serious. The end."

"If you cared to look at her, you'd see how serious it is to her."

Reese snorted. "Can we drop the Sam thing, already?"

I pressed on, "No, we can't. That girl would do anything for you. I knew that before you guys got together. She's always had a thing for you."

"Let's just say the feeling's not mutual and I have a thing for you." I could feel the muscles in his arms and back tense under my hands.

"No. I'm not doing this. I could never be with a person who so freely manipulates someone like Sam simply to hurt me. You're being cruel. You've got a girl standing over there who would give you anything."

He smiled harshly and squeezed me so tightly the air escaped my chest.

"Maybe she would."

My eyes tore from his and found Sam still unmoved and stricken. "You're unbelievable."

I pushed forcefully away from him. He stood there smug and still. I caught Sam's eyes for the last time, and sent an unspoken apology. Turning and stalking away I heard Reese call after me, "It could be you."

Chapter Thirty-One

BREAKING OUT

(PRESLEY)

Are you seriously having PB&J again?" Landon leaned back against my kitchen counter and wrinkled his nose at my dinner choice. "I swear, Pres, you gotta broaden your horizons."

"Well, there's nothing in this house!" I opened the pantry door to demonstrate my point. In Vanna White fashion, I gestured to the mostly-empty shelves. I grabbed a bag of soft white bread and closed the door. "My mom has never been a cook, which means I'm not much of one either. I don't mind. PB&J is luscious."

"It's not luscious. It's back-up food for when there's no better plan."

I shrugged as I unscrewed the lid from the peanut butter jar. "Well, this is all I've got. When you get any other brilliant ideas for my Skippy, let me know."

He hopped up on the counter. "As a matter of fact I do. When I was little, my mom helped us make chocolate peanut crunch truffles every year on Christmas Eve for Santa. He always ate every single one, so that tells you how good they are."

"I'm not sure truffles are the best dinner option," I said, shaking the spoon trying to release the glob of grape jelly that clung to it. It landed on the bread with a sloppy sound. Landon snorted as if to say, "And that thing is the best option?"

Instinctively, I turned to threaten him with my sticky spoon, only to realize that if I did chuck it at him, it would only go right through him and hit the cabinets behind. He was right of course; it was a pathetic dinner, but I didn't have the energy to remodel it. As a further blow, when I dug the plastic knife into the peanut butter, it snapped in half in my hand.

"Have it your way, then," he said, breathy and patronizing.

His smile was too yummy. I needed distraction. "Okay. Fine then. Let's get this evil plan to fatten me up started." I stabbed the broken handle of the knife into the unfinished sandwich and then slid the paper plate into the trash. "Tell me what I need for these alleged delicious truffles."

"Hey, if they are good enough for Santa, they are good enough for you. Do you have chocolate chips, butter, and Rice Krispies?"

I heard the crunch of tires on gravel and guessed my mom must be pulling up the driveway. The front door slammed and the tinkle of her keys hit the entryway table. Landon sat up straighter as if to make himself presentable. Miraculously, I found a half-empty box of Rice Krispies and the other ingredients I needed. I lost my grip on the cereal box and most of the cereal sprawled across the tile. I knelt down and started to scoop it back into the box.

My mom walked into the kitchen; Chase trailed, stuffing fries down his throat, humming loudly and noisily licking the salt from his fingers. The smell of drive-thru food followed her through the room. She threw a crinkly paper bag into the fridge and then turned on me. "Presley! What are you doing? That is disgusting. You can't eat that now; throw it away."

"Mom, I need it. It's an ingredient for a recipe I'm trying out."

"Recipe? Since when are you into cooking?" Gayle looked at me over the top of her red, square glasses as if I were a face she couldn't quite place.

"I'm not, really. Annoying school project," I said, veiling a smile. I kneeled down and retrieved the last handful of cereal from the floor and threw it in the box. Mom watched with a frown. "Don't worry about it, Mom. I won't make you eat any of my contaminated truffles of death."

"Hmm. Okay, but don't stay up too late, and I want it all cleaned up before morning."

"Yes, mother."

"Don't be smart."

"Yes, mother.

"I mean it."

I privately rolled my eyes at Landon. He bit his lip.

She made her way upstairs and then I heard the opening music to the local news. Mom always fell asleep to the news, and Chase was well into his nighttime routine, so I was glad Landon and I could be alone again. I gathered the rest of the ingredients and waited for instructions.

He taught me to mix and roll sticky balls of crunchy, peanutty goodness and how to make a double boiler. I dipped dozens of balls in melted chocolate and set them on wax paper in neat, shining rows. Admittedly, they looked delicious. Half an hour after we started, the last ball was dipped and the rumble in my stomach told me it was time to enjoy the fruits of my labor. I bit into the biggest one and the moan that escaped my lips betrayed me.

"Told you," he said, beaming a little too much for the occasion.

"I'm not worthy!" I whimpered through a mouthful. "This is the best thing I've ever eaten." I examined the last half of my truffle before I popped it in my mouth and licked the smudges of melted chocolate from my fingertips. Closing my eyes, I savored the taste. Then I heard Landon laugh quietly. I opened my eyes. "What?" I inquired.

"Nothing." He did a poor job concealing his smile. He found my eyes and a shadow of shyness passed over his face.

"*What* are you smiling about?" The curiosity was eating at me.

"Nothing! It's stupid." Inhibition was new for him.

"Oh, come on. You can't make a face like that at me and then say nothing about it. I know you're hiding something." I hopped onto the counter opposite him to signal I wasn't going anywhere anytime soon. He looked at me, wavering. I made my biggest pitiful eyes at him. He slid off of his counter and slowly walked to me, then stopped and stared at the rows of truffles lined up next to where I sat. I used this unusual closeness to examine his features more carefully. His mouth was slightly open and for the umpteenth time that day I found myself fixated on the softness of it.

"It's okay," I coaxed. "You can tell me—whatever it is."

His hand hovered over a truffle as if he were going to reach out and take one. Then he closed his fist. The confidence returned to his face and he looked at me.

"I just like that you liked these." His lips twitched into a boyish grin and I could tell his confession wasn't even a small part of what he really meant.

"And?"

"And . . ." he continued as his eyes traced the line of my hair, my cheekbones, my neck, finally settling on my lips. His voice was softer, "Something as small as you loving some food I showed you how to make, makes me happy. Bringing you some semblance of pleasure, no matter how simple, is the best bliss I can imagine."

I could feel the heat of his gaze on my lips. His eyes met mine, and in them I saw the impossible mix of satisfaction and pain. A flush of heat coursed through my body. I wanted to hide it. I was sure he could hear my galloping heart.

"So, you're enjoying this then?" I said playfully.

Seriousness smoothed his features and his eyes fixed mine with a look of surrender. "Yes."

A few beats of silence. My mouth curled into the faintest smile. "I'm curious then. If you *could* touch me, how would you?"

His face fell and I instantly regretted asking the question. Salt in the wound. "I'm sorry. I shouldn't have . . ."

"No. It's okay. I want to tell you. It's just that I spend ninety-nine percent of my time trying *not* to think of how I want to touch you. It's maddening, really. Now that I can't touch, it occupies my thoughts all the time. More than it should, I'm sure." He held his hands out in front of him and looked at his palms. "My body is gone, but my desires are stronger than ever. It's pretty much the worst torture I could imagine." He dipped his chin, probably trying to hide his emotion.

I didn't know how to comfort him. In any other situation, I'd have simply reached out and placed a reassuring hand on his shoulder, or slid next to him and put an arm around him. No, if I could have, I would have taken his face in my hands and kissed him until all of his hurt melted into me, absorbed and dissolved. But, I had only my words, which at that moment eluded me. Awkwardly, I pressed on, though.

"But if you could touch me," I continued, "what would you do first?"

He closed his eyes and his brow pulled into a pained expression. "Your hands, most definitely. I've watched them so many times. Holding your face when you are bored in class. Rubbing a knot out of your shoulders when you're stressed. Covering your lips when you're concentrating. They look soft. You don't know how many times I've wanted to reach out and feel them, hold them." He swallowed hard. "Feel them touch me."

My breath came out in a rush. I wondered what else he had noticed about me. I was flattered and aching.

"What next?" I gently prodded.

He softly covered his mouth with his fingers. A subconscious effort to stop speaking, stop revealing? It didn't work.

"Your neck." He looked at me apologetically, as though he'd been caught in the wrong. I smiled to reassure him.

"The other day when we came home from that run and I followed you inside, your hair was up. You leaned down to write that note to your mom. I saw a piece of hair escape and fall against your neck. I swear I could smell your skin, Presley. If I were me, all of me, I wouldn't have been able to resist kissing that place on your neck." He closed his eyes. "I don't know why I'm telling you this, but I've thought about that scenario so many times."

I knew my mouth had opened too far, but I couldn't close it. I couldn't move. I saw his mouth and imagined it on the back of my neck, and fine, tiny hairs all over my body rose and tingled as if he actually had kissed me there.

In one short discussion, we had rounded the bend. The air was thick with the intoxicating perfume of attraction and my whole body was singing with the way his words had caressed me.

In Landon too, the change was marked. His chest rose and fell with the roughness of his breath. His mouth was set and the charge in the air, palpable. I could see in his eyes that he would tell me anything I wanted to know.

"And of course there is the obvious." He eased the tension the tiniest bit with a playful chuckle.

"The obvious?" I asked.

"I've imagined our first kiss in so many different ways, Presley. I've wanted to do it a thousand times, I'm sure. But after all of this waiting and frustration I'm quite certain it would be your basic linebacker tackle. I'd kiss you so hard and long your lips would swell up."

I was sure I would dole out much of the same. Given the chance.

"Romantic," I teased.

"Straight up." He cocked an eyebrow.

"I think I need another truffle."

He leaned slightly closer to me, then bit his lip, laughed bitterly, and backed up again, less than an arm's length away.

I didn't like considering the thing that made us so different. He was here with me, but no matter how badly we both wanted it, we could only be so close. The disappointment was crushing.

In opposition to my dark revelry, Landon lifted his fingers just inches from my lips and smiled playfully. "And if I could touch you, I know what else I'd want to do. I'd kiss that little crumb right off your lip."

I had been trying my best the entire night to keep my heart and my hormones somewhat in check. Both plans were not going well. When he looked at me that way the walls came down. I privately berated myself. *Why get all worked up when I couldn't have him?* No matter how hard I tried to resist him though, all of my resolve was sweetly melting like the chocolate chips I had just warmed in the pan. I felt the heat bleed back into my cheeks. How could I let this happen? Why did I?

I struggled to avoid his stare because I knew that with one look in my eyes he would know it all. There would be no hiding the surge of need inside me. A need that could do nothing but remind me I could not have him. Not the way I wanted to. I considered what happens when a need exists that cannot be met. The only answer I could produce was suffering.

I met his eyes.

His expression hit me full force. He had his own gravity and I was reeling—trying to not be drawn to him.

I was slipping. His lips parted slightly.

"You're remembering aren't you?" My words cracked his expression, only slightly.

"Remembering what?"

"You're missing all of the parts of being human." Recognition glinted in his eyes. To live but not touch was living less than half a life. Ironically, again my impulse was to reach out to comfort him. Again, the gesture was killed before I moved.

He closed his eyes as if his mind were traveling familiar roads. He could not hide the recollections. I could see him folding himself inward, packing away and cramming in anything that would hurt too much. The sadness veiled his face and for the first time, I could imagine it under the mask of death.

That vision of him lifeless and cold, snapped something inside me. I impulsively felt more nervy. Wise or not, I needed to stop his hurting.

"Do you remember how it feels to be kissed?" I asked, the sound of my voice strained.

His eyelids fluttered open and I had never witnessed such sadness. The last trace of light drained from him and a hollow shadow settled on his face. I could not let him feel that way. I surprised myself by allowing my desire to violently well up and spill over. I let it come and felt myself recklessly swept into his current.

180

He rushed to me, closing the gap in a second. His lips were on mine. I could feel him against my mouth. Instantly, I was aware of the heat of his breath, the smell more sweet and addictive than I had imagined numberless times. He wrapped his arms around my back, crushing me to him as if to prove I was real—that this was real. My fantasy of what he would feel like was a thousand times rewarded.

I had been kissed before. But the sensation of his lips on mine was somehow more intense than I had ever experienced. We were welded, it seemed, soul to soul. Though my eyes were closed, I saw a brightness as if warming my face in the sun. I imagined our kiss like morphine, spreading through his veins and thrilled at the thought that I was the one providing relief to him.

How was this happening? I didn't waste one more second wondering. I had studied that face for weeks—fixated on the fullness of his lips. Lit up inside when I saw him look at me, physically craving to touch him. And now I could.

I pressed my lips harder to his and reached for his face. My fingers found his jaw, prominent and strong—but my touch startled him. Instantly, his lips tore from mine. He took two large steps back. His breath came in ragged gasps and he stared at me with a nameless look on his face.

I struggled to catch my breath, to process what just happened. It was simple arithmetic. I knew I was touching him and then I wasn't. I wanted to touch him again. I started for him, but he held up his hand in protest.

"Presley, no!" The urgency in his voice baffled me.

"What did I do?" I couldn't understand why he wasn't celebrating. I wanted to, desperately. I was bewildered and I knew it showed on my face.

"It's okay. You didn't do anything wrong." The words sounded uncertain as if he were convincing himself more than he was convincing me. He started to pace, looking like a caged creature.

"Landon . . . I . . ." I took another step toward him, but I was only met with him taking a huge step back. The rejection painted itself across my face.

"Pres, it's not you. I just . . ." He looked at me, his face a fusion of trepidation and regret.

It was the regret part I couldn't take. All attempts at playing it cool evaporated right then and there. I was embarrassed at how desperate I sounded, "Don't you *want* to be with me? Didn't you want what just happened?"

He looked through me. Then he held out his hands and stared into his open palms. He spoke so softly I almost didn't hear him. Then I realized he wasn't talking to me.

"I don't know what this means," he whispered. "I don't know what this means." He scanned the room with dark eyes, bottomless and empty.

"I'm sorry," he said. "I have to leave. Now."

"Don't go," I whispered, half-choked.

He turned and walked straight through the wall, which immediately swallowed him up, leaving a screaming silence I could not shut out.

Chapter Thirty-Two

HAPPY BIRTHDAY LANDON

(PRESLEY)

It had been five days since Landon kissed me then ditched me. How could he just leave me standing there with no explanation? For all I knew he'd changed his mind. Still, with each day that passed I wondered if he would ever come back.

Then, two days ago, Violet had stopped me on the front steps of the school to invite me to Landon's birthday dinner. Of course it was her birthday too, but she made it clear to everyone that she just wanted to celebrate Landon. Everyone who loved Violet knew what a hard day November 12th would be. No one had known what to say or do anyway. So we were relieved when she set the agenda herself.

There was to be a dinner with all of Landon's closest friends and family. I felt awkward, yet honored to attend, as I would be the only soul there who didn't know him. In life, that is.

They'd eat meatball subs (Landon's favorite), tell stories about him, share memories, and most shocking, view all of the footage anyone could find of him. Reese had sweetly agreed to assemble all of the clips into one presentation; a task I knew would be especially hard.

—

The cushions were deep and the leather soft on Violet Blackwood's sofa. I sat in the corner of the large L-shaped couch, with Garret and Kade on either side of me. Apparently, Reese had decided to behave for Violet's sake. He wasn't exactly warm and fuzzy toward me. In fact he hadn't even looked at me once since I'd arrived. While he monkeyed with wires and cords behind the massive flat-screen, Violet sat cross-legged in front of me, evenly stroking Rosie's sleek black coat. The rest of the friends filtered into the theater room and nestled on the thick rug or available spots on the sectional.

With good company, conversation, and full bellies, the mood was gratefully light. Only I seemed to notice the unnatural calm spread across Violet's face. I could see the effort she made to be present for what was about to take place. I too felt a storm building inside. Only days ago, I'd been with him, spoken to him, kissed him. It felt like the most monumental hypocrisy to sit in this assembly of mourners. At least I had the hope that he'd come back.

Reese moved to the switches on the wall and dimmed the overhead lights. The screen switched from screensaver blue to black. Then appeared the simple word that cut me wide open:

LANDON

Reese sat in a chair across the room. He leaned forward in his seat, resting his arms on his legs. I was glad I couldn't see his face. But more importantly, I didn't want him to see mine. In Reese's mind I'd never met Landon. Any show of emotion would probably seem unjustified to him.

The screen flickered and then Landon appeared on it wearing only a pair of obscenely tight denim cut-offs. They were so short you could see the white pockets peeking out from the leg holes. The room erupted into laughter and "Ohs" and "That is so wrongs." His thighs were paper-white, but his chest and lower legs were brown from summer. Rosie was on a red leash beside him, wagging her tail and looking thrilled to be in a Carl's Jr. parking lot with her master.

Garett interjected from my left, "Ha! I almost forgot how much he loved that dog."

Landon spoke to the camera as he approached the restaurant's tinted glass doors. "C'mon, Rosie. C'mon, girl." He pointed to the sign clearly posted in the window which read:

NO SHIRT, NO SHOES, NO SERVICE.
NO PETS ALLOWED.

"That's a bunch of malarkey if you ask me, Rosie." The camera zoomed in on the stupidly happy dog, and then onto Landon's bare feet against the sidewalk, up his hairy legs, over his naked chest and onto his mischievous face.

"Let's see if we can get you a burger, eh girl?" Rosie wagged her tail and looked up at Landon with abject admiration.

Landon walked into the restaurant, leading Rosie straight up to the counter. He took his sweet time appraising the menu, pausing here and there to consult Rosie on her choice of onion rings or fries, bacon or extra cheese. A pale and bespectacled boy stood behind his register and swallowed hard. His thin lips tried to form words, finally croaking, "Sir, I'm not sure I can serve you."

Landon stuck his neck out in mock astonishment. "What do you mean," he squinted at the boy's name badge, "Lloyd?"

Lloyd turned his head awkwardly and rubbed some chin grease on the shoulder of his purple polo shirt. "Well, it's just that . . ."

"Just that what?" Landon smiled. He put both hands on his hips, one hand clutching the leash.

I noticed the broadness of his tanned back and the gorgeous contrast of his neatly cut black hair against the skin on his strong neck. I'd never seen him shirtless.

Poor Lloyd gestured at Rosie who had entangled herself around one of Landon's legs. Landon followed Lloyd's gaze. "Oh what, you have a problem with my lady friend, pal?"

"Well . . ."

Landon shook his head and clucked his tongue. "It's because she's black isn't it? Man, just when you think this world has made a little progress, I come across a guy like you, Lloyd."

"No! It's not that, it's just that she's . . . you know . . ."

"No, Lloyd, I don't know!" Landon bent at the waist to scoop Rosie into his arms. The room roared as he exposed even more of his "assets."

He cradled her in his arms and smoothed her ears back—gazing into her black jellybean-like eyes. She snuck a small lick on his nose.

"Pay him no mind, Rosie, you hear me? Nobody is going to question our love. Nobody." Rosie believed every word.

"Sir, I just can't . . ." Lloyd was pinching and kneading the end of his nose. "We just aren't supposed to let . . ." He glanced nervously at the camera.

"Lloyd. Talk to me, buddy. What is the problem here?" Landon lifted his knee up high and perched a bare foot right on the counter near Lloyd's white knuckles. "Is it my outfit that offends you?"

I quickly covered, then uncovered, my eyes.

Lloyd fought with all the might a pimply sixteen-year-old could muster to *not* look in the general direction of Landon's embarrassingly short shorts. He failed. The cameraman zoomed to Lloyd's bewildered expression. I realized then that Reese was the cameraman because I recognized his sniggering in the background.

A few exquisite beats of silence and the look on Lloyd's face were all this group needed. Everyone rolled on the floor in fits of hysterical laughter, gasping for breath and wiping tears. They squealed and yelled as the screen showed a pot-bellied manager hustling around the counter to shoo Landon and Rosie out the door. He waved a plastic tray at them like he were fanning a flame.

Reading about their pranks in Reese's file was one thing. But seeing it on screen, I realized that pulling stunts like this were as common for them as getting dressed.

There were more video tales of Landon and his "sense of humor." The room filled with cat calls during the clip of him running straight through a Denny's in nothing but whitey tighties. I laughed and blushed as I watched his strong body navigate around a cart of dirty dishes and then a high chair in the aisle. His elbows pumped as he sped past a group of senior citizens gathered at the register, eating mints and picking their teeth. I thought I caught the faintest smile spread across the lips of the young cashier girl. I couldn't blame her.

I was glad to see even Violet laugh at the video of Landon hiding behind gas pumps at night and then exploding from behind them to scare whatever unsuspecting person was filling their car with gas.

I studied the faces of each person in the room. They were filled with painful joy. There was as much laughter as tears, and they mixed together into a bittersweet cocktail that the whole room was buzzing on. I laughed and cried along with them, only for a totally different reason.

I felt as if a thick rope were hooked in my chest and mercilessly pulling me to the screen. To the screen and straight through it. Through the walls and out. Out to wherever Landon was now. That was the difference between me and the rest of them. They were fixated, heart and soul, on that screen. It was all they could see of him now. But I knew better.

The class ring I'd found in the river that day hung from my neck on a chain. I pulled it from under my shirt and held it in my fist. I was sure it was Landon's and I'd worn it every day since he'd left. It was a physical reminder that he was real.

A blip in the screen again and Landon appeared in jeans and scuffed boots, plaid shirt with sleeves rolled to the elbows. It was night in front of a waning campfire. He was seated on a low stump, knees wide, and a black guitar rested on one knee. His head bowed low over the strings and the room took a collective breath at the soothing notes his fingers plucked out. He licked his lips before he began to sing and my heart squeezed when I saw that mouth. When his song reached my ears, my heart broke quietly into pieces.

—

The videos and dinner were over, but only a few people had gone home so far; the rest were gathered in the kitchen sitting on countertops and picking at leftovers while they visited with Violet's parents and each other. I hoped that in a group that size, no one would notice if I went missing.

I padded upstairs and shut myself in the bathroom. In the privacy of those walls I let the dam of my emotions break. I was unprepared for the tidal wave of emotion that broke over me when I watched Landon as he was, when he was living. As magnetic or more than Reese, he exuded confidence. He was dynamic and powerful. I could tell even through the screen that he brought life and energy into any room he entered. Everyone here tonight was still affected by him.

I hadn't even known he played the guitar. His song cut a bloody path through my heart. I wanted it gone. So I sobbed, knowing no matter how long and hard I cried, I would never be free of it. I mourned on that bathroom floor for the boy whose life was cut too short. I cried for Violet and Reese because I understood on a deeper level their loss.

The door cracked and Reese's voice floated in, "Presley, what's going on?" He stepped in, closing the door behind him. I scrambled to my feet grabbing a tissue to dry my eyes.

He looked me over, agitation clear in his features.

"What do you think you're doing?" The acid in his voice shocked me.

This was not the Reese that protected me in the halls from Megan and brought me four new tires. "You're going to upset Violet," he scolded.

"Which is why I came in the bathroom and shut the door," I countered.

"Why are you acting like this? You've never even met him," he spat. "I saw you during the movies, tears streaming down your face. I mean, Violet's a little puffy-eyed like everyone, but what's your deal?"

"I'm not sure why you think it's your business, but if you really must know, I'm sad for you and Violet."

"Everyone in that room is sad for me and Violet. But nobody's looking for attention like this." He may as well have slapped me. Is that what he thought this was?

"I'm not looking for attention," I assured him, gesturing to the empty bathroom. The tissue dropped from my hand and I bent to pick it up, straightening to meet Reese's face.

He dissected me with his eyes. "Something's not right." He glanced at my chest and I realized with horror that the ring I had carefully tucked under my shirt after the movie had slipped out when I bent down to retrieve my tissue.

As if he read my mind, Reese slowly and menacingly reached for the ring with two fingers. He held it for a moment before more closely inspecting the inscriptions on the inside of the ring.

"Where'd you get this?" he asked in a soft but threatening voice.

"I found it," I said, my voice cracking.

He ripped it from my neck, snapping the chain in two and leaving a stinging strip on my skin.

"You're crazy," I accused.

"No, Presley. I'm not the crazy one. You're the one walking around with my dead cousin's ring around your neck." He looked at me, clearly disgusted. "How do you think Violet would feel if she knew you had this? Or my aunt and uncle? This doesn't belong to you."

He stalked from the room, the chain from my necklace dangling helplessly from his clenched fist.

Chapter Thirty-Three

RUNNING HIGH

(PRESLEY)

> Please come home now.
> I need you.

For once I was grateful for one of Gayle's bossy texts. I was holding a cold washcloth to my eyes in Violet's bathroom. My face was still puffy and splotched, but a thin layer of concealer I'd found in a drawer masked it considerably. I made my apologies for leaving so soon and hugged my way out of the kitchen. Reese was stiff and avoided eye contact, but my insides were already so minced that I chose to ignore it until later.

Hoping Chase was okay, I drove home faster than I should've. I'd left Gayle set up with plenty of snacks and activities for Chase. He should've been fine. Taking the porch steps two at a time, I was anxious to see what I was up against.

A pale face appeared in the door's glass window, making me gasp.

"Geez mom—you scared me!"

She shielded her eyes from the porchlight with a shaky hand.

"Wait, what's wrong? You have a migraine?" Gayle hadn't had one of those in at least two years, but she'd had them frequently enough before that I recognized it now.

190

"Yeah," she croaked, as she squeezed her eyes shut. She traced her dry lips with her tongue then opened her eyes just enough to make eye contact. "Think you can give me a shot?"

"Yeah. Of course."

With my arm around Gayle's waist, we inched to the couch. Chase was seated at the kitchen table working on a puzzle.

"Be careful here," I cautioned as we navigated around her shoes on the floor. I set Gayle down and noticed the bottles of over-the-counter pain relievers on the coffee table along with empty cans of Diet Coke. Futile remedies for her migraines. "How's your vision?"

"Pretty bad—maybe fifty percent." Blurred vision and spots always accompanied Gayle's migraines.

"What time did you start seeing spots?"

"About three."

"Mom—why didn't you call me earlier? I would've come. You didn't have to sit here and suffer for hours."

"I didn't want to pull you from the party." She took a deep breath, trying not to puke, I assumed.

I threw a blanket over her and asked, "Where are your shots?"

"I'm pretty sure they're in one of those," Gayle sighed, pointing to three boxes stacked against the wall next to the entertainment center.

"We really need to finish unpacking," I said to myself. "Any idea which one of these?"

"Nope, just start looking."

I tore open the first box. Why anyone would pack bathroom and kitchen stuff in the same box was a mystery to me.

"Okay, which leg?"

"I don't care."

The piercing alcohol smell stung my nose and filled my head with memories of my childhood. I'd started giving Gayle her migraine shots when I was about ten. "You really need to man up and learn to give these shots to yourself," I admonished, rubbing her left thigh with the alcohol swab.

"I've tried a million times, but I just can't push the button."

I snapped the cartridge in place and pressed it against her left thigh. Crinkles appeared at the edges of her eyes.

"Just do it," she squeaked.

I pulled the trigger. *Pop.* "Okay, the worst part is over."

She lay motionless, covering her eyes with a limp arm. "You have some mail on the table there."

"Mail?" I said more to myself than to Gayle. I couldn't remember the last time I'd gotten anything in the mailbox.

Lying on the top of a stack of coupons and other junk mail was a plain white envelope with my name scrawled in handwriting I'd never mistake. It was perfectly slanted, elegant with uniform loops and lines. My dad's. The loser who'd just quit trying when I was only five. The guy who sent huge wads of money and gifts for birthdays and Christmas, but never visited. Maybe his wife didn't approve. Or maybe he was too busy with his wimpy CPA career to make time. The fact was, I didn't know, because we never spoke.

It wasn't my birthday, it wasn't Christmas. So what was the occasion? He'd addressed the letter to my Las Vegas home and it'd been forwarded to Truckee—just another testament of how clueless he was.

Gentle snores drifted from the couch and I glanced over to see Gayle with her mouth half open, her chest rising and falling in predictable intervals. Wasted from the shot, she'd be out for at least eight hours. Gratefully, it was late enough that Chase would be too.

Returning to my letter, I thought about ripping it up, but I was curious.

Dear Presley,

You must be surprised to hear from me this time of year. I know I haven't been the best at keeping in touch these last couple years . . .

Since when does couple mean twelve? Whatever.

Anyway, I've got some great news. You know that Heather and I have been married almost ten years now. I sure wish that the two of you could get to know each other. You have a lot in common. Did you know she went to school on a full-ride gymnastic scholarship to Texas Tech? You're still into gymnastics right?

Uh, not since I was twelve.

Back to the news. Heather and I have always wanted a family . . .

You mean like the family you walked out on?

Well, after ten years of trying (gross) *we'd pretty much given up on the idea. Seems like as soon as we stopped thinking about it, surprise! Heather turns up pregnant. She's due with a little girl around Christmas time. What a present under the tree that will be, huh? A baby girl. And a sister for you!*

There was more to the letter, but I'd read enough. A raw, malignant ache spread its tentacles through my chest. I fought to suppress it—to contain it, but couldn't. I closed my eyes, stubbornly fighting the tears that burned them.

"Presley." Gayle's voice was weak and cracking. She propped herself up on one elbow and peered over the back of the couch, obviously awakened by my crying. "What did your dad say?"

"Lay back down, Mom," I managed.

"No, Pres. What did he say?"

"Oh, nothing out of the ordinary." I wiped the tears from my cheeks. "Just that he's finally getting the family he's always wanted." I crumpled the letter into a tight ball and tossed it on the floor. I didn't wait for Gayle's reaction.

I left the house numb and ran to my Jeep. I floored it; the Jeep skidded precariously on the gravel from side to side as I backed down the drive. The loop around the lake had a speed limit of thirty-five; I took it at sixty-five.

I'd convinced myself for years that I didn't care about my loser dad. Added to that was Landon. I missed him so much. And I needed him at a time like this. If he cared for me like I cared for him, how was he enduring our separation? I tried not to think it, but for all I knew, he could have decided to take James's advice and move on. Leaving me behind.

Abandoned twice. It was too much.

I pushed harder on the gas until the speedometer reached seventy. Honking to make my presence known, I swerved around a truck and barely missed an oncoming sedan in the opposite lane.

"What are you doing?" a familiar voice boomed from the right.

My body jerked in surprise. Landon sat in my passenger seat, a look of horror and disbelief painted on his beautiful face.

"What are *you* doing?" I shot back, easing my pressure on the gas pedal.

"You are being a complete idiot, Presley." His voice was lower now, but still edgy. He gestured to the right. "Pull over up here, by that campground turnoff."

"I'm not pulling over." My throat was thick. "Why are you even here? I thought you were gone. It's been five days."

"I know. I'm sorry. I didn't leave you, though. You know I wouldn't leave you."

"No. I didn't know." Fresh hot tears ran down over the dried ones on my face.

Landon eyed the gauges, apparently still dissatisfied with my speed.

"Just slow down and pull over. You don't want to do something you'll regret. Stop the car. Please."

I pulled over and found an empty spot, which wasn't hard in the deserted campground. November wasn't exactly camping season in Tahoe. My headlights illuminated a thick wood picnic table and an empty fire pit. I parked and turned the heater on high.

"Wanna tell me what sent you on this suicide mission?" His eyes were searching, the shards of panic melting into pools of warmth and concern.

I was still mad at him for leaving, but his face held all the apprehension and concern of someone who cared deeply. And I knew that I could trust him. So I unleashed about my soon-to-be baby sister. I told him things that were revelations even to me. How I'd felt abandoned and betrayed. How I'd even felt angry with my mom for not trying harder to make it work with my dad and for not considering how growing up without him would screw me up. That I was jealous of anyone with an all-American family. I told him that I felt alone and afraid and wondered what my adult-life would be like without siblings to help with Chase. I felt screwed out of things that most kids had—family trips and sharing bedrooms.

We sat for the next few minutes in silence, and then he said, "I should've been there for you. I should have been there when you got that letter."

"Why did you leave that night? Why didn't you come back?" I forced myself to control my embarrassment and anger, at least until he could fully explain himself.

"There's nothing I can say that made what I did right. I shouldn't have left you. The only way I can explain it is that I was shocked. Completely confused. I'd spent five months unable to touch anyone. Then we broke every rule I thought controlled me with that kiss. I was afraid that James would be right. That somehow taking it to that new level would hurt you." His eyes searched mine and he held his breath.

"Okay," I said.

His breath came out and he seemed to relax a bit.

"If I look at it from your point of view, I can see how all of it would have been overwhelming," I admitted. I gripped the steering wheel and rested my head on it. "But seriously, five days?"

He shook his head, grimacing now. "I know. It took me a couple days to get brave enough to tell James what happened. He obviously wasn't happy about it. He's really on me to leave now."

I dropped my head back onto the steering wheel. "Great."

"Well, that's the bad news. The good news is, I think I understand what happened," he continued. "It's a little confusing, but

James basically explained it like this." He squared his shoulders to me and leaned in.

"Matter is matter. Even when you die, your spirit is still made up of matter. It's infinitely fine, invisible to the living, well *almost* all the living." He raised an eyebrow and smirked at me. "For some reason, you can sense me. James says, because of that, your energy, your matter—whatever we want to call it—it can interact with mine. Dang, I sound like Professor Dorktastic here, but do you see what I mean?"

My eyebrows knitted. I really was trying.

Landon sighed and struggled to clarify. "There is no such thing as nothing. I am not totally gone, Presley. Even physically, I am *something.*"

"Okay, I get that, but why am I the only one who can see you?" I wondered aloud.

"James has some guesses, but we don't know, exactly. The touch though . . . it can only happen when emotions run high. James said your soul sort of breaks through your body when there's extreme emotion. That allows my soul to touch yours."

I thought about that night. I'd wanted to comfort him more than anything. To imagine that feeling busting through the boundary of my body made absolute sense.

"I guess emotions were pretty high that night," I admitted with flushed cheeks.

"They were for me," he bit his lip. "Feeling pretty high right now, actually."

I could feel it too. Two magnets, charged and pulling.

"So, can you touch me now?" I asked shyly.

"Are you feeling emotional?"

I half-laughed and almost cried. For so many reasons. "Only slightly."

He laughed too. Then his eyes changed from friendly and playful to something more.

"Give me your hands." Landon took both of mine in his, and like lightning striking twice in the same place, I was breathless at the miracle. His hands were warm, solid. Heaven.

I closed my eyes, relishing this gift of touch that could pass at any moment. "I feel you," I said through uneven breaths.

He squeezed my hands. "Our emotions are heightened right now; that's when it can happen."

My heart sent thanks to the cosmos.

I opened my eyes and found his expression now back to playful, mischievous.

"Emotional for me, because I thought you were going to wrap this Jeep around a tree. And for you," his lips turned up slightly on one side and he cocked his head a little, "well, because you can't resist me."

My mouth gaped shamelessly open. "Are you seriously teasing me right now?"

"Absolutely not; that would be mean. I'm just stating fact." His eyes were bright. More joyful than I'd ever seen them.

I marveled that after everything he had been through, he wanted to play. Who could blame him? I didn't mind forgetting my troubles for a few minutes either.

My eyes narrowed. "I can resist you." I released his hands and folded my arms across my chest even though that was the last thing I wanted. The car was still running with the heater on, and the lights from the dashboard cast a greenish blue light on his face, which was still smiling smugly. Fog now covered all of the windows, creating an extra layer of privacy.

"Then let's have a contest," his mouth twisted into a wicked grin. "Let's see who can resist who the longest."

"But I thought you despised losing," I said, flippant.

"Oh, I don't plan on losing." He smiled but his eyes were serious. Leaning across the center console, he rested his forearm on the steering wheel and placed his other hand on my headrest, his face looming deliciously close to mine. His eyes consumed me. I stared back, struggling to think clearly, conscious of his warm breath on my face.

"You're weakening," he taunted in a soft whisper. "Don't fight it."

"You are so arrogant," I shot back with my best attempt at disgust. But his eyes caught mine in their spell, turning my face helplessly toward his.

"Confident, Presley. Confident is the word." He smiled again and his lips moved closer to mine.

His nearness was the best medicine. My pain floated away, distant and forgotten.

"Happy birthday, by the way. And thanks for finding me." Our eyes locked and a fluttering cord connected my heart to his.

"Thank you for forgiving me."

"Please don't ever leave like that again."

He reached up with both hands and cradled my face in their warmth. A fresh tear spilled down my cheek only to be softly swept aside by his thumb. His eyes searched mine and seemed to find what he was looking for.

It was impossible to tell who lost the contest. Our lips met in blinding relief to each other's ache. His fingers softly wound themselves into the back of my hair.

"Presley." My name on his lips, a perfect sound. The heat of his mouth found the curve of my jaw. One, two, three kisses until his lips were back on mine. My head filled with the same bright glow I felt the first time we kissed.

And then the world started to reel. Like I was trapped on a carousel spinning a thousand times faster than it should, pinning me in a sickening, unbreakable grasp. The windows blurred into a smear of fog and bluish light. Unimaginable pressure bore down on my body. I tried to lift my head but it slammed back down onto Landon's shoulder. I held on tighter to his neck and managed a feeble, "What's happening?"

And then we were in my kitchen—the spinning and pressure gone all at once. I sat on the counter next to trays of freshly dipped truffles—the taste of chocolate and peanut butter strong in my mouth, gaping at Landon, who looked as horrified as I felt.

Chapter Thirty-Four

ANSWERS

(PRESLEY)

Landon stood in front of me, only inches away. The spinning was totally gone, but my head throbbed, thick with pain. "What just happened? Landon?" I reached for him, but my arms were lead.

Landon cupped my face in his hands and scoured me with his eyes. "Are you okay? Pres, you're bleeding!"

He looked me over from the top of my hair, over my neck and down to my lap. He rubbed my arms and patted at every place on my body he could to make sure I was still in one piece.

I felt a warm trickle from my nose and wiped it away. "I'm fine." But I wasn't. I tucked my hands under my thighs to hide the trembling and breathed slowly to stave off the nausea.

"No. You're not." He pressed his palms hard against his eyes. "What did I do?" He slid his hands to his chin and talked over his fingertips. "I think I know," he said, his voice husky. "Back at the campground I was thinking of our first kiss."

"So?" His face blurred in and out of focus.

"Ever since my accident, if I'm thinking of something and the memory is really vivid, I can visit it again." He scratched at the back of his neck.

I studied him, incredulous, wondering how he dare have an itch at a time like this.

"What do you mean *visit* it again?"

"Like go back in time. Sort of." His eyes dropped to the floor.

I half-coughed and then leaped off of the counter and began to pace in small zig zags. "Why didn't you tell me about this?"

He continued to avoid my eyes. "Well, I figured you learning that I drowned last April was enough supernatural freakiness for one person." He paused and looked at the wall behind him before looking back at me. "Dead guy. Kissing a dead guy. I just thought that might be the limit for one mortal.

"James is always warning me about how all this could fry your mind. I had no idea I could take you with me." Landon's head sunk and he caught his forehead in the palms of his hands. "He's going to kill me."

These new facts boggled my mind. I absorbed their meaning and calculated the possibilities.

"So, let me get this straight. You just think of a memory and then you can go back to it?"

"Pretty much."

I asked the most obvious question. "So, why don't you just travel back to the night you died and change it?"

Landon's eyebrows shot up and his hands balled into fists. "I've tried. Like a hundred times, but it doesn't work that way. I can't travel to any time *before* my death. The furthest back I've ever been able to go is my funeral." His face paled.

"And I can only stay for a couple of minutes before I'm yanked to the present. It doesn't matter what memory, or how far back, it's always the same."

"What do you mean? What makes you return to the present?"

"I don't know. It isn't my decision. It's like you throw something sticky at the wall, but after a few minutes, it loosens and falls down. That's how it feels anyway. I try to hang on, try to stay, but it all begins to fade and I can't stop it."

"Listen, just a couple of minutes ago, you didn't even know you could bring me with you. You learned something new tonight. I don't think you understand all of the rules. I might be able to help you. Maybe we *could* go further, if you really focus . . ."

"No," he barked. "Absolutely not. This isn't safe."

The painful thud in my brain verified his conjecture with each beat of my heart. I tried to ignore it.

"We have to tell James." Landon looked apologetic.

"No! We can't. You know he won't agree with this. He wants to keep me away from anything that might upset me."

"Not upset you, Pres, hurt you."

"This didn't hurt me. I'm fine," I lied.

"I will not drag you around through time and space to tweak with stuff until it works."

"Tweak at *stuff*? Saving your life is not tweaking at *stuff*!"

"You know what I mean. There could be risks."

"You don't know that. You don't know anything."

"I know I'm not doing anything until I talk to James. You'll have to live with it. I won't risk you. I made my stupid mistake. It's not your obligation to erase that—especially when your involvement could hurt you."

I felt like the conversation was a filthy tangle of hair in hopeless knots. Knots that needed to be swiftly cut out, not fussed with and combed free.

"It's worth any risk to me, Landon."

"You don't know what you're saying."

"Yes I do."

"No, actually, trust me on this one. You really don't." His eyes were stone.

The edges of the wall began to blur and the room buzzed with energy. A slow swirl circled in my head, like water down a drain. I felt the breath squeeze from me just as I managed, "It's happening."

Landon's arms were around me in an instant. "Don't let go of me, whatever you do."

I wrapped my arms around his neck and buried my face in his chest. The pressure and the spinning hit me like a crushing wave. It took all of my breath, all of my sense of direction. It even took my physical sensation. I could no longer tell if I were holding on to Landon. There was just the sickening weight of what could only be endured second by second.

And then it was over. We were slammed back into the seats of the Jeep. The heater hummed and blew warm air, and the fog from my breath still slid in droplets down the windows. A slow stream of warm blood trickled again from my nose and over my lip.

Landon held my face in both hands and wiped at the blood with one shaking thumb. "Pres, are you okay?" He grabbed me and pulled me into a crushing embrace. I could hear in his voice the pain and regret cracking him in half. Though my head exploded in blinding white-hot pain, I had never felt more hope or possibility in my life. This changed everything.

Chapter Thirty-Five

NEWS TO ME

(PRESLEY)

Landon followed me into my house. Gayle's couch was empty. Curious, I followed the weak light from the kitchen and found her at the table, resting her forehead in both palms.

It took only seconds, from the hiccup of her breathing, to realize she'd been crying. To my surprise, a half-drained bottle of wine sat on the table in front of her. I groaned. *Since when did Gayle start drinking wine straight from the bottle?* She looked up and I was frightened at her appearance. The skin around her jaw hung slack and the hoods of her eyes weighed heavily down, reminding me of my grandmother's face. "Mom, what is it?" I probed. I sensed something more than a headache plagued her.

Gayle closed her eyes and her nostrils flared slightly. She took a deep breath and held up the crumpled letter, now mostly smoothed out. She let the breath out slowly and opened her sad eyes. "I've done something very, very bad. I'm scared to admit it." Her words caught in her throat.

Dread pulsed through my gut. "What do you mean? Where's Chase?"

Even through her stupor she looked stung. "He's fine. Upstairs with a video."

As if on cue, Chase's hum filtered down the stairs. Relief washed over me.

Gayle stared intently at the spot on the table in front of her. She seemed to need it for strength to say what she needed to say. "I haven't been truthful about the reasons your dad left. The reasons why I *asked* him to leave."

I didn't know what I had expected her to say, but definitely not that. All my life I'd freely accepted the ideas my mother fed me: that my father was bad. That he left us because he was weak.

"You *asked* him to leave? But I thought . . ."

"I know, Pres. I know what you thought." Her eyes shifted. "I'm sorry."

She dropped her head and sobbed.

My voice quavered and rose in timbre. "Why would you do that?"

Gayle began to rock slightly. She crossed her fists in front of her and buried her chin in her chest. "He let it happen. He didn't watch you closely enough. He fell asleep and let it happen right in front of him." Her eyes begged me. "He should have been there. He shouldn't have let you fall in the water."

"What water?"

Gayle continued rocking.

"Mother! What water?"

Gayle's eyes squeezed shut so tightly, the skin around them looked flaky and ready to crack. "The pool."

A distant cold horror flickered in my mind.

"He was supposed to be watching you! He was asleep when you wandered out and fell in." She shook her head. "Only three years old. Didn't even hear the splash of the water."

Gayle's voice rose in pitch to an airy whisper. "Your tiny face, Presley. It was blue and so still. You died. You died! He *let* you die!" She choked on sobs.

I stared, horrified, into Landon's face. Gayle was so distraught, she noticed nothing.

For the third time that exhausting day, tears erupted in my eyes. "I drowned?"

Gayle looked up at me. Pleading. "You died."

A pregnant silence hung in the air. So much to process at once. *I died. And it was my dad's fault.*

"They revived you. Barely. You were in the intensive care unit for weeks after the pneumonia set in. It was touch and go . . ." Gayle pressed the back of her hand to her lips and seemed to fight to regain composure.

I didn't know what she was talking about. Some of my earliest memories were of fights and screaming matches. My mom throwing things, doors slamming or being jerked from my bed in the night to go stay at my Aunt Lily's.

Gayle had always told me they'd split because Dad couldn't handle Chase. But really, she couldn't handle my dad. Because of what happened to me.

I hated them both. Her for driving him away. And him for letting her.

And what about Chase? If anyone needed a father, it was him.

No matter how badly Gayle treated him though, nothing excused him for twelve years of absence. But the shame he must have felt from the accident. The shame my mother must have inflicted upon him. More answers to why I hadn't seen him. He probably felt undeserving. Mortified. I couldn't forgive him for leaving, but at least I understood more the reasons why.

Finally I said, "That's why you made Dad leave? Because of a terrible accident?" I quaked with rage.

Gayle slid down in her chair, seeming to actually shrink before me. Her voice sounded small and simple. "I couldn't bear the sight of him. How could he let that happen? I couldn't look at him. Speak to him. I couldn't forgive him for what he did to you."

"He didn't *do* anything to me!" I was an atom bomb. "You couldn't forgive him? And for what? Not being perfect at all times? Like you? You think he let me fall in there on purpose? How could you be so single-minded? How could you punish him for that?"

"Presley, you don't understand . . ."

"No, mom, I do! You took my father away. You took him away from me and from Chase. My whole life I thought he never loved us. That Chase's autism was too much. You robbed us of what could have been. Because you couldn't forgive."

Gayle's lips trembled. Then she was very still. "I did."

"Well," I said, my voice deadly calm. "I think I understand what you felt."

Gayle looked up, hopeful for the first time.

I continued then, my voice composed. "Because now I know how it feels for forgiveness to be impossible."

I strode by, snatching the letter from the table. I ran up the stairs and burst through my bedroom door, Landon inches behind me.

James stood at the foot of the bed. He looked at us both with sympathy.

"And that, Presley, is why you can see dead people."

Chapter Thirty-Six

EXPOSURE

(LANDON)

Presley sat on her bed, knees pulled tightly to her chest with her back against the wall. Her eyes, masked in a faraway look, worried me. I kept to the other side of her room, sensing she needed space.

James never sat down in the presence of a human—always careful to maintain a clear barrier between the living and the dead. Sitting, to him, was something the living did—something to provide rest to the body, which of course he no longer needed. Instead, he moved near the door, another subtle sign that he viewed himself as a temporary visitor to this world, nothing more.

He explained what he had learned with gentle gravity, like a doctor delivering terminal news.

"Presley, because you have crossed realms," he paused and began again. "Because you have experienced death, brief as it was, your spirit has an enhanced sensitivity."

Presley blinked, but her eyes registered no spark or connection to James's words.

"It's not common, but some guides have seen it before." James's hands remained still at his sides. "When people have died and then return again to life, they can gain this increased power—the ability to sense spirits."

Still nothing from her. I took over. "Pres, I know you've been through a lot. And now this news about your Dad. The timing couldn't be worse." That got her attention.

"You think?" The muscles around her mouth strained as she held back tears. "I don't have anyone now. My mom wasn't much of a mom to begin with, but this!" Her eyes flooded and spilled over. "Gayle pushed him away. I could have had a dad this whole time. And Chase." She covered her mouth with the back of her hand and struggled to compose herself. "But you know the worst part? Even though my mom was the reason he left, he sure didn't have a hard time staying away, did he? What kind of father allows himself to be bullied right out the door and never comes back?" She laughed a mirthless laugh. "Screw him."

I moved next to her and placed a gentle hand on her back.

Presley sobbed, "And I *drowned*? I can't believe she never told me." She snatched a tissue and wiped her nose. "I guess it makes sense why I can see you. I guess it's good to know why . . ."

She hugged her ribs and curled into herself. "I don't know what to think. I don't know."

I risked a glance at James. His face was hard. It took me aback.

His voice came out soft and measured, "*This* is what I've been trying to get you to understand the entire time." James pointed at Presley with a slender finger. "Do you see now? Think of what she's had to grasp in the short time she's known you. The dead among the living. Vigilum. Time travel. How much do you think she can endure before she breaks?"

Every word James said confirmed it, and looking at her bent, shaking, her ribs spreading and collapsing with each sob, I knew none of this would be happening if it were not for my disregard of all the warnings James had given me. Reluctantly, I let my mind tiptoe back across the line of past denials and fully admitted my fault.

James considered Presley, his face doleful. Then he finally shook his head and rounded on me. "You think this love will work?" His voice was almost a whisper, but it struck me. "That you have a second chance at life? All of your decisions have been based on what feels good to you. None of this has been in Presley's interest. It gives me no pleasure to be harsh, but you need it. Your actions have been incredibly selfish, Landon. How can you see it as anything more?"

I felt like I was trying to tread water and each statement was a weight tied to my feet. My head dipped below the surface.

"The dead don't receive second chances," James said with finality.

All of his words smarted, but his judgment of my selfishness injured me the most. I had to admit that when I first met Presley, I only wanted to know why she could see me—what that had meant for me.

But it wasn't long before it became much more. In fact, only knowing her a few days, I found myself caring deeply for her. My change from selfish to devoted happened almost imperceptibly. It was hard for me to imagine a time without her. She was in me, all around me—all that was before me. And though James said the dead don't get a second chance, I had to take issue with that because I had Presley. If she wasn't a second chance, what was?

True, it was a messed up situation—complicated. And maybe James was right; maybe it couldn't last forever no matter how much I wanted it to. But, I couldn't swallow everything he moralized.

I cared for more than myself. And I knew that Presley cared for me. This simple truth was like breaking the water's surface and taking a life-saving gulp of air.

I squared with James, confident. "You know what it's like to love. Tell me you wouldn't do the same thing if you had the chance."

James cocked an eyebrow.

I continued, my sureness bolstered. "Tell me if you could have spent one more minute with your wife and your boy, holding them, touching them . . . tell me you wouldn't have taken that opportunity in a second."

James's countenance blackened. For the first time in my dealings with him, I saw true darkness in his eyes. It was startling.

"You don't know what you are talking about," James accused, each word frosted with a grave, quiet rage.

But I knew James's story. Early in our relationship, in an effort to empathize with me, James had shared how he had lost his wife and son. It was in the late 1800s. James and his wife, Lucy, and their seven-year-old boy, Michael, were traveling from Illinois to Oklahoma in a wagon to gain some land in the newly opened territory. The journey started out almost ideal. The weather was temperate, and they found plenty of clean water for the livestock and themselves. The trail was cooperative. Lucy collected wild flowers each day along the way and put them in a dented tin cup of water each night at dinner. James had purchased an inexpensive harmonica for Michael to occupy him along the journey. He would drive his parents insane practicing "Polly Put the Kettle On" over and over. By all counts, they almost considered the trip a long holiday.

Then Michael got sick with cholera. And mothers hold and comfort their sons even when they know it will do no good. She died three days after he did.

James's eyes swam with the memories of his family. His chin quivered and his voice grew thick.

"I had a wife. I had a child. That is love." He swallowed hard and stabbed an accusatory finger at me. "You, my friend, are a boy." He gulped again and cleared the emotion from his throat. "You put her in harm's way again and again and you call that love?"

Out of respect for the pain that was obviously still raw for him, I paused for a moment before I countered.

"Presley and me together—yes, it's difficult. Problematic even. But we choose each other. You have to give Presley some credit; she knows what she's doing. I'm not forcing her."

James cut in, "Yes, but if you truly loved her . . ."

"Don't feed me some cliché crap about if I truly loved her I'd set her free. I can't set her free. And I can't keep her. It's *her* choice. But if it were my choice, I'd hang on forever and never let go. I love her too much—I can't be without her."

I looked at Presley who had calmed down considerably, but her eyes still teemed with pain. The pain was for me. The pain was for her.

I took her hand and brought it to my lips, kissing it.

"We may not be married, or have a child, or even share the same realm, but I love her. I know you can understand that." Presley squeezed my hand.

James considered me, teetering a bit where he stood.

I went on. "You say that my life here is over. I say it isn't. I know it isn't the same life I had; maybe it's a half-life in many ways, but it's a life with Presley. And I will fight for every second of it."

My eyes speared into hers as I addressed James. "You tell me if the tables were turned, if you had been the one that died and not your wife and boy, if you had the chance to be with her for one more day, to touch her . . ."

I slowly, painfully, severed my gaze from Presley to face James. "You look me in the eyes and tell me you wouldn't have done exactly what I'm doing."

James sagged.

Except for an occasional cried-out hiccup from Presley, the room was quiet.

At last James loosened. He closed his eyes and tipped his head back. "You're right. I would have fought for any amount of time I could have had with Lucy and Michael. I would have done anything."

I sat up taller, gratified with my point, now proven and put my arm around Presley's shoulder.

"But it doesn't matter." James's eyes seemed to apologize. "In this matter, if you neglect to make a choice, the choice will be made for you."

Presley's visage cracked, and a small vein of puzzlement spread across her brow. My own heart sunk from James's tone. A sudden dryness in my throat caused my voice to come out hoarse. "What do you mean?"

James found the chair near the foot of Presley's bed and heaved himself into it. Then he folded his hands in his lap and studied them. "I'm almost certain your time here is nearly gone. No matter how hard you fight for it."

Presley's mouth gaped, wordless. My eyes locked onto hers.

"I never told you. I had my reasons," James said. "But if you don't decide to either use or forsake your passage, you will be taken from here. You will lose your right to choose."

I was furious with James for not telling me sooner. But my head clouded. I couldn't think clearly and contemplate losing Presley at the same time. I took her in my arms and held her to me. I could bring myself to say only one word. The only word that mattered.

"When?"

James gave a weak shrug. "It could be at any time. I've never seen anyone stay as long as you have. You are months past the longest I've heard of." All of the business was drained from his face. It was clear from his harrowed expression he took no satisfaction in delivering this blow.

"Well, if I'm the longest you've ever seen, maybe that's a good thing. Maybe it means something?" I brightened a bit.

James nearly cut me off. "No. No, Landon. There is no escaping it. Just as there is no escaping death. We may dread it, we may run from it." James paused before delivering the final blow. "The time to pass through comes to all."

Presley's eyes narrowed. She gently freed herself from my arms and stood. "Then what about the Vigilum? They stay. If the time comes for all, and there is no way around it, then why are they still here?"

My head whipped back to face James. A slow anger seethed in me. Partly out of confusion, and partly out of frustration with him for disclosing only the information he wanted me to know. Not all of the information available.

"James, I need you to come totally clean. What are the rules here? Not just the rules you want me to know, but everything," I said.

James sighed and turned his head, avoiding our gazes. "It will bring no good to you. I'm doing you a kindness by keeping information from you that will cause ill effects. Trust me on this."

"No." Presley's voice was hard and earnest. "You spout all of this bull about free choice and then when it comes time to make some choices, you won't give us all of the information we need. That's no kind of choice. If you believe in free choice, then let us be free to make *any* choice. Not just the ones you can swallow."

James shook his head and raked his hands through his hair, a very human-like gesture, one that I'd never seen him do before.

"Fine. You want to know the rules? These are the rules." James's speech spilled out, clipped. He jabbed a finger into the upturned palm of his other hand, almost like a coach scratching out a play.

"All spirits have a space of time to choose to move on. The amount of time it takes for each spirit to do so varies greatly. It could be instantly or it could take, as in your case, Landon, months. People have different reasons for staying. Some aren't prepared to separate themselves from their family."

I flinched.

James continued, "Some are shocked to find there is an existence after death and are afraid to pass through, either from fear of the unknown, or fear of punishment for the deeds they performed in life.

"Not all souls require a guide," James continued, "Those who anticipate an afterlife make the transition more easily. Those who have no knowledge of an afterlife or who possess extenuating circumstances usually require more guidance."

I laughed humorlessly. "Like me. Extenuating circumstances. That's one way to put it."

"Yes. Guides like me come to assist because it's what's best for the spirit."

"Why?" Presley questioned. "Why is moving forward necessarily what's best? And if they are going to be taken anyway, why bother sending a guide to hurry along the process?"

"Because it is better for the spirit to decide." James said, seeming agitated. "It eases the transition. In my world, action and choice are valued." He paused and regarded me. "Leaving oneself to be acted upon is not the way."

I considered James's words. The theory rang slightly true, but I couldn't apply it to myself. "But I feel like I am making a choice. A choice to stay with Presley. Why isn't that valued?"

"It will be recognized and addressed. But not valued."

"What do you mean?" I asked.

James raised his eyebrows. "Don't you see? Choosing to stay will make you Vigilum."

The statement was like a deafening blast. My ears rang from the impact of it.

"You choose to act against progression." James's eyes pierced me. "You choose to go back, not forward. This life and the next are about advancement and development. By choosing to stay with Presley, as pleasing as that choice may seem, you choose wrongly."

I fought for footing. "I don't see it that way. Choosing to stay won't make me Vigilum. I would never become that."

"How do you know?"

"Because! I would never deceive or manipulate people or prey on their fears to gain passage. I don't need it. I don't want it. I'll have Presley."

"Will you?"

I looked at her. A twinge of something I couldn't identify passed her face and in turn pricked my heart.

Was it doubt? It couldn't be.

Presley interjected. "Of course he'll have me. I'll always be with him."

"Are you sure?" James probed.

Presley took offense now. "Yes!" she snapped.

"You are prepared at this moment to decide to never be married? To never have a child? To grow old while Landon stays perpetually seventeen. To be with someone that nobody else in your life will ever have the opportunity to interact with? Do you realize the life of isolation you are choosing?

"And even beyond that, I know it seems a long way away to a young person like you, but when you decide at your death to give up your own passage to remain with Landon, you will be separating yourself from your family members who have and who will pass on. You will not see your mother. You will not see Chase. Chase, if you did not know, will be whole. You will have the opportunity to know him as he would be without his afflictions."

Presley's nostrils flared against oncoming tears. James had hit his mark.

"And you," he said solemnly, addressing me now, "You will not see your sisters or parents. Reese. The babies born to your siblings. They will be beyond your reach and you will have no claim to them at all. The two of you will be an island unto yourselves."

At the very least I had to admit that we were young. We didn't know it all, and maybe James had thought of things that we hadn't. It didn't mean we changed our minds on the future we wanted with each other, but the truth had to be swallowed and digested no matter the bitterness.

James proceeded softly, "Are you prepared to ask that of her?"

I was silent. I looked at Presley with less certainty. It wasn't that I loved her any less, it was just that James's probing had caused me to consider my love for her more deeply.

James continued gently, "If at any time in Presley's life, she decides she wants a family, a different path, with more people in it—which I'm sure none of us in this room would blame her for, then you will be left alone, Landon. You will be left with no one. And I can tell you that decade after decade of that will make you reconsider your willingness to become Vigilum. At that time, your desire to pass on to a place where you can move forward with others like you will become like a sort of starvation. You may not be able to help yourself. You'll steal a passage any way you can get it to end your suffering and isolation.

"Consider the Vigilum you know. They'll stop at nothing. Even those that fear their punishment grasp at any chance to move forward. They discover that the plan was right. Their idea was wrong. That stagnation is the worst sort of torture.

"You and Presley, no matter your love for one another, will crave growth. My greatest fear for you both is that the realization of your mistake will warp into resentment toward each other. You very likely will take the pain and isolation and channel it at one another. That would be a tragedy, indeed."

Presley and I looked at each other with an agonizing distance, contemplating our destiny. No matter how we manipulated it, it seemed irrevocably broken. A price had to be paid, one way or the other.

The air in the room hung static. It seemed any word I said would put me on one side of the line or the other—an action I wasn't prepared for. An impossible choice. Stay with Presley and wreck ourselves in the long run. Or leave now and ruin all we had. The worst part of it all was that at any second, the choice could be taken away and none of it would matter anyway.

"I can save you." Presley's eyes flashed wildly from James to me. "It's the only way."

A storm brewed on James's face. His brow clouded over and the full power of his gaze was on me like lightning. "What is she talking about?"

"James—" I began.

"I went with him," Presley cut in. "We kissed and we traveled back to the first time we touched. He was able to take me back."

James closed his eyes. He seemed as though he could crumble and blow away from the slightest whisper. "I can't say I'm surprised. You've broken through every other limit."

"I knew you'd be angry" I said.

"I'm not angry," James said softly. "I see I have no control over what you and Presley do. Perhaps it was wrong of me to so tightly govern things in the first place."

"I've already told her I won't do it. It was an accident in the first place; I want you to know that. I wasn't trying to use her to change anything."

James's face softened slightly.

Presley said, "Haven't you two ever thought that maybe *my* being able to go back with Landon was meant to be? If I could do it again, and this time make it to a time *before* Landon died, I might be able to prevent it from happening. How could either of you deny me that—you can't just make me sit by, powerless."

"We can and we will because it could kill you. Actually, it probably will," James explained, dispassionately. I'd never seen him look so tired.

216

"It won't." Presley's jaw was set in determination.

"It might," I said. "Presley, you were bleeding. We only traveled back a couple of weeks and you were hurt. Imagine what several months could do."

James arched an eyebrow, but remained silent.

"I'm fine! It was nothing," she said.

For the first time since meeting Presley, I looked to James to back me up. Sure, in a perfect world, where every ending is happy, I'd love for her to save me. To save us. But loving her taught me there are worse things than not getting what I want. And loving somebody with my whole soul and then hurting them was one of them. I would never let her try, no matter what. My eyes begged James. "Tell her, please."

James swallowed and addressed Presley. "Your body, in its current state, is not designed to cross the gateways of time. Bodies like mine and Landon's can do it effortlessly, with no unfavorable consequences. Frankly, I'm surprised you survived. Had you broken the connection with Landon, you would have died instantly. You beat the odds this one time. But it would be folly to believe it could happen again."

"I did it once, I *can* do it again." Her voice was hurt and childlike.

"No, you can't," James said tenderly. "I know you would if it were possible, but you can't. I don't say it to hurt you. If there was a way I could fix all of this I would."

Presley's eyes shone with tears. "I wish I could believe that."

Chapter Thirty-Seven

CREEPER

(PRESLEY)

Violet and I sat cross-legged on her living room floor, buried in ivory and gold ribbon and a garden of silk flowers. I'd just finished my fifth centerpiece of the day and my back ached from sitting for so long. I stood up to stretch and noticed my fingers were freckled with hot-glue-gun burns.

"How many of these did you say we need?" I asked, making an effort to sound curious, not burned out. We'd spent the last two weekends knee-deep in all things wedding for her sister, Becca. The Blackwoods certainly had the money to hire these things out, but Becca had a very specific "vision" for the wedding and wanted to inspect everything.

Violet was in the middle of tying an elaborate bow around a vase. She paused for a brief moment and stared beyond me with a concentrating expression. "Well, five hundred guests, ten guests per table, so that's fifty tables. I've finished six and you've done, what? Five?"

I groaned within myself. Each one took like an hour. "So thirty-nine more."

"We're making progress though," Violet smiled.

I returned her smile. After the kindness she'd shown me, helping out with the wedding was just a small token of my appreciation. And how could I tell her that my real issue wasn't the time invested in crafting wedding décor, rather every hour I spent arranging flowers and creating fancy bows was time that I couldn't spend with Landon?

"Oh shoot," Violet said. "We're out of gold. Will you grab the ribbon box from upstairs? In my room, right inside the door. I'd do it but . . ." she gestured to her hands entangled with intricate loops and knots of ribbon.

"Of course," I said, just as Becca walked into the room. She thanked me for all of my help, then began to chitchat with Violet as she picked the finished pieces up one by one and turned them in her hands.

I'd been up and down these stairs several times since the first time when Violet had shown me the school pictures. It was still depressing to take the Blackwood portrait tour. Something about knowing Landon would never have another picture taken of him. Ever.

The spools of ribbon were easy to find, lying in the box near Violet's door—just like she said. I picked up the box and circled back toward the stairs, but paused at the only closed door in the hall. Large, dark mahogany. It was Landon's room. It had to be. In the handful of times I'd hung out with Violet, we'd gone all over the house, but never into this room. My breath quickened.

I could *open* the door.

I tuned my ears to the banter downstairs. I could hear Violet and Becca engaged in some kind of playful debate with Frank. Something about his geriatric mind clouding the facts of the argument.

"Geez, Vi. I'm not *that* old," he said.

"Dad. Your favorite food is prunes. You wear suspenders. You're old," Violet said.

I shifted the box to rest on my hip, freeing a hand. One eye on the staircase and one eye on Landon's door, I gripped the knob and twisted.

Landon's bed was unmade.

I stepped inside and softly closed the door behind me. The room was surprisingly large—twice the size of Violet's. A baby grand piano stood in its own alcove. Not just an alcove, a recording room, judging from the microphone booms hovering over the piano, speakers, cords, and other audio equipment.

"Are you kidding me?" I said.

Several large and crowded shelves hung on the wall adjacent to his bed. I stepped closer for a better look at the dozens of trophies and pictures displayed there. I surveyed trophies from his early youth to his high school years. Three bronzed snowboarding statues larger than the rest lined the top shelf.

"Seriously? California Triple A State Champ. Three years running?" I laughed derisively. Based upon the team awards I'd seen at school, I guess I shouldn't have been so surprised.

I wandered to his dresser where there appeared to be more mementos from his obscene sports accomplishments.

"The freaking X Games, Landon?" I lifted one of the golden medals that hung on the wall above the dresser and traced the large X with my thumb.

"Super Pipe. Sounds dangerous." I shook my head and hung it back in its place. As I did so, a word caught my eye. *Olympics.*

A framed newspaper article hung near a row of medals.

Hometown Hero to Compete in Upcoming Winter Olympics

Truckee High snowboarding and alpine ski champ Landon Blackwood dominates in five qualifying events securing a spot on U.S. Olympic Alpine Ski Team.

I took the article over to his bed and sat down to read. I learned that he was one of only fifteen Americans chosen to compete on the men's alpine team. He was just ten months away from the games when he died.

I almost wished I had never opened the door and walked into his room. Grief squeezed my heart. Suffocating deprivation. I'd never stand at the bottom of the mountain to cheer him on. I'd never lay on his bed and listen to him compose, note by note. He wouldn't be at the Olympics in two months. Neither would his family. Neither would I.

Lately we'd been in a standoff. It'd been two weeks since James dropped the bomb and now Landon wanted to give up his passage. He was crazy if he thought I'd let him turn Vigilum for me. How could he be so shortsighted? If he'd let me try to save him, we could have a real life together. But he won't even talk about it.

I hated wondering every time we parted if it will be the last time.

Landon's letterman jacket hung on his bedpost, an empty shell. I reached for it, and hugged it to my chest, breathing deeply, searching for his scent. It smelled clean, foreign to me. Bottled.

The Landon I knew smelled warm and earthy. I slipped into the jacket. If he were still here, maybe he would have draped it over my shoulders on a chilly day. Wearing his jacket felt natural and right. Something any girlfriend would feel entitled to do.

"You look cute in that."

"Geez! You scared me!" I jumped up from the bed, blood thudding in my veins. "What are you doing here?" I asked.

Landon flashed a crooked grin, stifling a laugh. "I was going to ask you the same thing."

"Were you spying on me?"

"It's *my* room." He laughed, obviously enjoying my discomfort.

"I didn't think you came here anymore."

"I don't, but I wanted to see you."

"So you *were* stalking me."

"Hey, you're the one rifling through my drawers and wearing my clothes." His eyes flashed mischievously. "It's whitey tighties, by the way, but you probably already know that."

"I wasn't rifling through your drawers."

He smiled, brows raised. Expectant.

I exhaled forcefully and looked around the room. "This is just embarrassing. I'm sorry."

He crossed the room and laced his fingers with mine. He lowered his head, his lips found mine and he murmured against my mouth, "Don't be sorry. I love having you here."

The hollow feeling I'd had filled with warm relief at his touch. I unlaced my hands from his, and braided my fingers in his hair, pulling him closer to me. It felt like kissing someone new. So many surprising secrets. Secrets I wanted to know more about.

I reluctantly pulled away. "You play the piano." I nodded toward the recording room. Composition sheets lay scattered, crumpled or scribbled on, all over the floor.

"I did."

I walked over to the piano, expecting he would follow me, but when I turned back he hadn't moved from the foot of the bed. His eyes were reluctant.

"Is this okay?"

He shrugged and smiled shyly.

"Come on. Get over here, you closet genius, you."

He rolled his eyes and made his way to me.

"Tell me about all of this," I coaxed, gesturing to the piano and the mess of handwritten sheet music. "Looks like Beethoven was your roommate."

His nose crinkled. "Not quite Beethoven."

I picked up a particularly complicated looking piece and studied it. "Could have fooled me. I played when I was younger, and I would have never attempted anything this advanced." I squinted at the pages. "How do you even begin to create something like this?"

"It's not as hard as it looks, honestly. I just started with a theme or whatever mood I was in."

"What's this piece called . . . schizophrenia?" My eyes blurred at the repeating hills and valleys of sixteenth notes.

"I wrote that after my last X Games. My interpretation of speed. Riding the edge." He leaned in. "See where it slows down here? That's when I'm airborne." His eyes glinted.

"I can totally see that." I leaned over the keyboard and clumsily plunked out a couple of measures.

"How long did you play?" he asked.

"Until my mom went back to school. Then I had Chase practically full-time."

He looked at me a few seconds longer than I was comfortable with. Then he grinned.

"Sit down," he said. "Play something for me."

"Oh yeah, right." I laughed. "Heart and Soul or Chopsticks?"

"Don't be modest," he said, as he gently pressed down on my shoulders. "Sit."

I slid to the front of the bench. He reached around and softly lifted my hands from my lap and placed them on the keys. I could feel his breath at my neck as his hands hovered over mine like a warm shadow. "Like this," he whispered in my ear.

He guided my hands in a simple, but soulful chord progression. A song that was unique, completely his own.

I closed my eyes, relishing the sensation of envelopment. His hands pressed earnestly onto mine as the tempo increased, sending ripples up the backs of my arms. And then the song resolved, like a river that emptied into the ocean. His hands rested over mine as the last vibrations dissipated from the instrument. In one fluid motion, he pulled me up to join him.

He leaned in and rested his forehead against mine, stroking my cheek with the back of his fingers. He closed his eyes. "Your timing is just so bad, Presley. I swear if I would have met you last April, I would have been right here with you, probably in this room. Not at the river with my friends."

It was hard not to feel frustrated with him and his "what ifs" and "if onlys" when I had a tangible solution. "You say my timing is horrible. I say it's perfect." I lifted his chin, forcing him to look at me. "We already know you can take me back in time. You have to let me undo this." It was hard to swallow around the lump in my throat. "What we have is worth the risk."

The door suddenly swung open and Violet stood on the threshold, her eyes round with shock. "Presley?"

Landon immediately parted from me, but stood close by, his reassuring hand at my back.

Violet quickly strode past me and yanked the keyboard cover shut. "Landon is the *only* one that played this." Her face crumpled. "And we don't come in here."

I remembered I was still in his jacket and started to shrug out of it. Landon said in a low voice, "Presley, just keep calm. She'll be okay. She'll get over it."

"Vi, I'm sorry," was all I could say. I hurried back to Landon's bed to replace the jacket on the post and bent to straighten the blankets.

"No! Don't touch it! Please." Violet choked back tears. "We leave everything exactly how it was." She looked at the piano and back to me. "I don't understand why you would do this."

So many times I'd wanted to tell Violet that Landon was still here. But never as much as now. If I could just tell her that he was standing two feet from her. "Violet, there's something you need to know—"

"Presley, don't! It won't help. She won't believe you. You'll just make it worse," he pleaded.

I glanced at him briefly, but in that snap of time we conveyed an understanding.

Violet waited for my explanation, tense and incredulous.

I continued. "I was trying to learn more about Landon . . . so that I could be a better friend to you. So that I could understand more of what you're going through."

Violet softened, her shoulders sinking.

"It's just that you don't tell me much about him. There's a huge part of you I don't even know."

"Yeah, you'll never know," Violet said. She hugged her ribs and looked down at the floor.

"Just take her out of here, Pres," Landon said. We shared one last look. His eyes were troubled.

"Hey, I've still got some centerpieces left in me if you want to keep going." I crossed over to Violet and put my arm around her shoulders to comfort her but she was stiff and resistant toward me.

She led the way down the stairs. I followed, purposefully averting my eyes from the Blackwood portraits. I'd intruded enough.

Chapter Thirty-Eight

Vows

(LANDON)

Of course I'd go to my sister Becca's wedding. James knew better than to try to convince me otherwise. It was near Christmas and signs of the season were displayed all around the historic lakefront lodge with swags of evergreen and lights. The room felt medieval with its lofty knotty pine ceiling and a heavy beamed balcony rimming all but one side of the grand hall. Massive stonework covered the last wall and in the middle of it an oversized fireplace. Its flames made a luminous backdrop for the altar. A huge glittering Christmas tree stood off to one side, adorned with ivory poinsettias. Floor-to-ceiling windows along the western wall offered a stunning view of the lake and its snow-covered beaches. Outside, fir branches hung low, weighed down by thick blankets of snow.

My dad, always the overgenerous softy, spared no expense. A string quartet welcomed guests with music as they trickled in and found their seats. I stood on the balcony, hidden from Presley, who was seated near the back. She likely knew I'd be at the wedding, but strangely we didn't talk about it. It was painful and awkward. I planned to stay out of sight though, because I wanted Presley to be herself around her friends, which would be impossible if she had to split her attention between my world and hers.

The last of the guests took their seats and I noticed someone approach the quartet and give them brief instructions. The musicians sat taller in their seats and shuffled sheets of paper on their music stands. Straightening his tie and looking dignified, the clergyman took his place near the groom as my mother, radiant with emotion, was led by an usher to her seat in the front row.

A prelude began to play and the bridal party lined up and made their way in pairs down the aisle. The bridesmaids were dressed in champagne—an "untraditional" Christmas color, according to my sister. In my loafing around the house, I'd been privy to many mind-numbing planning sessions with Becca and her bridesmaids.

Violet was especially stunning in her dress, her olive skin and midnight hair pulled elegantly low on her neck. Reese, looking very Hollywood in his impeccably fitted black tux, guided her to the aisle. I noticed Violet looking pale, and Reese leaned in and whispered to her. She swallowed hard and nodded. Barring the brief piano incident, this was the first time I'd been this close to her in a long while. I should've been more mindful of our proximity. Perhaps watched from a window. An outsider. Because that's really what I was now.

Becca's arrival was at last announced by the quartet's wedding march. She smiled through tears and grasped my father's arm. He was doing a horrible job of holding back his own. The mood in the room was almost manic. Immense joy, mingled with profound feeling seemed to have everyone there smiling, then crying, then smiling again. My heart pulled as I saw Becca's groom beam at her and take her by the hand.

"All be seated," the clergyman directed. His eyes were kind. "By request of the bride, we'd like to take a moment to remember her departed brother, Landon. Family members will be coming to each row with red roses. Please pin one on in remembrance of him."

Quietly, many of my younger boy cousins flooded the audience, and handed out roses. The flowers passed from hand to hand and I watched with choking emotion as family members and friends solemnly pinned Truckee-High-red onto one another. It was especially hard to watch my grandmother's chin tremble as my grandfather fumbled at her lapel, at last securing her rose. She lifted the bloom to her lips and kissed it, then lowered it and patted it just like she used to do to my head after she kissed me. A surge of grief pounded me.

Becca, now finished pinning roses on my parents, returned to her groom where he handed back her red bouquet.

The ceremony was meaningful and brief. Love saturated the room and well-wishes were palpable. Almost audible, as if saying, *Live well. Live long. Be happy.*

After the couple kissed, the reception started adjacent to the wedding room in a sparkling lakeside ballroom. Light from a massive chandelier glittered warmly from the windows and glassware. Lively conversation reverberated through the music and the tinkling of flatware against china. All seemed happy except Reese.

I'd watched him through the ceremony. His eyes had landed on Presley's more times than I wanted to count.

Now he seemed more relaxed somehow, and for that I was glad. His features were more his own, and less puppeted by Vigilum influence. Whether they backed off or Reese had fought for better control of himself, I couldn't tell.

But he looked longingly at Presley. Harder to admit, she looked at him a few times too. I saw their eyes meet and a smile faintly appear on her lips. A rowdy, likely intoxicated aunt, found Reese and pulled him to the dance floor. Thank. The. Heavens. Presley gave him the thumbs up and returned to the chaotic business of the table where she sat. She was seated with my brother Eric, his wife, and their four children—a trial on anyone's patience, but Presley was . . . sweet.

She had her hands full cutting meat for the toddler next to her who wolfed it down faster than she could supply it. She laughed heartily when my two-year-old niece rejected a bite and spit a lump of macerated beef back onto Presley's plate.

Then she offered to hold my cousin, Sara's newborn son, so she could eat. When Presley reached for the baby, every sound in the world collided into silence. I had a vision of her years from now, taking her own baby into her arms. Admittedly, it was an unlikely thought for a seventeen-year-old guy to have, but in light of all I was forced to consider about my and Presley's futures, my thoughts often traveled nontraditional paths.

Her brows furrowed at his helplessness. Her nose brushed the downy hair on his tiny head, likely taking in that unmistakable baby smell. For a moment she was a mother. A radiant mother to a beautiful baby I could never give her.

And then Reese appeared and sat next to her. He kissed the baby's head while Presley watched adoringly. They smiled at each other and somehow in that moment, I knew she had forgiven him. How could she not? She knew his bad behavior was poisoned by Vigilum. I knew she'd never be so naive as to dismiss his choices; they were still his, but her mercy could help her turn a blind eye. Especially when she considered all Reese had been through. She was too good not to forgive.

I watched it unfold right in front of me—the hope return to Reese's eyes, the gentleness return to hers.

Then I knew he could make her happy someday.

I knew she could love him.

All of the pain and confusion I brought to her life could be gone with one decision. Her stupid but incredibly loving offer to travel through space and time to save me could be a distant memory. She could be happy, safe, and in love if I just removed myself from the picture.

It was like our love was a balloon. And I just let go of the string and watched it float up, soaring further away by the second. I didn't want it to go away. I didn't even let go of the string.

It was cut.

It was cut by the truth.

She could be happy without me.

Chapter Thirty-Nine

Awkward

(Presley)

Reese offered to walk me out. Stepping into the December mountain air, I shivered and wished I hadn't refused the heavy coat Gayle offered me when I left the house. Reese shrugged out of his tuxedo jacket and tenderly wrapped it around my shoulders. The reception was winding down but the sound of the music still drifted out to the softly lit stone courtyard, which felt private walled in by trees. Blankets of snow lay on lighted branches and produced an enchanting glow that was more beautiful than the chandeliered ballroom.

Reese caught my arm and turned me gently to face him, placing one hand on the small of my back. "I didn't get to dance with you tonight," he said playfully.

"You'll freeze out here."

"Trust me, I'm not cold." He grinned.

He took me in his arms and we swayed comfortably.

"Presley, I really need to apologize to you."

"It's okay. You don't have to say anything."

"Yes. I do."

I'd wanted to apologize to him about Landon's ring, but I couldn't think of any explanation that made sense. So, I never brought it up and I was relieved that he never did either. Maybe he never would.

"You were right about a lot of things," Reese said. "Especially about Sam. I used her to hurt you. I don't know what came over me;

I just couldn't get a grip." He searched for solid ground, for justification, then shook his head.

It seemed like Reese was back to himself. His eyes were clear and his countenance was bright again. I felt sure the Vigilum had backed off. It wasn't hard to decipher why—the closeness Landon and I had developed must've convinced them that Landon's passage was theirs for the taking—his decision to stay with me appeared sure. Blackening Reese so that I'd choose Landon was no longer necessary.

Pitiful. Reese had been the Vigilum's pawn without even knowing it.

"So, how's Sam doing?" I was uncomfortable asking, but I was worried about her.

"Well, not great. We went on a drive and I broke it off with her. She kicked me out in a snowstorm five miles from home." He laughed a little.

"You deserved that. Every mile."

"And worse." He looked down and scraped the toe of his shoe along the paver stones. "I did my best to make things right with her, but I feel horrible about the way things went down. At the time, I didn't let myself think about her really being into me. It sucks getting your heart broken like that." His eyebrows rose, looking resigned. "I hope she'll forgive me eventually."

"She has a pretty big heart. I wouldn't be surprised if it's sooner than you think," I said, reflecting on the generosity she seemed to show to everyone she knew.

Feathery snowflakes drifted down, lighting upon Reese's dark hair and broad shoulders, making me feel like we danced in a powdery dream. A flake landed on my bottom lip and Reese's eyes crinkled a bit at the edges when he smiled.

"You've got something there," he said. "Let me." He placed his thumb softly on my lip, and the snowflake immediately melted under his touch. He paused and contemplated me, and then drew his hand back. "I have a confession."

"Uh oh. That sounds scary."

"It kind of is, actually. Well, more creepy than scary. Like I said, I don't know what got a hold of me those weeks."

"I'm listening."

He looked off to the side and then back at me. "I looked through your phone. I was being an idiot."

My knees weakened. I wondered if he'd seen the picture of Landon.

Under non-Vigilum circumstances, I would've been a lot less forgiving of Reese's prying. Although, was I much better? I'd stolen his school file, after all.

"Find anything juicy?" I asked, pinching the back of his arm. Hard.

Reese jerked his hand from around my back and briefly rubbed the spot I had pinched. "No, but that's all the punishment I get?"

"Well, what were you expecting?"

"I don't know, a slap across the face. A kick to the shin."

"The wedgie of a lifetime?"

"One can only hope," he smirked, twirling me dramatically but then pulling me in close. His playful eyes grew serious. "That night in your room when I had your phone, I felt like I needed to know who the other person was."

"Reese . . ."

"No, just hear me out. I don't need to know now because it doesn't matter. And I'll give you all the time you need to figure out what you really want." His eyes gazed soulfully into mine. "I know what I want," he said, his mouth set. "I'm going to keep loving you. I couldn't choose any other way, even if I wanted to. What you do with that is up to you. And how I deal with your choice will be my problem."

He said he loved me. And I believed him. My personal choices were so much clearer when Reese was in a Vigilum headlock, although it was heartbreaking to watch.

Reese stopped dancing and softly took my face in his hands. He bowed his head, touching his forehead to mine. "I don't want you to leave."

"I know." I was tempted to stay. Under other circumstances, Reese would be everything I wanted. But I had Landon. And because of that, the warmth of Reese's touch and his breath on my face felt wrong.

"Walk me to my car?" I broke from him, hoping he would think the trembling in my voice was from the cold.

When we approached, I was surprised to find Landon leaning against the driver's side door, hands casually inside his pockets. His face was calm. Unreadable.

I'd never had the two of them in such close proximity. I looked in Landon's eyes, searching for emotion. He gave me none. My stomach hollowed.

Landon stepped aside as Reese reached to open the door for me. As I moved to get in, Reese grabbed my hand. "Pres . . . I'll wait for you."

I smiled and said, "I'll see you soon."

The drive home was quiet. Landon's face was turned from me, gazing out the window at the starless night. He didn't look at me, but broke the silence and said, "I'm glad you forgave him."

"I don't know what to say." I gulped hard, feeling guilty, though I hadn't technically done anything to warrant the feeling. "It wasn't what it must have looked like."

"You're not in trouble, here. I'm just glad that you forgave him."

Not trusting my voice, or even the thoughts in my head, I changed the subject from Reese. "Did you see the wedding, then?"

"Yes."

Another stretch of silence. Issues with Reese aside, Landon's distance didn't seem entirely unreasonable. I imagined he was grateful to have witnessed his sister's wedding, but sad that he wasn't standing in the groom's line with Reese. This was the first he'd seen of Violet and his parents in weeks and that likely reopened all kinds of wounds. My dance with Reese surely poured salt into them.

"It must've been hard tonight."

"Mmm. I can see everybody's moving on. Looks like people are managing to find happiness without me." He paused—again without looking at me. "And that's a good thing."

I didn't like the unsettling weight of his words.

"Are you coming over tonight?" Normally I wouldn't even ask.

"If you want me to," he said continuing to stare out the window.

"Of course. Why wouldn't I?"

"I'll come then."

Chapter Forty

ALREADY GONE

(LANDON)

I'd known for two hours that this would be my last night with Presley. I thought with derision how James would be thrilled. He was right. I'd been selfish. Staying would only deprive Presley of a real life. And if I'd only give her the chance, she'd move on and be fine. If not with Reese, then with someone else. The irony was sickening. I'd finally learned what it meant to truly love someone.

And it meant letting Presley go.

True love doesn't always mean a happy ending, I admitted.

Presley stopped in the living room to exchange a few pleasantries with her mother about the wedding. The status of their relationship was beginning to thaw, especially since Gayle had encouraged Presley to reconnect with her dad. I didn't really listen to what they said. Their words were just noise to me anyway.

My decision felt staggering and disorienting. I'd committed to a path with Presley. I'd convinced myself that we could be happy together. And now, unexpectedly, I was about to depart from that road.

Part of me felt like a coward for making this decision on my own because Presley had a right to know. But the rest of me finally understood what James had been trying to teach me for the past several months: that love means doing what's best for the one you love, even if it's not what's best for you.

I had no idea what was ahead. James had assured me several times that moving on was natural progression and that happiness and comfort awaited. But he was always elusive with the details. The only thing I knew for sure was that Presley would not be a part of my immediate future.

She finished up with her mom and discreetly signaled with her eyes for me to follow her up the stairs. I stood paralyzed at the bottom of them, internalizing that once I took the first step, it would be the beginning of the end. She paused at the landing and turned to me, her expression searching.

People who love someone more than themselves make impossible decisions all the time.

Young mothers separate themselves from newborns when they know someone else can care for them better.

Soldiers kiss their wives then take the front line.

Families tell the doctor that it's finally okay to pull the plug.

I reminded myself of those braver than I and placed my foot on the bottom step.

Inside her mostly dark room, Presley busied herself for a moment, tidying up. I smiled sadly. *Such a cute and hopeless little slob.* Just one of a many things I'd miss about her. She half-straightened the blankets on her bed and sat cross-legged on them in a square of moonlight, patting the mattress, inviting me over. For her sake, I crawled out of the abyss of my self-pity and laid next to her. She melted into my side, and laid her head on my chest.

"It was a rough night for you," she said, compassion in her voice.

"It was."

"I bet it was hard to see so much of your family gathered in one place."

"I hadn't seen my grandma since my funeral."

"I thought the red flower gesture was really sweet . . ."

"Can we not talk about this?" I reigned back the unintended bite in my tone.

She rose up on one elbow. "Landon, if you are mad about Reese, let me explain . . ."

"I already told you, I'm glad you two made up."

"Well, you're not acting glad. And that makes me think you need to hear me out." She arched her eyebrows and dared me to protest. She could be so feisty and stubborn. Two more things I'd miss.

"You don't have to explain yourself to me," I began, using a bit more caution with the next statement. "It would be okay if you felt more for Reese than you're telling me."

I searched her eyes carefully, hoping to find an atom of relief on her face. Some small sign that she was willing to at least consider a relationship with him.

"Why would that be okay with you?" she asked, hurt evident in her voice.

I shrugged pathetically, not knowing what else to do. It's not like I could tell her that she'd need him to help pick up the pieces once I was gone.

"I care for Reese. He's been a good friend to me, but that doesn't mean . . ."

"Can we just be one hundred percent honest?" I interjected. "He's in love with you. Just so we're both absolutely clear."

Presley exhaled forcefully. "I'm sure someone else will come along next week to take his mind off of me."

"That won't happen," I said flatly.

She rolled her eyes.

"Look, it might be true that in the past girls have been somewhat disposable to him. But it's not that way with you. I can tell he genuinely cares for you. I know him better than anyone. The way he looks at you, Pres—if you could hear the way he talks about you when you're not around."

Her breath quickened and I fought back the pain that was tearing its way through my chest as I watched her eyes glisten. She hastily turned her head and looked out the window. As much as the words choked me, I took the opportunity to drive my point home.

"Reese would take a bullet for you, Pres." I gently cupped her chin and turned her face to mine. "He would love you forever if you'd let him."

A deep crease appeared between her brows. "But I choose you." A tear spilled over, making a shining trail down her cheek. "Why are you even talking like this? You're scaring me."

"No, Pres . . . don't be scared."

"You tell me how to feel then," she said, her face a mix of confusion and despair. "It feels like you're trying to talk me out of loving you. Like you're trying to let me down gently." Her eyes darkened.

"I don't want to be played with. You can't use Reese as some shiny distraction. He is many things to me, but he's not you and my love for you will always be stronger than whatever I feel for Reese." Her words were pure and solid. They cracked what was left of my heart right down the seam. She swallowed hard. "Is it that you don't love me anymore?"

I should have left the wedding and found James as soon as I knew I'd be leaving her. He would have provided me an extra measure of strength to follow through with what I had to do.

Though I'd been intentionally vague with her to avoid outright lying, subconsciously, she perceived the truth. I should've known every second I stayed was as good as butchering both of our hearts. Yet I could not bring myself to say the words to her. I could not walk out the door. Not yet.

"Come here." I pressed myself up, cradling her in my arms. She pressed her head to my chest as I smoothed her hair away from her face and kissed her forehead. "I will never stop loving you," I said, wiping away each of her tears as they fell. "You'll always have my heart. Don't you ever doubt my love for you."

She sat up tall in my lap and cradled my face in her hands. Her eyes feverishly confronted mine. "Then stop talking like this. It hurts me."

"I know. I've never meant to hurt you. I'm sorry." It killed me that she thought I was reassuring her, when I was really trying to say goodbye. If I could only make her understand that my departure was the ultimate proof of my love. But I knew she'd never accept that. The most I could do was speak the most vital truth to her. "I will love you forever, Presley." Her dark eyes, still rimmed in moisture, glinted before I kissed her.

Every kiss before this one had been a wild celebration of a miracle I never thought possible. They were kisses of youthful exploration and playfulness. Expressions of affection and passion. Kisses between a boy and a girl.

This kiss was different. A punishing kiss. It burned inside my bones. A poisonous kiss that slowly slayed me, but left me wanting more. How could I ever part my lips from what I never wanted to stop loving?

So I didn't. I expressed in every breath, in every embrace, the depth of my love. I knew I could never tell her I was leaving her because she would only hear, "I don't love you." I couldn't bear to see her that way. So I held on to her and kissed her like she was my salvation. Hours later, in the quiet of her sleep, I wondered if she was.

I stood at the window and contemplated while snow fell outside. Maybe there was no other way for me to learn to love like this than to have her and then choose to give her away. Was that the purpose? Was my time with her some orchestrated schoolyard from a higher place? I wanted to be grateful for what I'd learned. But I just couldn't be.

Chapter Forty-One

No One Wins

(PRESLEY)

I woke up and knew he was gone. The house had a dead-aired empty feeling.

Before, when he stayed with me, he always waited for me to wake. It's not like he could leave a note on my pillow or text me later, so it had been important to him to say goodbye face to face. A perfect gentleman.

This empty bed, this hollow feeling—it wasn't Landon.

Bewilderment took me from my bed and pulled me to the window. Everything outside was blanketed in virgin snow—the whole world pale and bluish in the slanted light of sunrise. Landon was there, near the edge of the meadow dressed in the same clothes he had on the night before; his form a stark contrast to the unbroken whiteness around him. I could tell by his stride, shoulders rounded, footfalls purposeful yet leaving no tracks that he was leaving. And not coming back.

A chemical alarm rippled over my skin. I burst from my bedroom, took the stairs three at a time and exploded from the front door, halting, toes curled at the edge of the porch.

"Hey!" I screamed. The sound of my voice echoed harshly through the still, white clearing.

He stopped, his back still toward me. Slowly, he turned only his head. "Get back inside," he said sharply.

"What?" I scrambled down the porch steps, my bare feet slipping on the icy coating.

"You'll freeze to death." He turned his head away again.

I shivered in my pajamas and marched through ankle-deep powder toward him, rapidly closing the gap between us. "Where are you going?"

"Where I belong."

I rounded on him, my jaw set and my chest painfully heaving from the icy air that filled my lungs. He met my eyes for the briefest moment, but I wished he hadn't. His gaze was empty and gave me no reassurance. He looked ahead toward the path he was traveling moments ago.

"No." I choked on the word. "I thought you understood. I told you last night I don't want to be with Reese."

"It's not about Reese," he said, his eyes half-hooded and his voice cool. "We just aren't a good fit."

His words impacted me like a whistling bat to the face. "You're not making sense. Last night you're in love with me and today you're leaving me forever?"

"Yes."

"Coward."

His eyes snapped back to mine, a flash of emotion evident. Finally, something. Maybe I hadn't lost him. Maybe he could be reasoned with. Maybe I could find out what was causing this and make it better. Make it go away.

"I can't believe you would do this; just sneak out while I'm asleep without even saying goodbye."

"I'm not getting into this with you," he said as he turned from me and continued walking toward the forest. "We've been here before . . . it can never work."

"It was working. It was for me. What's changed?"

He didn't answer, but continued walking, his pace a little faster.

"What? Are you sick of me?"

"No."

"Is it your family? Is it too hard that I can be around them and you can't?"

"No."

The gap between us was widening and I struggled to keep up with him, even with the help of adrenaline pumping through my body.

"Oh, I get it. Your babysitter James finally got in your head," I said desperately.

He stopped abruptly and faced me. "This was *my* choice." His eyes were hard again. "I'm sorry this is difficult for you. But you need to be strong. It's what's best."

"You don't get to decide what's best for me—you should've talked to me about this." My arms gestured wildly. "And you know . . . I am so sick of everyone telling me what's best for me. You. James. My mom. How about I decide what's best for me?"

"Oh, like holing up in your bedroom with me and completely isolating yourself from everyone in the real world? Like dismissing your friends and avoiding your family? Starving every *real* relationship you have?" He took a step closer to me and I shrunk back. "Throwing away the chance to get married, to have a family of your own? That's what's best for you?"

He swallowed hard and his lips formed a firm line. "Grow up, Presley."

"Okay. Yeah, because getting wasted and jumping in a frozen river and getting yourself killed was super mature."

A knot of muscle worked in his jaw. "You're right. You just proved my point perfectly." He stared at me gravely.

I felt my hold on him dissipating. Like sand on the road getting blown away to somewhere nobody cares about.

"Just come back to the house with me and let's at least talk about this." I reached out and took his hand. It was warm against mine which was starting to shake from the cold, along with the rest of my body.

"I'm sorry for leaving without saying goodbye, but I knew this would happen. There was nothing I could say that you would accept. I'm sorry for everything. For bringing you into my world." He bowed his head briefly and then whipped it back up to look me deeply in the eyes. "James was right. I should have never put you through any of this. The Vigilum, the secrecy between you and Violet. The isolation I've caused. This is not healthy."

"Like my life was healthy before you? Taking care of Chase twenty-four-seven, a mom who doesn't give a crap, no dad? Yeah, that's an awesome life."

He squeezed my hand. I was grateful for his touch.

"But that won't be your life forever. I know you're talking to your dad again. You'll be in college next year. Start hanging out with your friends again. Make plans."

"No. You are my plan." I shamelessly cried. The tears stung against my frozen cheeks.

"Make amends with your mom. Go visit your dad. I know they're not perfect, but they're family. And they won't always be there. Make it right while you can."

I knew there was truth to what he said, but I didn't care.

"And Reese. I've never seen him care for someone like he cares for you. "

I felt Landon's grip start to fade.

"Let him in, Presley. I know he can make you happy."

He still held my hand but I felt nothing. Our connection was gone.

He was really leaving. The last drop of hope left me, stripping my insides bare—everything down to the bone. For the first time I felt the intense burn of the snow on my bare feet.

"It's time now, Landon," James emerged from a copse of trees, his hands in his pockets and his face placid.

Landon let go of my hand and took one step back. "I love you," he mouthed, as James extended his arm and ushered Landon to his side.

I collapsed to the snow, my strength finally gone. "Landon!" I sobbed. "You don't have to do this. Please James, don't take him from me."

Neither acknowledged my pleadings. Landon forged ahead, not looking back, while James fell in line behind him blocking my view of the love of my life.

"Please stay!" I screamed, knowing he wouldn't.

Chapter Forty-Two

WORSE THAN DEATH

(LANDON)

You should listen to your girlfriend, River Boy."

It'd taken all my will to keep moving in spite of Presley's pleadings, so this unexpected voice from behind tore me from my focused departure. I whipped around and saw Liam towering over Presley.

I looked to James, confused. Because I'd made up my mind to leave, I hadn't anticipated any interference from the Vigilum. After all, it was my undecided passage they had sought and it was no longer available. I was surprised Liam would confront me, given that I still had James's protection.

I remembered how James had commanded the Vigilum away with only words the night they'd tortured me and my confidence swelled. I appraised James. His jaw was set; he met my eyes and nodded firmly.

I turned back to Liam. "Sorry, man. I'm already gone."

"Really?" Liam laughed flippantly. "You might want to reconsider."

Presley cowered away from Liam, unable to take her terror-stricken eyes from him.

"James. Can they hurt her?" I was a breath away from charging Liam, but my instincts warned me to keep still.

"They won't. Keep moving. If we leave, they leave," James assured.

"I wouldn't do that," Liam said with an unnatural calmness. "See, your sister was hard to get to. There was only so much grief we

243

could grow in her. Reese somehow found a way to man-up and be decent."

"But Presley." He licked his lips and smiled. "We can be much more . . . creative. So easy to manipulate someone who can see dead people. We have you to thank for that tidbit, Landon."

Presley scrambled using her hands and feet to inch backward through the snow.

"It's alright. He's calling your bluff," James encouraged, though I thought I detected a hint of nerves in his voice. "Keep to the plan," he said.

I couldn't tear my eyes from Presley. I wanted to trust that James was right. But if there was any chance he was wrong, I couldn't just leave her there.

"Landon, you know there is no alternative. The sooner you go, the sooner they'll leave her alone."

As I saw her there, cowering, all I wanted was for her to be safe. And if my leaving was the only way that could happen, then I'd have to find a way to do it.

I turned my back on her but before I took my first step, Presley's scream tore through the air. I spun to see her thrown on her arched back, ribs spread skyward, her body seemingly paralyzed.

I rushed Liam.

"I'll kill her, I swear I will," Liam warned.

At his side, Presley jerked upright out of the snow, her toes dangling inches above the ground. Though her arms hung useless at her sides, she gasped in rapid, shallow breaths, panic alive in her eyes.

I halted.

"James!" I screamed.

"Let her go," James commanded. His voice was cool and even, yet his anxious eyes locked onto Liam.

After the night the Vigilum tortured me, I was afraid they would do the same thing to Violet or Presley. But James had assured me then that physical manipulation was only possible against the dead. We both sickeningly realized, as Presley thrashed inches above the ground, that he was wrong.

"This is not a negotiation." Liam's eyes were black and his gaze matched James's in intensity.

"That's not how it works; you know that," James said, his voice level. "Your power lies with the undecided. Landon has made his choice. You can't extort forfeiture."

"Watch me," Liam seethed. His black eyes widened slightly, and instantly Presley cried out.

Impulsively, I lurched at him. His eyes flickered from James's to mine and as Presley fell to the ground in a crumpled heap, an unseen iron vice closed around my neck. Pain exploded behind my eyes, distorting my view of Presley. Even through the blur I could tell her lips were grey and her breath ragged. She attempted to stand and walk, but took only one step toward me before collapsing again into the snow.

I was powerless to help her.

"You ready to deal now, River Boy?" Liam said through clenched teeth. A moment later, the choking pressure on my throat loosened enough that I could think straight, though my limbs were still paralyzed.

"How do you think this is going to end, Liam?" James stepped guardedly forward.

"You're asking *me* to think. How about *you* think? Maybe you should've thought harder about how things would end up for me."

I wondered why Liam was speaking to James so personally. But James said nothing.

"Oh this is rich," Liam gloated at James. "You haven't told him anything."

"What's he talking about, James?" I asked.

James hesitated. "I was Liam's guide."

"Guide?" Liam spat. "Is that what you think you were?"

"Why didn't you tell me this?" I shot at James. I was blown away that he never shared that he had history with Liam. James and I had our differences these last months, but my trust in him had been unbreakable. Now, at the worst possible time, it cracked.

Liam seemed to relish in my shocked state. "Let me elaborate," he began bitterly. "I may not have been some varsity-lettered, golden boy like you, but I deserved more than the ten minutes he gave me. Hell, he gave you eight months." His eyes narrowed. "You think he's your perfect guardian angel? Always has what's best for you in mind? He threw me away like trash." His voice broke. "Ditched me."

"You're right," James answered bleakly. "I did abandon you. It was wrong. At the time, I thought you were getting what you deserved. Now I realize it's not my place to administer justice."

Liam's face remained hard. "Your conversion does me no good now."

Liam turned on me and the choking pressure returned. "And this jerk. What's he deserve, huh?" Though Liam was speaking to James, his malevolent eyes bored into mine. "This idiot who thinks the universe should bend to him because he found a girlfriend? He deserves eight months of your time?" Liam's clenched fists began to shake at his sides, and the tendons strained at his neck. The noose tightened, punishing me with incomprehensible pain, and I began to wonder if it were possible to die twice.

And then it was over. I fell to the snow, my strength drained—helpless to do anything but lift my eyes to Liam's.

"You will give me your passage or I will kill her," Liam promised. Then he glared at James. "You owe me this."

James sidestepped cautiously toward Presley, who was now hunched over on her knees and shaking violently. He knelt on one knee beside her and placed a careful hand on her back.

James told Liam, "My wrongs against you are inexcusable. But I won't allow you to harm this girl."

Arms limp at his side, Liam swayed slightly and in a husk of a voice said, "So that's it then. You're sorry, but you won't help me. Nothing's changed."

James draped Presley's arm over his neck and lifted her from the snow. "Nothing can."

"Then let the blood be on your hands," Liam said.

Dark figures began dropping out of trees that formed the perimeter of the meadow. They fell silently as more emerged on foot, appearing from the shadows. The most Vigilum I'd ever seen gathered in one place were the dozen or so present the night Liam tortured me outside my house. There were easily three times that many now and more were coming.

"Presley, I need you to run," James commanded.

"I can't," Presley sobbed. She staggered on her feet as James positioned himself in front of her, crouching protectively.

The horde converged, forming a tight circle around us.

A handful of Vigilum broke from the crowd and ripped James away from Presley, pinning his arms behind his back. James thrashed fiercely against their hold, while Liam closed in on Presley.

Standing before her quivering frame, Liam extended two pale fingers and softly raised her chin. He cocked his head slightly to one side and studied her. He smiled with one side of his mouth; there was a palpable pause. Without warning, his hand swiftly clamped around her neck. Her eyes bulged and a strangled gag escaped her mouth.

Liam wasn't bluffing. He was going to kill her.

James was outnumbered and overpowered. I frantically calculated options. The only advantage I had was that all the Vigilum, including Liam, were solely focused on watching Presley's life slip away. I struggled to pull myself up from the ground, strength slowly bleeding back into my limbs. James noticed me and made meaningful eye contact.

Praying James would know what I meant, I mouthed, "I have to try."

Confirmation flashed in his eyes and he nodded. James, seizing upon our last hope, roared and miraculously broke free from his stunned captors. He sprung at Liam, Vigilum clawing at his back. James clamped both arms around Liam's neck and yanked back mercilessly.

I poised myself to lunge for Presley, who had been knocked from Liam's chokehold.

The hungry pack ripped James away from Liam. They piled on top of James, gnashing their teeth and tearing at him. Pinned with his face forced into the ground, James flashed desperate eyes and managed through strangled gasps, "Take her as far as you can. Hide her."

He took a last crushing blow to the head and fell limp. A desolating regret ravaged me. I should've listened from the beginning.

With James unconscious, Liam shifted his attention to me, his eyes wild.

"Forget your passage. You're going to watch her die."

Liam wasn't bluffing. He'd kill her if I didn't do something. Gratefully, I stood three steps closer to her than he did. I lunged and threw myself on top of Presley, who was now lying face up in the snow.

She knew. Her eyes flooded with relief and trust. I held her frozen body to mine and buried my face in her neck.

"You can't let go," I said. "Promise."

"I promise," she whispered.

Chapter Forty-Three

Lost

(PRESLEY)

It was the cold that forced me to open my eyes. The packed snow against my face was biting and starting to burn. My head spun sickeningly and my brain thudded against the walls of my skull. Bright, nearly blinding light added to my disorientation and just as I began to wonder if my eyes were malfunctioning, I saw shocking red spread slowly into the snow I lay on. Startled at the amount of blood flooding from my nose, I tried to lift my head. The throbbing exploded into searing pain and my stomach rolled with nausea.

"Frank! Frank!" a panicked voice called. With great, painful effort I turned to see the frightened face of Afton Blackwood. She knelt beside me in the snow, her hair a glowing crown of gold from the sun filtering from behind her. "Get over here, Frank! Someone's hurt!"

Why did she refer to me as "someone?" Was my face truly that unrecognizable? Were my injuries so bad that she wouldn't know me? And how had I gotten hurt in the first place?

My breath quickened. Something was desperately wrong. I wanted to scream because my mind wouldn't work—wouldn't recall the fact I needed, the thing that nagged and pulled at the edges of my memory. Landon.

He'd saved me from Liam, but where was he now? My eyes darted frantically. I seemed to be in an outdoor crowd—spectators at some kind of event. A fence made of sponsor banners marked the boundaries of a ski run. Directly across from me on the other side of the run, I could see Violet and Sam, bundled in beanies, and thick knitted mittens. They looked uphill toward the run as they jumped up and down and screamed, "GO! GO!"

I followed their gaze to the group of skiers racing down the slope at a breakneck speed. The leader was mere feet ahead of the rest.

"Sweetheart, are you alright? What happened?" Frank Blackwood knelt at his wife's side, gently taking me by the arms to support my upper body. My head helplessly lolled to one side.

"We need to get the paramedics over here," he directed Afton. She rose and quickly disappeared into the crowd.

One by one, people nearby took notice of me and encroached around me, blocking my view. "Help me up, please," I begged Landon's father.

"No. No, you shouldn't move. Just hang tight until the paramedics—"

"Please! Please, you don't understand. You have to help me up!" I mustered my strength and rose onto shaking legs. Frank immediately stood and put a strong arm around my ribs, helping me maintain an upright position. But he didn't look happy about it.

"I really think you should stay down until they get here . . ." His words were just white noise. I knew Landon had to be near. He wouldn't leave me and I couldn't have gotten here without him. Wherever or *whenever* this was. Maybe he was looking for me too, but just couldn't find me. Then, Violet's cheering floated across the crowd with the one word that stopped my heart: "Landon!"

"You can do it!" she screamed. "Hustle down; you got this!" she shouted over Sam's head.

As confused as I was about where or when I might be, I knew one thing for sure—Landon had to be alive. Somehow, he had managed to bring me with him back to a time before his death. Even more mind-blowing, I'd survived it.

The skiers blew between us, obscuring Violet for a brief moment. I scrambled to the front of the crowd, with a critical desire to find

Landon. Frank trailed behind me, still issuing warnings to stay put. I stopped listening.

Landon, the clear winner of the race, judging by the maniacal celebrating that Sam and Violet were engaged in, swept in a large arc, spraying a fan of glistening snow into the sunlight. He threw down his poles and ripped off his helmet and goggles. I saw his face—unquestionable proof he was alive.

Overpowering love and relief engulfed me. I felt I could have fallen back into the snow to lie down and die, and all would be well because Landon was okay.

He was more than okay. His face flushed with exertion and his smile gleamed victoriously. I stumbled toward him, pushing people out of my way, finally breaking through the crowd.

"Landon!" The exertion of calling to him sent a fresh slice of pain through my head.

A tangle of cameramen appeared and encircled him, spouting congratulations and peppering him with questions. I staggered forward, again trying to pierce the barrier of people blocking me from my goal. With the ringing in my ears and the sickening thud in my head, I could only hear pieces of what they were saying. "X Games . . . Winter Olympics . . . youngest qualifier. . . "

"Miss, miss!" A gloved hand closed over my arm. I turned to see three men dressed in orange jackets, cargo pants and mirrored glasses, leaning toward me. Two of them held some kind of woven stretcher between them. "Can you tell us how you were injured?"

I knew they wanted to help me, but I just wanted to get away from them. They were only keeping me from Landon.

Violet and Sam tumbled through the crowd and met Landon at his side. Violet beamed. "You did it little brother! This is your moment!"

"Little brother? I thought you two were twins." A pretty blonde with a leopard scarf and leather gloves shoved a microphone in Violet's face.

"Well, I'm seven minutes older," Violet kidded.

"Miss, you are bleeding pretty badly." The paramedic again. "Some from your ears. That's not good, we need to get you to lie down. Another paramedic appeared and draped a scratchy gray blanket over my shoulders. It may as well have been made of lead because in my weakness, the weight of it nearly pulled me down to the ground. "Let us help you," one of them said.

I broke from his grip and threw off the blanket. My voice was thin, but I managed to call for Landon again.

At that moment, Violet met my eyes. Relief poured over me. Everything would be okay now that she knew I was here. She would remember everything.

But she didn't. In fact, no recognition glimmered in her eyes at all. Rather, confusion She whispered something to Sam and then Sam mirrored the same perplexed expression when she saw me. Together, they discreetly pulled Landon in the opposite direction of me, the cameras and journalists following him like satellites.

I followed them, my feet feeling like wood and with the last burst of strength I had I reached my arm between two interviewers and grabbed hold of Landon's sleeve. He whipped his head around to face me and as the blackness began to close in around me I saw a flicker of light in his eye. Faint, but there.

Immediately, Violet positioned herself between me and Landon. My hand fell helplessly from his sleeve and as my legs gave out, the paramedics caught me, wrapped me in the blanket again, and began to position me on the stretcher.

Violet shook her head at me as the paramedics secured me to the stretcher. She leaned into Landon and I heard her say under her breath, "This is the biggest moment of your life and she's upstaging it."

"No, she's not." Landon firmly moved Violet aside and stood over me. The crowd grew quiet except for the manic clicks of camera shutters.

That beautiful face. Finally. The blackness encroached further until the edges of my vision were stained and darkened but I willed my eyes to stay open so I could look at him.

"Landon, please come over this way; let them do their jobs," Violet pleaded as she pulled again on his arm. "You've worked your whole life for this. Please. Let them do what they need to do."

The only warmth I could feel was the tears leaking from my eyes and running down my temples. "Landon." I wanted to say more. So much more, but I didn't have the strength to.

Landon looked into my eyes, his seeming to swim with memory, but hesitation. After a short beat of time he shook his head minutely and turned away. Violet and Sam and now his parents at his side, led him a few yards away where he was again engulfed by press and spectators. Only Frank looked back momentarily, with pity in his eyes. Nothing more. "Poor thing. Must be a mental issue."

Like the last tremulous leaf clinging to a tree upon winter's approach, my will to fight detached and floated down and away to a place I couldn't seem to call it back from. From the deep chasm of my pain though, I summoned it back for the last time. Just one more try. And then it would be finished. I was sure.

It was nothing more than a whisper, but I sent it out, hoping somehow, my words would find Landon's heart and somehow, some-way he would know. "I love you, Landon Krew Blackwood."

The paramedics finished securing the straps over me and lifted me from the ground. As my eyes began to close, I used the last slit of light to look at the top of Landon's hair, the only part of him visible to me. My eyelids grew impossibly heavy and finally the darkness claimed me.

Epilogue

What are you doing?" Violet's voice drifted through my semiconsciousness. "She isn't your responsibility, Landon."

At his name, my eyes snapped open. The sun, piercing through the cold blue sky like an eye of white fire, blinded me and I squinted away from it.

"Son, stop for a moment, will you?" This time, the voice was Frank's.

"No." Landon's voice, clear and strong. Music. It strummed my broken heartstrings and the feeling vibrated through my whole body, replenishing strength to my limbs. I struggled against my restraints.

"Son, just tell me what you're trying to do here."

Landon was marching with purpose through the snow, his whole family and several other people trailing behind him. He swatted at them. "I don't know, Dad," he cried. "Just . . . give me a minute, will you?"

"But you don't even know her." Afton dug her small feet in the snow, trying to keep up with Landon's long, strong strides toward me. "That girl is probably sick," she said kindly. "She could have learned your name from anywhere. She needs help." She stumbled once, but quickly recovered. Her voice issued out stronger now. "What is it you think you can do for her?"

Landon halted and rounded on everyone. "Just *stop*!" I could hear his breath trembling. His fists balled at his sides. "Everyone just leave me alone." His voice broke on the last word. "Please."

Violet's face flushed red with frustration, but she didn't say anything. Sam at her side, held her back with a cautious hand.

Slowly, Landon turned and met my eyes. His immediately welled with moisture and the bewilderment on his face changed his usual expression into one I barely recognized. Slowly, he stepped toward me until he stood over me, his body slightly angled as if he were prepared to run at any second.

One paramedic addressed him. "Do you know this girl?"

Landon exhaled forcefully and slowly shook his head. "I'm . . . not sure. I might." His breathing picked up pace as his eyes scoured my face.

I didn't know how he could have gotten to this place in time, whole and alive. I didn't know how he could have brought me with him. I didn't know why he didn't know me like I knew him. But I knew our love hadn't been for nothing.

With everyone watching, I had limited things I could tell him. But I had to take the moment to do something. I gave him a little smile which seemed to take him off guard. But I thought I detected the slightest glimmer in his eye. A reconnecting of some sort. A dawn of recognition. His eyebrows pulled together and conflicting expressions chased across his face. Something akin to disbelief, and hope. Finally, he spoke. "Presley?"

I smiled and let out a sob. I wanted to reach for him, but my arms were still restrained. So I reached for him with my eyes and with my heart. "I didn't let go, Landon. I held on just like you told me to."

At last his face smoothed into a smile. Removing his gloves in a hurry, he leaned in and brushed the hair from my face with his warm fingertips and then cupped my face between his palms. His eyes poured into mine and he leaned over to whisper against my lips, "I won't let go either."

Book Club Questions

1. Caring for a loved one with autism is grueling. Was Gayle justified in putting so much of Chase's care on Presley's shoulders?

2. Marriages sometimes don't survive after a child dies. Do you sympathize or disagree with Gayle's choice to leave her husband after she almost lost her child in his care?

3. Was Gayle justified in keeping Presley's true past a secret?

4. Do you think Presley and Landon's situation or predicament were the result of freedom of choice or destiny?

5. If Presley would have chosen Reese, how would the story have changed? If Landon would have used his passage, how would the story have changed?

6. This book explored some heavier themes such as death and caring for loved ones with disabilities. Did any of these themes make you uncomfortable?

7. In a movie version, who would you cast for the parts?

8. How do Presley, Reese and Landon change and evolve throughout the book? What events trigger those changes?

9. How do you imagine Landon different before his death? How do you think death might have changed him?

10. Who is the most relatable character in the book?

11. Were you hoping for Presley to choose Landon or Reese? Why?

12. How did you feel when Landon said, "True love doesn't always mean a happy ending." In what cases do you agree or disagree?

13. What did you think of the ending?

Acknowledgments

Together we'd like to thank our beta readers whose time and keen insights proved invaluable: Sara Cecchini, Kacey Nielsen, Ana Mahoney, Michelle Larkin, Carlee Cutler, Jaune Curtis, Kristina Lords, Lisa Jurvelin, Shayan Vahdati, Apryl Larkin, Shawna Tibbits, Sarah Swindel, Kim Larkin, Janet Cole, and Shaunna Sanders.

Thank you also to Bobbi Schwarz, Brock Shinen, Kiki Comin, and Barry Thomas.

Finally, a huge shout out to the Cedar Fort Team. To Hali Bird for recognizing the potential in BEYOND from the beginning (and for your supernatural editing powers). To Priscilla Chavez for creating a cover that took our breath away. To Vikki Downs for your marketing prowess. To DeVin Ortin for your technical genius. And to Jessica Romrell for your sharp editing eye.

Catina Haverlock

Thank you, Mom, for teaching me to love reading. I remember sitting on your lap as a toddler while you read to me *The Monster at the End of This Book* and *Oscar Otter* "just one more time." Dad—thank you for teaching me the importance of service, honesty, hard work and compassion. You are so loved.

To my co-author and sister, Ang...I had the time of my life creating this story with you. I've never laughed so hard! Epic writing sessions. Your James impression! I can't! Let's do it again, sometime!

Ashli Hamilton—I don't think I ever told you, but our conversation (when *Beyond* was just an idea) at a diner across the street from Disneyland changed everything. Your extreme enthusiasm for the concept gave me the confidence to write this story.

Much gratitude to my book club girls: Sarah Swindel, Susan Frank, Marie Wallwork, Jeannette Miller, Emily Boles, Shawna Tibbets, and Shannon Dixon. Everyone of you claimed no surprise when I shared the news of our publishing deal with you. Excitement, but not surprise. Thank you for your faith.

To my children: Adam, Zac, Ellie, and Crew. You are my purpose. There were too many nights of fast food, I know. Too much time on the other side of my bedroom door when deadlines were the boss of me. Thank you for your belief in me and in this story. I couldn't have done it without your patience and support.

Finally, thank you to my husband, Scott. "It's too good not to get picked up," you told me several times. You were confident when I doubted. Thank you for laughing at the funny parts and gasping at the scary ones. So much fun to read to you! You're my biggest fan, and for that, I can't love you enough.

ANGELA LARKIN

I'd like to thank the first reader I ever knew, my mother, for reading to me and for never limiting the number of books I could check out from the Stead library. Also, thanks to my dad, who always smiled at me like I was somethin' else. You made me feel like I could do anything.

To my sister and co-author, Tina, thank you for calling me that day on the I-15 and telling me about your idea. And later, for inviting me to help you write it.

To Kacey Nielsen, I'm not sure I truly believed until you read *Beyond*. Because if someone so smart and funny liked it, I knew we had something.

Thanks to each friend who ever told me that I should write a book. Eventually, I believed you.

Certain people influenced the course of my life at an early age. Mrs. Watts, you showed me what excellence is and that the world is full of stories.

To my kids: Afton, Evan, Jemma and Luke. I thank you for your understanding and encouragement as Mom flew to writers conferences and spent so much time in front of the computer. This process taught us that we can do hard things!

Lastly, I want to express gratitude to my husband, who fanned the flames of my interests and talents, even when I was up to my eyeballs in diapers and playdates. I'll never forget the day you brought home a new laptop and told me to write. I'm glad I listened.

About Catina Haverlock

Catina worked her way through college as a newspaper and television journalist. Itching to stretch her creative muscles, she convinced her university to create a dating game show, which she hosted. After spending most of her adult life in Las Vegas, Catina traded in tumbleweeds for earthquakes and now lives with her husband and four children near San Diego, California. If she's not home, chances are you can find her at the beach, Disneyland, or In-N-Out.

Scan to Visit

www.beyondthenovel.com

About Angela Larkin

Photo Credit: Kiki Comin

Angela Larkin spent much of her childhood under a blanket with a flashlight, secretly reading past bedtime. She's been a gold miner, a pool cleaner, a mannequin dresser, and a teacher. She's lived a true romance: meeting her husband in a case of mistaken identity. They recently moved with their four children from the sparkling city of Las Vegas to the shade of the North Carolina Pines.

Scan to Visit

www.beyondthenovel.com